The Personal Assistant

ALSO BY BECKI WILLIS

STANDALONES
The Widow's Baby
Keep Your Doors Locked
The Stalker
The Personal Assistant

THE
PERSONAL
ASSISTANT

BECKI WILLIS

Joffe Books, London
www.joffebooks.com

First published in Great Britain in 2024

Cover art by Nick Castle

ISBN: 978-1-83526-686-1

CHAPTER ONE

Lexi

Big Moments in life didn't always come with warning signs. No standard label saying *Caution: Everything you do from this point forward will change your life forever.*

Unlike in the movies, there weren't always telltale signs of what was to come.

No scenes in slow motion.

No sound effects.

If I had known this was a *Big Moment* in my life, I would have done things differently.

But this wasn't Hollywood. I didn't see the signs. And I didn't know that my life would forever be defined into two distinct categories.

Before, and After.

* * *

I'll be the first to admit: I had become a creature of habit.

After an anything but conventional childhood, the adult me liked schedules and routines.

On a normal day, I would dress for work and head across the street to my favorite coffee shop, where I would order my usual coffee from my usual barista. With to-go cup in hand, I would scan the street before taking my faithful four-block route to J.M. Creations.

But that day wasn't normal. Instead of walking to the studio, my boss had called a rideshare that whisked me off to a new art gallery across town. Bluntly put, Janine Morrow had sent me there to spy on them.

To be clear, that was her word, not mine. I preferred to think of it as checking out a new business in town.

I know, I know. It was the same thing, but to me, the word 'spying' had too many negative memories. Never mind that my visit included a semi-disguise. That didn't mean I was actually *spying* on the upscale art gallery.

As far as disguises went, mine wasn't much. My normal work attire was a simple sundress topped by a thin, light-weight cardigan. My normal hairstyle was a simple ponytail. Today, I had on a short-sleeved dress, my blond hair was left long and free, and I had traded my hobo-style purse for a sleek little handbag barely large enough for the essentials. The purse alone was proof of my disguise.

So, there I was, standing in the middle of Ocean Art Gallery, looking at some wild, swirly painting the artist called *Music in Motion*. I was more impressed with the sculpture beside it, something in bronzed plaster depicting musical instruments stacked one upon the other.

I wandered about the airy space, taking several discreet pictures with my phone so I could report back to Janine. None of the featured pieces were of the same caliber as hers. Getting the talented Janine Morrow an art exhibit there should be easy enough. Even if the new gallery rejected her for some reason, they posed no threat to her stronghold over the market.

I typed out a message but just before sending it, I remembered Janine was in a meeting. She had told me to call a rideshare when I was done and meet her back at the studio.

Knowing that still didn't keep me from pulling my keys from that tiny little purse as I moved toward the exit. That, too, was habit.

I only remembered the rideshare as I stepped into the salt-flavored air that was Galveston, Texas. I pulled the app up on my phone.

All it took was a split second. My attention was divided for exactly that long, but it was enough time for someone to run past me, yank the purse from my hand, and race down the street.

Later, I would grudgingly admire the thief's speed and agility. The person hadn't even hesitated. Just snag, grab, and run. Once upon a time, I could have pulled off the same simple heist.

Times had changed. I was still relatively new to the area, and I didn't know this part of town at all. Plus, part of today's semi-disguise was a pair of low-heeled pumps. They weren't made for sprinting down unfamiliar sidewalks.

Even so, I took off in pursuit. I rounded the corner just in time to see my assailant disappear around the other side of the block. He or she wore nondescript clothes, black or dark blue, and sneakers.

Figures.

I knew a moment of uncertainty. Should I give up or push forward?

Common sense told me I didn't know the neighborhood. Didn't know if the next corner led to an alleyway or to a busy intersection. And the overhead sun was brutal, baking layer upon layer of heat into the sidewalks, while humidity from the Gulf sucked the breath from my lungs. Risking scorched feet and a heat stroke wouldn't bring my purse back.

Instinct urged me to keep going. The purse itself wasn't important. It was too tiny for anything other than my credentials, a debit card with maybe twenty bucks left on it, and a tube of my favorite lip gloss. Getting my driver's license reissued would be the biggest inconvenience of all.

If I continued, it wouldn't be the purse I went after. I would be going after the person who snatched it.

This, I was certain, wasn't a random act of convenience. *Woman steps onto the sidewalk, woman isn't focused on her surroundings, woman's purse is just there for the taking.* I was certain this had been a targeted attack.

I had known it for a few weeks now. Someone was following me. I hadn't been able to see them yet, but I knew the signs. That tingling feeling along my scalp. That awkward self-consciousness. That searing heat of someone's gaze upon my skin.

I felt my feet slowing. Instinct or not, going any further would be useless, and perhaps dangerous. I didn't know the area. I didn't know the escape routes or the hidden pockets where someone could jump out at me.

Whoever stole my purse had been waiting for me to leave the gallery, and the moment I did, they had flown into action.

This stunt hadn't been about stealing my purse.

This was about stealing my sense of security.

* * *

The first thing I noticed when I reached the studio was the cardboard box sitting on my desk. I saw that my desk surface had been rearranged. Among other things, my cup of pens, the one Janine had given me with 'Fabulous Assistant' emblazoned on both sides, was missing.

Dang it! I hope it didn't get broken when the delivery man brought the box!

I opened the top drawer of my desk, searching for the box cutter, before realizing the box was already open. Curiously, I leaned in to see what it held.

I imagine that the confusion in my voice matched the look on my face. "Janine?" I called. "Why are all my things in this box?"

I heard a faint sniffle as Janine uncurled from the couch at the far side of the loft. As I watched her cross the space between us, I realized she had been crying.

"Janine? Is something wrong?" A touch of panic crept into my voice as a half-dozen scenarios ran through my mind. Had someone died? Had her show been canceled? Had she lost the lease on the building? Were we relocating? "Tell me, and maybe I can fix it."

"I'm afraid you can't. Not this time." She attempted a brave smile.

"I don't know about that. You always say I have magical powers when it comes to fixing problems." A smile hovered around my lips as I tried injecting a sense of false confidence in us both. "Let me pull out my magic wand and go to work. Tell me what we're up against."

"I'm sorry, Lexi. This just isn't working."

I was still confused. "What's not working? The new schedule we set up? That's okay; we can still tweak it." I would have grabbed my planner, but it, too, seemed to be inside the box. I motioned toward it with my thumb. "What's with the box, anyway?"

"I thought it would be easier this way. I've gathered all your things for you."

An uneasy quiver fluttered in my stomach. "I can see that." My words came out as slow and dulled as my thoughts.

Something very bad was happening here, but I was too shocked to compute the truth.

"I truly am sorry, Lexi. It's nothing you've done. But I have to let you go."

"Let me . . . go?" That last word came out impossibly high. "What . . . what do you mean?"

"This is no longer working." Janine made a motion with her hands.

"You're firing me?" Another high note, this one filled with disbelief.

"I truly am sorry. You'll find your last check, a generous severance pay, and a letter of recommendation inside the box. In fact, I've already spoken to a colleague who is looking for an assistant."

That was it. That was all she said before turning her back on me. I knew her well enough to know this was her final word on the subject. Nothing I could say or do would make a difference.

In stunned silence, I took the box and left. I walked back to my apartment on auto pilot, too numb to process what had just transpired.

Like J.M. Creations, my living space was located in The Strand Historic District in downtown Galveston. Tucked in the far corner of the second floor, it overlooked a brick-paved alley and was accessed by a steep, narrow set of stairs. Even with its leaded-glass entrance, the stairwell would be dark and oppressive if not for the wonders of LED lighting.

By the time I dredged myself up the steps and opened my front door, my arms ached from the weight of the box.

My heart ached from the weight of reality. I had lost my job. My purse. What little sense of security I had managed to garner over the past few turbulent months.

The box fell to the floor with a thud, rattling the contents inside. I collapsed into my favorite chair, utterly drained of all energy.

I sat there until the walls inched closer, squeezing the very air from my lungs. The apartment was already small enough, even before the gloom pushed its way in. I had to get out. I had to stretch my legs. I grabbed my faithful hobo purse, the one with all my paraphernalia, and all but ran out the door and down the steep stairs, bursting into the fresh, humid air of the Texas Gulf Coast.

I needed the tang of salty sea air and the roar of the Gulf. The seawall fronting the ocean was too far by foot, but Galveston Channel was only a few blocks away. I took off at a fast pace, desperate to find what tranquility I could among the swooping sea gulls and the pungent bouquet of live seafood, fresh off the boat. I even forgot my ages-old habit of watching my back.

Hearing a blast from a ship's horn, I wondered if I could sneak aboard. It didn't have to be one of the luxurious cruise ships in port. It could be a container ship. A bulk carrier. A tanker. Anything to take me away.

Stop it, Lexi. I used a stern tone in my silent rebuke. *You can't keep running. Galveston was going to be different, remember?*

I slowed my pace, allowing the words to penetrate. When I made the move to the shore six months ago, I decided that this was it. This was the place I would call home. No more moving from place to place, trying to outrun my past. I couldn't — I wouldn't — allow something as simple as losing my job set me back. Not this time.

Making my way down to the pier, I took in the sights and sounds of the busy ship channel. Restaurants and bars lined up alongside anchored yachts and pleasure boats. *I could get a job down here,* I thought. *With so much activity, I'm sure someone is hiring.*

I slipped my phone from my purse to search for job openings, and that's when it happened. That's when my phone slipped out of my fingers, through the pier railing, and down into the murky, muddled waters below.

"No!" I cried aloud. "No, no, no!" I made a symbolic show of falling to my knees and reaching toward the water, but there was nothing to be done. My phone was gone.

CHAPTER TWO

Lexi

By the time I roused the next morning, sunlight stole through the slits of the Venetian blinds, casting slices of buttery light across my rumpled bed covers. The sounds of life — cars driving past, voices mingled with bursts of laughter, a shouted greeting, the cry of a little child — drifted up from the street below.

Realization flooded in with them.

You have no job. Janine fired you.

I roused enough ambition to pull myself from bed, take a shower, and get dressed. It was my usual routine: a quick scrub with a loofah sponge, lathering my hair with lemony-fresh shampoo before blowing it dry, and applying nude lip gloss and a few swipes of bronzer. Out of sheer habit, I put on a yellow sundress topped by a shrug woven of multi-colored threads. Just before slipping into sandals, I remembered I could wear flip flops, instead.

The thought sobered me as I left the apartment. Even though it was two hours later than my normal routine, I headed toward Galveston Gusto.

Heeding an old habit that had wormed its way back into my life, I quickly scanned my surroundings the moment I stepped onto the street. SAR was something my father taught me long ago: Scan, Assess, React. I had tried breaking the habit. I wanted no ties, no habits, and no connection to the man who had raised me.

But the first time I felt those prying eyes on me, the old habit returned. Like it or not, SAR was part of my normal routine again. And after yesterday's purse-snatching, it was a necessity.

Being late this morning had its perks. No prying eyes, and the coffee shop wasn't nearly as crowded. The breakfast crowd had cleared out, and it was still hours before afternoon coffee breaks. Only a handful of people occupied the normally bustling shop.

"Hey, Lexi," Raven greeted me. The barista was one of the few people on the island who knew me by name, so I counted her as my friend.

"I wondered where you were this morning." She grabbed a to-go cup, hand poised on the second. "Two to go?"

"Just one today," I answered, hoping my voice didn't reveal my heartache.

After a restless night, exhaustion had temporarily dulled the harsh reality of losing my job. But now, ordering only the one cup of coffee, a fresh wave of pain came rushing back.

Janine, my employer and my friend, had fired me. The thought was as depressing today as it had been yesterday.

"If you're still serving the sausage pastries, I'll take one of those, too," I told Raven as she prepared my solo order.

"Anything else?"

I shook my head. "That's it this morning."

Paying for my order, it occurred to me that I should keep an eye on my finances. Janine paid me a generous salary and had been equally generous with my severance pay, so my bank account wasn't anemic at this point. Future expenses would change all that, especially if I went any real length of time without a job.

I vaguely remembered Janine saying she had spoken to a friend about hiring me. But since my phone was currently laying at the bottom of the ship channel, any potential new boss wouldn't be able to reach me. I had stopped last night to buy a pay-as-you-go phone. In my father's world, it was best known as a burner, but I refused to think of it as such. For me, it was a temporary substitute until I replaced my smart phone. I needed to contact Janine now and inform her of my new number.

I wasn't ready to hear her voice just yet, so I opted for a text. Sinking into the first chair I came to, I settled at the small bistro table, gathering my wits. With unsteady fingers, I typed out a simple message.

Lexi's new phone number.

Too impersonal, I decided. I deleted and tried again.

I have a new number! Please give this to your colleague.

Too peppy. It sounded like I didn't have a care in the world. Like her betrayal hadn't hurt to the bone.

A third attempt wasn't much better. After deleting that message, too, I gave up and tucked my phone away. I deliberately cleared my mind, determined to think of nothing but how tasty my sausage croissant was this morning. I closed my eyes, concentrating on each burst of flavor. Buttery flakes of pastry. A nicely seasoned pork patty with subtle undertones of smoky paprika, sage, and cumin. A hint of spicy chorizo.

Focusing on my breakfast was the only way to stave off reminders of the day before. The day I lost my job, my friend, my purse, and my phone.

Sausage croissant, I reminded myself. *Flaky, smoky, savory. Flaky, smoky, savory. Flaky, smoky, savory.*

My concentration broke as I felt someone's gaze on me. Opening my eyes, I looked around until I saw him. Instinct told me it wasn't my stalker. A nice-looking man at a back table watched me with a hint of amusement upon his face. I assumed it had more to do with my absorption in my meal than it did with my ravishing, good looks.

It was petty of me, but I let my gaze roam over him in appraisal before sniffing disinterest and turning back around.

Never mind that he was actually very attractive. I knew his look. Starched white shirt, starched jeans, boring tie, scuffed cowboy boots. Clean-shaven face and closely clipped hair. He didn't need a badge to taunt his profession. He was a lawman, through and through.

In my father's world, that meant nothing but trouble.

As much as I hated to admit it, part of me still shared that mentality. I was raised to avoid the law at all costs. Lawmen, my father convinced me, weren't to be trusted. They wanted to stifle our way of life. They cared nothing about our freedom. If the law caught up to us, he said, they would take him away and stick me in foster care. He made it sound like a fate worse than death.

That was years ago, I told myself. I was old enough now to form my own opinions. Old enough to know that few things my father taught me were the truth. Old enough to understand that rules and laws were necessary, and that my father was a bad man who lacked regard for either.

Still, some habits were harder to break than others.

Ignoring the amused man, I tried concentrating on something new. My croissant was almost gone. What little was left wouldn't taste nearly as good now, knowing the lawman was laughing at my expense.

I considered my distrust of his kind. What was fact, and what was my father's twisted version of truth? And what, I wondered, would have happened if the law had caught us back then? What if I had been thrust into foster care? Would I have been spared the heartache and horrors of life with my father? What if I had lived with a family who appreciated me for me and not simply what I could do for them?

"It doesn't matter," I muttered to myself. "No amount of wondering and wishing can turn back the hands of time."

I don't know how long I sat there. I was killing time, wanting to be anywhere other than my apartment. It was the same size as it had always been: a modest-sized space with the standard kitchen/dining/living area all in one, a single bedroom, an old-style bathroom, and two meager closets. Yet it felt smaller today than it had yesterday. Today, it had to make room for heartache and sorrow, and for the oppressive thought of my new normal.

I didn't leave Galveston Gusto until I became aware of someone lingering near my table, hoping to snag an empty seat. A quick look around told me that it must be noontime. No more than two people occupied any of the tables, but it was just enough to create a lack of seating.

"Here," I said hastily. "You can have my table."

"Are you sure?" she asked. She was already piling her shopping bags into the chair opposite me.

I was embarrassed to have lingered there for so long. What must Raven think? What must the amused lawman think?

But he, of course, was no longer there. Raven was elbow deep in sandwiches and drinks, much too busy to pay me any mind. Other than the grateful shopper already seated at my table, I slipped out of the coffee shop without anyone noticing.

My steps were heavy as I crossed the street to my apartment. I was in no mood to browse through the boutiques and small shops scattered throughout the historic district. Budget concerns aside, I felt no desire to shop, even if it meant returning to my apartment.

I trudged up the stairway. Even before I reached the door identified as 2D with antique brass letters, I saw the note wedged into its jamb.

A flash of panic ripped through me. *I've paid the rent, right? Surely, I'm not being evicted on top of everything else!*

I jerked the note from the door, relief flooding through me when I realized it wasn't bad news. If anything, it was the only spot of good news I had had in the past twenty-four hours. I quickly unlocked the door and carried the note inside to read again.

> *I understand you are looking for employment. Your former employer provided a glowing letter of recommendation. If interested, call this number.*

I turned the note over in my hand. It was written on fine stationery but had no name and no address. Just a few simple words and a phone number.

I debated for a full two seconds before pulling out my new cell phone and dialing the number.

"Samson Shipping," a professional-sounding voice answered. "Would you mind if I place you on a brief hold?"

Before I could reply, classical music tinkled softly in my ear. I hated classical music.

Why no, I have nothing better to do, I groused silently. *I can stay on hold all day. Really, think nothing of it.*

Okay, so I was a bit of a smart ass. I figured I had earned it.

The voice returned, making me feel about two inches tall when I heard the sincerity in her apology. "I'm so sorry about that. The phones have been ringing all morning. How may I help you?"

"Uhm, this is Lexi Graham. I believe Janine Morrow contacted you on my behalf?" I hated the way my voice made that funny little hitch when I said her name. My mind still had trouble catching up with the reality of my situation. My closest friend had fired me.

Somewhere in the back of my scrambled thoughts, I had to wonder, *Does that make Raven my closest friend now? I don't even know her last name.*

"One moment, please, while I transfer you."

After another brief hold, the line picked up. "Lexi! Yes, of course!" a man gushed. "We were hoping you would call."

"Uhm . . . okay?"

I didn't always preface every sentence with 'uhm' nor did I often sound so uncertain. But this was such a surreal situation. Losing one job and being mysteriously offered another within the space of one day was a little much for my sluggish brain to comprehend.

"Would you be interested in coming in for an interview tomorrow morning? Say, around nine?"

I caught myself just before saying uhm again. "Of — of course. Nine sounds fine."

"Perfect. We'll look forward to meeting you." He rattled off the street address.

"Likewise. And . . . thank you."

"Thank you, Miss Graham. We'll talk tomorrow."

It wasn't until I hung up that I realized a few key points.

I had no idea who or what Samson Shipping was.

I had no idea what the job was.

I had no idea what the man's name was who answered, or why he sounded so pleased to hear from me.

And I had no idea how my potential new employer knew where I lived.

CHAPTER THREE

The Milkman

There was no moon to illuminate the night. He liked dark nights like this.

His car was parked one street over. Dressed all in black, the man leisurely walked the block and a half to his destination. He had scouted the area a half-dozen times. He knew exactly which houses had motion detection lights, which had alarms. Which had a safe escape route.

Avoiding the front porch light, he slipped around to the back of the house. He knew the owners didn't have a dog, nor did they have an alarm system. He knew only one car was parked beneath the rear carport; the husband was in the middle of his overnight shift at the warehouse.

Getting inside the house was easy enough. Even the deadbolt didn't pose a problem.

The light beneath the microwave gave off a dim glow. It was just enough to keep him from bumping into a kitchen chair, shoved at a careless angle beneath the table.

He had been inside before, so he knew the layout. Kitchen, dining room, living room. The stairs were in the living room. And the bedrooms were upstairs.

The house was carpeted throughout, keeping his footsteps muffled. He even knew where the tattletale squeaks were on the staircase. He could make his assent stealthily.

She would never know he was in the house until the time came. And by then, it wouldn't matter. He made certain there was no landline, and he had used a cell phone jammer to disable any calls. It was a precaution he always took on these visits.

The man paused outside her bedroom door, breathing in anticipation of the pleasure. Just a few more minutes, and his fantasies would play out.

Stepping into the room, he heard the woman's soft snore as she slept, oblivious to his presence. He watched her for a few moments before bumping his knee against the side of the mattress. She stirred but didn't awaken.

He pushed harder. She mumbled a protest and turned over on her side, still asleep.

"Graciela," he called softly. "Wake up, Graciela."

Her back to him, the woman slid a hand across the bed and croaked groggily, "Henry?"

"No, Graciela. Henry's not here."

She came awake immediately, quickly sitting up in bed. Her dark eyes were wild as she peered through the darkness, searching for the voice.

"Who — who are you?" she demanded. She clutched the covers to her, as if a few layers of cloth would protect her.

"A friend," he said. His voice was soft, and almost friendly. "Don't be afraid, Graciela. I'm not going to hurt you."

"What do you want?" Her eyes went to the monitor beside her bed, which was unexpectedly dark. "My baby!" It was as much a gasp as it was a scream. "What have you done to my baby!"

"Nothing. I haven't done a thing to the little fellow," the man assured her. "Come with me, and you can see for yourself."

"What do you want? Is it money? My purse is there, on the dresser." She made a wild gesture with one hand, still clutching the covers to her with the other. "Take it! Take anything you want, just please, don't hurt my baby!"

The man sounded affronted. "I would never hurt little Enrique."

"How — how do you know his name? Who are you?" Her voice became increasingly hysterical.

"I know all about you, Graciela. I know that Henry is working, and that your little baby boy is across the hall, sound asleep in his crib. I peeked in on him earlier. He's all tucked in, nice and tight."

"I swear, if you've hurt him!" They both knew it was an empty threat, but she screamed the words with conviction.

"I assure you, I haven't. Let's go see, shall we?" His manner was bizarre, borderline friendly. He acted as if having a total stranger wake her in the middle of the night was the most normal thing in the world.

Graciela scrambled out of the bed. When she would have darted past him, he caught her hand. "Wait for me, Graciela. Let's go wake him together."

Graciela's body trembled as she managed the short walk to the nursery. Her knees barely supported her weight, but she had to reach Enrique. She had to make sure her baby was safe.

She let out a whimper of relief when she saw her baby, all snug and safe in his bundled blankets.

"Pick him up, Graciela."

It sounded like a command, but Graciela gladly did so. Tears dripped from her face as she bent over the crib and picked up her son. She gathered him close, rocking his sleeping form to her chest.

"Sit down," the man said. When she would have taken the rocker, he stopped her. "Not there. There." He pointed to the floor.

Confused but grateful that her baby was safe, Graciela did as she was told. Her movements were smooth as she lowered herself to the floor and sat cross-legged, without as much as jostling little Enrique.

Ah, to be young and graceful once again! the man thought wistfully.

As Graciela rocked nervously on the floor, she dared to ask, "What — what do you want from us?"

"Just a moment of pleasure," he told her.

Repulsed by the innuendo, the young mother's face filled with disgust. Instinctively, she held her son closer to her, twisting slightly away.

"That's good, Graciela. A mother should protect her baby. But I mean you no harm. Truly," he assured her.

She cringed when he moved forward, but he reached for the chair, not her. He slid the rocker across the carpet, placing it between her and the door. Then he lowered himself into the seat.

"Feed him," he instructed.

Her forehead wrinkled. "But . . . he's asleep."

"Wake him up." Some of the friendliness slipped from the man's voice.

"I just put him down an hour ago!"

"I want you to feed him."

"But—"

He cut off the woman's protest. "You'd deny your son?"

"Of course not! But he ate less than two hours ago. I don't think he's hungry yet."

"We'll let little Enrique decide that." He leaned forward in the chair and spoke in a slow, distinct voice. "Wake the baby up," he told her harshly, "and feed him."

With tears streaming down her face, Graciela unbundled the newborn and patted his tiny cheeks, trying to tease him into waking.

"How do you plan to feed him with your shirt on?" the man asked.

Graciela visibly swallowed. "Could you, uh, turn your head?"

"No."

She stared at him, trying to gauge his intentions. Other than his comment about pleasure, he gave no indication that he planned to rape her. Yet he wanted her to lift her T-shirt

18

and expose her breasts to him. Was he prolonging the inevitable? She shook her head, silently begging this stranger not to do what she feared he might.

"Don't make me angry, Graciela," the man warned. "What kind of mother are you?" he spat. "Feed. Your. Baby."

Whimpering, Graciela pulled Enrique to her breast and tentatively raised her T-shirt.

"Take your shirt off," he instructed.

She started to argue. The nightlight was behind him, so she couldn't see his face. But she saw the way he leaned forward. Felt the heat of his eyes as they bore into hers. With her free hand, she pulled the T-shirt up and over her head.

"There's nothing to be ashamed of, Graciela." The man's voice was gentle again. "You have beautiful breasts. What you're doing is as nature intended. Now, wake Enrique and let him nurse."

She shook so badly, Graciela feared she might drop her baby. She cradled him in her arm as she aggressively jiggled his cheek, not stopping until she saw the tiny slit of his eye open.

"Hey there, little guy," she cooed through her tears. "Can you wake up? Come on, wake up and eat for Mommy."

Despite her efforts, the baby was sleepier than he was hungry.

"I-I don't think he's going to wake up," she said, looking up at the man in the rocking chair.

"Start undressing him."

Horror distorted her pretty face, and she released a long stream of Spanish curses.

"I'm not going to molest him!" the man snapped in irritation. "It's the fastest way to wake an infant. If he's not bundled up nice and toasty, he'll wake up. Start by taking off his blanket."

Keeping her eyes warily on the man, the mother did as instructed. Without the buntings, and with a few more tweaks to his cheeks, the baby squirmed.

"Put him to your breast."

It still wasn't enough. Enrique's mouth didn't open, and his eyes were drooping again.

"Wake him up. Feed him!" the man bellowed.

The loud voice startled the baby. He looked ready to cry, but Graciela quickly slipped her nipple into his mouth. When he had trouble latching on, she kept trying until she felt the tug of his tiny mouth against her skin. She worried that her milk wouldn't come down, being as nervous and tense as she was, but at least he was trying to nurse. Maybe it would be enough to appease the man and he would go away.

"Beautiful," the man murmured. "Just beautiful."

Graciela said nothing. Silent sobs racked her shoulders as she sat cross-legged on the floor, naked from the waist up, nursing her infant as some madman who had broken into her home watched.

"That's my momma," he purred. "Beautiful. Just beautiful."

Smiling, he softly hummed Brahms' 'Lullaby' and lost himself to pleasure.

CHAPTER FOUR

Lexi

I was surprised to see that the address for Samson Shipping was nearby. In a city of over fifty thousand residents and a land mass of over two hundred square miles, I somehow managed to exist within a six-block radius. I had only visited the Walmart once since moving here. It was about five miles away, situated along Seawall Boulevard.

Walking to Samson Shipping wasn't out of the question unless I factored in the heat and humidity of the seaside city. Moisture from the Gulf of Mexico thickened the air with its muggy breath, temporarily stealing mine whenever I first stepped into its greedy clutches. It always took me a moment to adjust, leaving me to wonder if it would forever be this way. Did residents ever get used to the humidity? Did it linger all year round, or was this a handicap of summer? From what I had seen, summer here started in April. I was afraid to ask when it might end.

A brisk breeze blowing off the water kept the day from being miserable. Yet. There was still plenty of time for that to change.

I didn't want to show up for my interview sweaty and bedraggled by the Texas heat, so I chose to make the short drive in my faithful old Subaru. It wasn't much in the way of style and good looks, but at least it had a good air conditioner.

One of the best features of my apartment was that it came with its own parking space. Since I could walk to most everything I needed, I seldom vacated the coveted spot. Making an exception this morning, I hoped the space would still be there when I returned. I knew from experience that people didn't always honor the alleyway's *No Public Parking* sign.

A few blocks later, I pulled up to the curb of an old warehouse that looked like it had been there since the days of bustling steamboats. If I hadn't been following the directions on my GPS, I might have missed the unassuming sign identifying this as Samson Shipping.

"Here goes nothing," I said, leaving the cold air behind as I stepped from my car.

Aside from the ornate door with its heavy leaded glass, the entry to the building was less than impressive. *It's a shipping company, Lex. What did you expect?* I chided myself.

The ordinary vestibule where I stood featured standard tile flooring and bland walls. An elevator dominated the space. As I stepped forward to press the call button, I saw a long hallway stretching out on either side of the entry.

Which way am I supposed to go? I wondered. I didn't relish the thought of hiking down either corridor, only to discover I should have taken the elevator up.

So, when the doors slid open, I did just that.

I went up.

I made the right choice. The second floor was more open, with a decent entry and a large wall graphic that identified this as Samson Shipping. A pen and ink drawing, splashed here and there with pale watercolors, dominated the wall, depicting the waterfront shipping district and therefore clarifying the nature of the business.

"Ah, you must be Lexi!" A man approached from my left, his body language shouting a welcome as I stepped off the elevator. His smile was friendly enough, but I noticed it never quite reached his eyes. "I'm Simon Brewster. We spoke over the phone. Please, follow me."

I trailed behind him, noticing a half-dozen or more work-stations. They weren't quite offices, but glass enclosures made the spacious cubicles almost appear that way. I saw three people behind their desks and another at the coffee station. I lifted my hand in a wan greeting, noticing that few seemed to notice my presence.

Simon led me to the very end of the hallway. His office, I noticed, was surrounded by four walls. Three were paneled in a rich cherry veneer, while the fourth featured floor-to-ceiling windows, allowing plenty of light to flood through.

"Have a seat," he invited, waving toward the wingback chairs fanning the front of a massive desk. "May I get you something to drink? Water? Coffee? Soda?"

"I'm fine, thank you," I replied demurely. Was Simon Brewster the owner of Samson Shipping? The president? There wasn't a nameplate on his desk. *Is this even his office?*

He seated himself within the folds of the leather executive chair, its over-sized proportions dwarfing his small frame. *He looks like a Simon. A little shorter and narrower than average. Well dressed and well groomed, even though I'm no fan of slick-backed hair. Maybe it's to hide a receding hairline. It accentuates his sharp nose and even sharper eyes. Are they dark blue, or are they black?*

Good or bad, I had a tendency to size people up when I first met them. Like SAR, my father had taught me the importance of trusting my first impressions. It was another habit that was hard to break.

While I made my silent assessment, Simon glanced over the sheet of paper he held. "Ms. Morrow states that you're excellent at juggling responsibilities. She says here that you handled her office affairs, scheduled her calendar, arranged art shows and exhibits, and kept track of expenses and profits. Very impressive."

"Thank you." I didn't add that it was easy to do when you loved your job as much as I had loved mine.

"She also states that through no fault of your own, it was necessary to terminate your business arrangement. She feels any employer would be fortunate to have you as part of their team, which is why we contacted you so promptly." Simon flashed me a smile. "We heeded her words. We didn't want someone else snatching you up before we had a chance to hire you."

I knew I should feel flattered, but all I felt was betrayal. If Janine was so pleased with my work, why had she abruptly let me go? I kept her books. Paying my salary hadn't been the issue.

"It is my pleasure to offer you a position here at Samson Shipping," Simon continued. Passing me a piece of paper, he encouraged me to look at it. "I believe you'll find that to be a generous starting pay."

I held in a gasp. Janine had paid me well, but it was nothing compared to Simon's offer.

"Y-yes," I stammered. "This is a very generous offer."

"It's salary, of course, so you won't have set hours, per se. I think we'll all benefit from a more flexible schedule, and you can take time off as needed. Within reason, of course." He flashed that smile again, the one that never found its way to his eyes.

"Of course."

"We have an agreement, then?" He looked quite pleased, as if we had hammered out contentious details and both came out as winners.

"Wait." I finally found my voice. "I don't even know what the job is!"

"You'll be Lillian Samson's personal assistant, of course."

I stared at him in surprise. *Of course? Why of course?* And who was Lillian Samson? Nothing about this interview made any sense. Nothing about these last two days made any sense. Maybe I was going crazy.

"I need more details than that, Mr. Brewster."

"Please, call me Simon. And I do apologize. Sometimes I get ahead of myself." His fake smile was getting old. He seemed to think it was charming, which made exactly one of us.

"Lillian Samson is the owner and CEO of Samson Shipping. She acquired the business when her husband died and has been instrumental in growing the company into a multi-million-dollar success. Due to . . . health concerns . . . Sam, as everyone calls her, doesn't get out as much as she once did. Among other things, you will assist her with errands and personal concerns."

"Health concerns? I'm not a nurse, Mr. Brewster."

"Simon," he reminded me. "And Sam hardly needs a nurse."

"I'm not a personal companion, either." For the kind of money he was offering, his idea of personal concerns might mean something more than the average assistant provided.

Simon looked appropriately dismayed. "I'm afraid I'm still doing it. I'm putting my foot in my mouth, aren't I?"

I had the oddest feeling he was doing it intentionally, although that was preposterous.

"Sam can explain better than I, but sometimes, she gets so bogged down in the day-to-day aspects of running the business, that she forgets to handle personal correspondence, social obligations, shopping, errands, and so forth."

I found myself nodding. "Many of the same things I did for Janine."

"Exactly! You'll have other responsibilities, of course, especially once you get a feel for what is needed. But for now, you'll be Sam's helper."

"You mean I'll be a well-paid, glorified Girl Friday."

For the first time, his smile looked like it might be sincere. "What's in a name?" he countered with a flick of his hand.

"Doesn't Mrs. Samson want to meet me first?" I asked. "We may not be compatible."

"Sam gets along with everyone," he assured me. "And she has full confidence in Ms. Morrow's judgment. I have no doubt the two of you will become the best of friends."

Been there, done that. No more mixing friendship with business, I silently vowed. This will be a job, nothing more. A very well-paying job, and enough to tide me over until I found something to my own liking.

"If you have no further questions, I'll get your benefits packet and terms of employment. I encourage you to take them home, look them over, and bring them back when you report to work. When would you like to start?"

When I did something, I believed in jumping in with both feet. "I have nothing pressing on my calendar," I told him. "I can start whenever you like."

"How about day after tomorrow? That will give you a day of orientation and the weekend off, before digging into the job next week."

"Yes. That's fine."

Simon reached across the desk to offer me his hand. "Wonderful! Welcome aboard, Lexi Graham."

I took his hand and shook it, mumbling my appreciation. Something about this entire situation still felt surreal. Perhaps even too good to be true.

I should have looked harder for those warning signs.

CHAPTER FIVE

Lexi

I took care of reissuing my driver's license before looking over the paperwork Simon had given me.

Samson Shipping offered an impressive benefit package. Comprehensive health care, dental care, and a generous expense account were just the beginning. There was also a credit card to purchase fuel, a courtesy card that would get me into the most exclusive spots in Galveston, reimbursement for using my own vehicle or, better yet, the option to drive one owned by the company. Simon had dropped that enticing tidbit just before I left. He said it was better than slap-footing it. When I looked puzzled, he flashed his fake smile. "Slap foot against pavement," he said.

At the time, the generous offer sounded wonderful, but I wasn't so sure. My brain hurt from absorbing it all.

Not for the first time, I wondered what my exact job would be. These benefits seemed like something for an executive within the company, not an assistant. The same could be said for the salary.

I nibbled on my lower lip. Was this company legit? Was this *job* even legit? Long ago, I learned that when something seemed too good to be true, it usually was.

I had to ask myself: if Samson Shipping was offering to pay me a fantastic salary and give me such impressive benefits, what was the catch? Because there had to be one. Offers like this didn't come along every day.

Simon said they were a multi-million-dollar company, but with practices like this, it wouldn't stay that way for long.

"They have to be doing something illegal," I decided aloud. "Whether they're dealing under the table or flat-out breaking the law, there is definitely something fishy going on."

An even bigger question to ask myself: was I expected to take part in illegal activities?

And how did I feel about that?

I wanted to say, unequivocally, that I would never agree to such. I had turned my back on that lifestyle. I was starting over. I was a law-abiding citizen now. I was done with my father's way of life.

My newly developed conscience nibbled at me.

Was turning my head to their deception any different? If I took this job, knowing in my bones that there was something very wrong there, wouldn't I already be taking part?

"Didn't you just hear yourself, Lex?" I chided. "Already, you're qualifying to what degree they break the law."

The law-abiding Lexi was right. I had done just that. Not two seconds earlier, I was thinking there was something fishy going on, whether they were 'dealing under the table' or flat-out breaking the law. But wasn't tax evasion breaking the law?

It wasn't up to me to decide the scale of justice when it came to obeying laws. Technically, evading taxes on a hundred dollars was the same as evading taxes on a hundred thousand. Both were stealing. Both were against the law. It wasn't my place to justify one but condemn the other.

That still left me with a dilemma. I knew turning down the job was probably the right thing to do morally, but not financially. A job flipping burgers might keep me off the streets, but another offer like this wouldn't just land in my lap. Assuming I did take the job, how far was I willing to go to keep it? It wasn't like I had never broken the law before, but there was this whole new starting over issue to consider.

It made my head hurt, deciphering the thin line between right and wrong. It wasn't always easy to see.

Growing up, I was taught that it all depended on the angle I chose when looking at that line. If a crime was committed against me, the line was in one place. If I committed the crime against someone else, the line was in another. The boundary, I grew up believing, was negotiable.

Early on, my father taught me that every single one of us had something that someone else wanted. If another person wanted it badly enough, it gave us bargaining power. Sometimes, it even gave us the power to shift the line between right and wrong.

"Whoa. Where are you going with this?" I asked aloud.

I shook my head, flinging my father's memory from my head.

Thoughts of my father always haunted me, but over the last few weeks, they'd plagued me more frequently. Maybe it was because I was doing my best to follow the straight and narrow, and because my father always had a way of derailing things for me.

Maybe it was because we had lived along the coast once before, up in New England. My father had been working a new angle to an old scam, and of course, he had needed an accomplice. Perhaps the unwanted memories of him blew in with the breeze. Perhaps they were triggered by the sound of the ocean. The animation surrounding the docks. The mournful cry from the big ships. The salty sting of sea water, burning into wounds not yet healed.

Or maybe it was because someone was following me. Someone had stolen my purse. If anything brought back unwanted thoughts of my father, it was that unsettling feeling of being watched, the need for my SAR mantra again, the survival instinct to get away, as fast and far as I could. To just run, despite my vow not to.

Maybe that was what this was about. My father was mocking me from his prison cell because this time, I swore it would be different. I *needed* it to be different.

I reluctantly admitted that another possibility existed. Maybe memories of him resurfaced because, deep down, I didn't believe I deserved this fresh start. After all I had done, I didn't deserve a do over.

What if this job with Samson Shipping was some sort of divine test? A chance to prove, if only to myself, that I was better than my father. That his blood might be running through my veins, but that didn't mean his twisted sense of morals were.

Needing to get out of my head as much as I needed to get out of my apartment, I risked losing my parking space again. I knew very little about my new hometown, and now was as good a time as any to familiarize myself with it. Everything beyond the wharfs and The Strand were still foreign to me.

I knew that Seawall Boulevard boasted the usual suspects: condos, hotels, restaurants catering to every palette and every pocketbook, souvenir shops, and countless stores that sold almost everything under the sun. It even had a historic board-walk named the Pleasure Pier.

Prompted by hunger pains, I stepped out of my normal routine and went for broke. As reckless as it seemed, today, I was trying out a new restaurant.

After a surprisingly delicious lunch, I spent an hour driving around Broadway, admiring the old mansions that lined the main drag from the ocean's edge to the causeway. I gaped at the huge old churches, the heavy influence of Victorian elegance, and the sad negligence of the twenty-first century. While waiting at a red light, I studied a gigantic bronze statue sitting smack dab in the middle of the intersection.

I wandered off Broadway, onto side streets brimming with more Victorian-style homes. None of them compared to the grand mansions a few streets over, but they had a beauty of their own. Some were restored to their former glory. Some were left to the mercy of the harsh salt air. Others were suspended somewhere in between, as if contemplating whether to fall down or rise to the occasion.

Even the cemeteries here were fascinating. Mausoleums and crypts protected the above-ground burial sites. Steel vaults, no doubt, protected those dug into the ground. I shivered when I thought about what a massive flood or hurricane could do to an island cemetery, so I concentrated on the oldest of the headstones and mausoleums. Many were true works of art, all the more so because they had been chiseled by hand. I read somewhere that the Old City Cemetery was at least two hundred years old.

As morbid as it sounded, I had always been fascinated by cemeteries. I liked the permanency they represented. Not because they housed dead bodies — that would just be sick — but because they gave their occupants a final resting place. A forever home, you might say.

It was something I had never had. For that reason, cemeteries brought me a peculiar comfort. I vowed to visit again when I could get out and stroll among the rows, reading the old stones and imagining the former lives of the people buried below.

Now, however, I had a new mission. It occurred to me that while Janine may have approved of my casually chic wardrobe, my new employer might expect something more professional. It wouldn't hurt to add some new pieces to my closet.

"Does that mean I'm taking the job?" I asked myself. I took a deep breath and made a decision. "For now, yes. I'll take the job. If I start to feel uncomfortable, or if they ask me to do something I feel uncertain about, I can always quit. There's no harm in padding my bank account until then."

Earlier, I had spotted a boutique that piqued my interest. The attractive window display suggested they had the look I was after. Professional, but not stuffy. Stylish, but not dressy. Something I could pair with the clothes I already owned to give them an elevated look of success. Something . . . grown up.

Yes, that was it. I parked and went into the store. I wanted to look grown up. It wasn't the same child who once trailed behind my father, guilelessly following his orders. This was the *new* me.

"There you go," I muttered beneath my breath, "thinking about him again. Focus, Lexi. Focus on finding a new wardrobe for your new job."

There were only a few other patrons shopping that day. Two of them were women a couple of decades older than me, making me rethink my style decisions. But one of the women had her cell phone to her ear as she thumbed through the selections, and from what little I could hear of the one-sided conversation, she was some sort of executive.

Maybe I was on the right track, after all.

The other woman had come in after me, but there was something vaguely familiar about her. I was certain I didn't know her. I knew very few people here in Galveston. Embarrassingly few.

I decided maybe I had seen her at Galveston Gusto, the one place I frequented most often. Or perhaps she worked at the little café down the block from my apartment. But she wore a badge and lanyard around her neck, and I didn't think they wore those there. I tried getting a better look at her badge without being obvious.

Uh-oh. Busted.

The woman caught my eye, offering me a tentative smile as she pulled a blouse from the rack.

"Great choice," I said, nodding to one of the ugliest creations I had ever seen in my life.

"You think?" She looked doubtful.

I shared her hesitation, but she had caught me looking, so I had to lie. "It brings out the blue in your eyes. You have lovely eyes, by the way." I had already told one whopper, so what was another?

"You think so? Why, thank you, shugah," she said with a wide smile.

She took the blouse to the register and paid for it. I discreetly watched, still curious about her. Her eyes sought mine as she reached the door and wiggled her fingers in farewell.

Where had I seen this woman before? It bugged me that I couldn't remember. I watched to see what kind of car she drove.

Blue minivan.

Figures, I thought with a grunt. Not only was she older and frumpier than me, but she drove a *minivan*. Not even one of the fun, sportier versions. This was a full-out minivan, the kind soccer moms and old people drove.

Okay. Maybe I really should try another store . . .

Doubts aside, I ended up buying two pairs of slacks and a lightweight blazer at the boutique. Then, wonder of wonders, I visited two more stores.

Believe me when I say that wandering in and out of legitimate businesses was still a new experience for me. In my past life, I had been more of the dart-in-and-grab-it sort of girl. It may or may not have included stopping at the cash registers. Today, it even gave me an odd thrill to go over my intended wardrobe budget. The old me would have used the five-finger discount.

Amazingly, when I pulled into the alley, I saw that no one had stolen my parking space. It was a Wednesday, meaning lighter traffic and fewer people ignoring the *Private Parking* signs.

As I stepped out of my car, I did the SAR routine. I didn't see anyone, but unease slithered across my skin. I grabbed my bags and hurried out of the alleyway and into the building.

The tension eased from my shoulders as I spread the newly acquired clothes across my bed. I felt a stirring of pride, knowing I had made good choices. Many of the new pieces worked with those already in my closet. I now had two weeks' worth of clothes that touted the woman-on-her-way-up vibe I was going for.

Now, to find out what my new job entailed, and where my aspirations of going up would lead me.

CHAPTER SIX

Lexi

I arrived ten minutes early, eager to make a good impression on my new boss. I was surprised to see that behind the glass-enclosed cubicles, other employees were busy at work.

"Am I late?" I asked with a crinkled brow. "I thought you said to be here at eight thirty."

"I did," Simon assured me, flashing me his faux smile. "But we're a shipping company, so that means early-morning deliveries, early-morning departures. Since you're not directly involved in the logistics side of the business, there's no need to miss your beauty sleep." He threw a glance my way, and I saw one of his rare, sincere smiles. "Not that you need it, of course."

"Thank you," I murmured demurely.

Inside, I was fuming. Was he *hitting* on me? Would this be *that* kind of job? Because if I had to sleep my way to the top, I would gladly wallow at ground zero. In my estimation, that was about where Simon rated. He had that *ick* vibe about him.

"We'll start with a tour," Simon said, seemingly oblivious to my discomfort.

In a blur of information overload, he led me down hallways, in and out of offices, pointed toward maps and charts, stopped at cubicle doorways, and almost left me as I drooled over the break room's selection of freshly-ground coffee beans. I met chipper Cindy the receptionist and remembered just two names of the cubicle dwellers: Howard with the bad haircut, and Donna with the dimples. I knew where the bathrooms and lounge were located, and I thought I could find my way to the boardroom. Otherwise, the last forty-five minutes had been too much to remember.

"Ready to go up and meet Sam?" Simon finally asked.

I refrained from rolling my eyes. *Finally!*

We stepped into the elevator and were whisked effortlessly away. This was a different elevator from the one I had taken earlier. This one was accessed by code and was on an entirely different level than most. The walls were burled wooden panels, the handrails were polished brass, and the floor appeared to be marble, even though I briefly wondered about the weight of natural stone.

This was obviously a private lift. I noticed there were no floor numbers, just two discreet buttons. Simon had pressed the top one.

Look at me, my very first day, and I'm already on the way up! A song from an old sitcom played in my head, something about moving on up.

The elevator eased to a gentle stop, and we exited into an elaborate foyer. The decor echoed that of the elevator. The difference was the gilded mirrors on the walls and the fresh floral bouquet taking center stage on the narrow entryway table. Two tapestry-covered chairs resided against one wall, separated by a floor lamp. It, too, was brass, with a cut-crystal globe.

Everything about the foyer screamed wealth. A feeling of unease crept over me.

"Right this way," Simon said, indicating the polished double doors. "Sam is expecting us."

We entered without knocking, stepping into yet another entryway, with yet another set of doors facing us.

Good Lord, how many doors did this woman hide behind? And why? Three possibilities went through my head. One, Lillian Samson went above and beyond to display her wealth. Two, she had something to hide. Three, she thought she needed protection.

A fourth possibility was: all of the above.

What had I gotten myself into?

At least the French doors ahead had glass panes. They were opaque and probably made of reinforced leaded glass, but they didn't block out the light.

Simon stepped around me to open the French doors, motioning me forward.

My unease skyrocketed. Belatedly, I recognized the first warning sign. I felt as if I were stepping into the lion's den.

Subconsciously, SAR kicked in. I scanned the apartment. I saw nothing of obvious concern, but something nagged at me. I assessed the lush furnishings and the over-the-top accents. Yet, like a fool, I didn't react. Not the way I should have. I should have gotten the hell out of there, right that minute.

I should have run.

The massive living room gave me a sense of déjà vu. I had never been there, but the feel of the place was eerily familiar. I knew the way the furniture was grouped together. Leather club chairs placed casually around the gas fireplace. An intimate grouping clustered near the floor-to-ceiling windows overlooking the bay. I knew the main seating area. Two couches — one of leather, one of brocade — on opposite sides of a Persian rug. All flanked by armchairs with ornately carved side tables and antique lamps. I knew the expensive vases. I knew the museum-quality artwork.

I knew the look, at any rate. I knew my new boss had the same tastes as my father.

And I knew that my stomach hurt, along with my head.

I suddenly felt claustrophobic in a room twice as large as my entire apartment.

Breathe, Lexi, I told myself. *Get a hold of yourself. Tons of people have the same tastes. Tons of people have this same style of decor. Breathe. This isn't your father's house. He has no influence here. Just breathe. He's not here. He's locked away now.*

Despite the five-finger discount, I hadn't always grown up a pauper, and certainly not in my teen years. The grab-and-dash thing was more like an exercise, which came in handy when we were on the run. Evading the law wasn't exactly cheap, you know. Especially with my father's extravagant taste for the finer things in life.

My father called himself an *artist*, but in truth, he was a con man. He could run a scam with the best of them and for the most part, it afforded us a life of wealth. Sometimes, the wealth was nothing more than an illusion, but more often than not, we had money. It just wasn't ours.

With his swarthy good looks and a vague resemblance to a couple of celebrities, my father was known to impersonate both a movie star and a famous musician. We hid behind the star treatment and the luxuries it provided, claiming a need for privacy.

Once, he even pretended to be a prince visiting from a foreign country. I, of course, was his young princess daughter. Playing a princess might sound like a fairytale come true, but *you* try sitting with your back ramrod straight, perched on the edge of your seat for minutes on end. It turned out to be my most challenging role of all. I had to learn all about proper etiquette, proper speaking, and, of course, keeping an ever-proper appearance. It was more nightmare than fairytale.

Before his world came crashing down around him, my father was living large. He had an apartment much like this one, filled with expensive baubles and antiques that held no sentimental significance at all. Their value was measured in social status. He could host a dinner party and drop casual comments about picking up this signed masterpiece in Milan, that ivory bust in Greece, or the diamond-studded pincushion in a quaint little antique shop along the Rhine. They were nothing but props in his game of subterfuge.

He was addicted to money. He was addicted to the power he thought it gave him. He was addicted to the over-the-top lifestyle and to the underside of the law that made it possible.

"Lexi?" Simon's concerned voice pulled me back from the rabbit hole. I had zoned out for a minute there, lost within the tunnels of my father's underground world.

"I-I'm sorry," I stuttered. "It's . . . a lot to take in."

"Impressive, isn't it?" It was another of his rare sincere smiles. His eyes glittered in appreciation, and with something I suspected was greed. I wasn't clear on his job title or even his position here at Samson Shipping. I assumed he was second in command, but what if he were heir to the throne, so to speak? Would all of this be his one day? That could explain the look.

I found enough of my voice to murmur, "It's really something."

It was vague enough to sound like a compliment. I hadn't meant it as such. It was something that brought back bad memories of bad times. Something that set my nerves on edge. Something that repulsed me.

Something I will be working in every day.

The pain in my head intensified.

The pounding tempo almost drowned out Simon's next words. "If you'll step this way, I'd like to introduce you to the CEO of Samson Shipping."

We turned right, into a wide hallway. "Powder room," he said as we passed the first door. At the second, he said, "Your office." I only caught a brief glimpse as we proceeded down the hall. "It connects to this, which is Sam's office."

The door was open, welcoming us inside. My eyes quickly assessed the room. It was a generous size and slightly less pretentious than the living room. At least this space was brighter, with light-colored walls and plenty of light. The windows faced the street and were covered with a gauzy fabric of pale green. With a bird's-eye view of the city and the ocean beyond, I vaguely wondered if the elevator had skipped a few floors. In the center of the room was a massive desk, cluttered with two computer monitors, papers, file folders, discarded candy wrappers, and an elaborately carved cigar box. A cigar smoldered nearby, giving off hints of sweet, smoky leather and old library books. The smell took me back to my childhood when my father smoked. He gave up the habit in later years but kept a box similar to this one on hand, if for no other reason than to impress clients and colleagues.

The unwanted memory was the only explanation I had for failing to notice my new boss. I mean, how could I *not* notice the woman?

Before I could school my face into a neutral expression, I'm certain my shock was evident. Lillian Samson sat behind the desk, which, considering her size, no longer looked so massive. She was easily the largest woman I had ever seen.

I told myself not to look. To focus on her face, not her body. There could be a medical reason the woman was so large. Perhaps she had a metabolic disorder of some kind, or mobility issues.

At least she didn't try to camouflage her size behind dark, somber colors and nondescript clothes. Instead, she wore the multi-colored floral pattern with confidence.

An old saying drifted into my mind. "If you got it, flaunt it." I had to admire her attitude.

I forced my eyes up and remembered to smile, still trying to overcome my shock.

"Lexi, may I present to you the CEO of Samson Shipping, Lillian Samson."

"It's Sam." The woman's voice was rough but not unfriendly. Particularly since I had just ogled her with something akin to morbid fascination. She was used to it, I was sure, but it didn't excuse my rudeness. She thrust out her hand, which was strangely small in comparison to her body.

I took her offered hand, finding her grip strong and sure. "Lexi Graham. It's a pleasure to meet you, Mrs. Samson."

"Sam. Call me Sam." Her gravelly voice made it an order, as her icy blue eyes bore into mine. For a moment, it felt like some crazy challenge. A test of sorts. Then she broke out in laughter and shook my hand so hard, my entire arm wobbled.

"Well, now, Lexi. Take a load off and tell me about yourself." She motioned to the chair in front of her desk.

I already had the job, so there was no reason to sell her on my finer points. "There's not a lot to tell, really. I put myself through college, double majoring in business and office management, with a minor in art. I've worked in a variety of positions, my last being with J.M. Creations, as I believe you know." I hoped my rambling introduction sounded more impressive than my actual work history. It was hard to build much of a resume when I kept moving, trying to outrun my father's shadow.

"Yes, and after reading Janine's glowing recommendation, I knew you were just the person I was looking for." There was that look in her eyes again, that hint of a challenge. I shifted in my seat, suddenly not so confident about having the job. Maybe I should have talked more about my academic record or my work ethics. Maybe I should have embellished my employment record, although any employer worth their salt would have already checked it out.

"You're a friend of Janine?" I asked, shifting the focus away from myself.

"More of a patron," she corrected, "although I'd like to think that extends to friendship. I have several of her paintings, one of which is in the formal dining room."

I had never seen this woman at any of Janine's art exhibits, so it had to have been a private sale. An online purchase, perhaps. I tried to remember if I had ever seen her name on an invoice.

"Either way, her word is good enough for me. If Janine says you're okay, then you're okay."

It seemed a reckless way to hire an employee, but who was I to argue? I wanted a job, and Sam had one available. No negotiation needed.

For the briefest of moments, I wished my father were here so I could rub it in his face. Not everything in life was a trade-off. Not everything was a game, played with kings and pawns. I had gotten this job on my own merits, no bargaining required.

The wish was fleeting, not to mention foolish. Not even I needed validation badly enough to wish for my father's presence!

"I appreciate that," I told my new boss.

"I trust that Simon provided you with an information packet and your employment contract. Any questions about the paperwork? You're free to go over it with your attorney if you like."

I hid my scoff. Attorney? The only attorneys I knew — the ones from my father's world — were as crooked as a winding mountain road.

"That's not necessary. I've already signed it and given it to Mr. Brewster."

I had almost forgotten he was in the room, until the man spoke from behind me. "Please, I insist you call me Simon. We'll be on the same team. No need for formalities."

Foolishly, I ignored the little voice inside my head. The voice that asked why I needed a contract in the first place, especially one that included a non-disclosure clause. The voice that balked at the thought of being on the 'same team' as these people.

I would live to regret my oversight.

CHAPTER SEVEN

Lexi

Despite my jump-in-with-both-feet mentality, I swear my feet were getting cold.

I spent Saturday trying to settle my nerves.

I went for a walk. I made a long loop, going left from my apartment for two blocks, crossing the street, and coming back in from the right. It left me hot and sweaty, but every bit as stressed as when I started. More so, given my SAR obsession.

I thought the roar of the ocean would do the trick, so I tried strolling along the beach. The rideshare deposited me at the water's edge, where a couple of hundred other people and I vied for the sand between the seawall and the sudsy waves. Because it was the weekend, there were too many tourists out and about, and it seemed every single one of them had either a blaring radio, a barking dog, or a crying kid. Some had all three.

I came back home and gave a hot bath a try. I even added some bath salts Janine had given me in a little gift basket one time. The package claimed they had therapeutic qualities to relax achy muscles, reduce stress, and create inner healing. I reminisced about the day she gave them to me. I had pulled a muscle in my back while loading some of her pieces into the delivery van, and she insisted I take the day off to recuperate. Janine was thoughtful like that, giving me random presents for no reason at all, or little surprises to brighten my day. But using the salts made me think of my friend, so then I ended up depressed, as well as stressed.

I tried reading, but the romance was too sappy and over the top for me. And for some crazy reason, the hero in the book brought to mind the lawman I had seen in Galveston Gusto. Sure, the guy was good-looking, but he had been laughing at me. Plus, he was the *law*, of all things.

With a hard pass on the romance and its irritating hero, I slammed my e-reader case shut.

I tried watching a highly lauded movie. I found it on pay-per-view and settled onto my couch with a bowl of popcorn and a cola. Unfortunately, the movie was about organized crime, which was too close for comfort to be considered entertainment. My nerves couldn't take any more, so I turned off the television and found a bottle of Jack Daniels. I poured a generous amount into what was left of my cola, thinking it might be the thing to help.

The first glass didn't do much for me, but the second one settled my nerves enough that I gave a third glass a try.

I fell asleep before I could try a fourth.

Sunday was my scheduled day to clean the apartment. According to one of my many self-help books, housework was a good way to reduce stress.

Through the years, I had read a lot of those types of books. With a past like mine, I probably should have been in therapy, but when I broke away from my father, I made it a clean break. Professional counseling was out of the question, but I could manage a self-help book here and there. I usually bought them at a used or half-off bookstore, so I was always a trend or two behind on that front. Still, the outdated methods were better than no method at all.

Some of the books said it was good to stick to a regular schedule. I may have overdone it a bit and become, dare I admit, *too* predictable. But I found it comforting, and it was one of the few objectives I could complete, much less excel at.

What the book didn't say was that strenuous housekeeping was also a good way to pull a muscle, so I ended up in the tub again. That time, I knew to skip the salts, even without reading it in a book.

The previous week had definitely thrown me off my carefully orchestrated schedule. It was no wonder I was a nervous wreck. What better way to find comfort, I mused, than with a meal? My favorite deli, the one where I bought my normal soup and sandwich combo, closed early on Sundays. I had to hustle to get out of the tub, into clean clothes, and over to the shop before it closed.

Before you think I had become too obsessed with this keeping a normal routine thing, you should know I sometimes mixed things up by ordering jambalaya instead of soup. And if I really went out on a limb, I snubbed the sandwich all together and went for a salad. Call me crazy.

SAR didn't reveal anyone following me on the way to the deli. I had ruled out reading a book or watching any action-type movie again that night, so there was no reason to rush back. Since I was already bored at home, I opted to eat there in the deli.

I had gotten my phone replaced but I was still learning how to use it. Some of the buttons and apps had changed. As someone opposed to change, I didn't handle this well. I was busy trying to figure it all out when someone bumped into the edge of my table.

"I'm so sorry, shugah," the woman said. "Sometimes, I can be so clumsy!"

It took me a moment to answer. It was the same woman I had seen at the clothes boutique. The one who drove the minivan. Was it strange that I should see her twice in just a couple of days? Because it felt strange.

She didn't seem to recognize me, so maybe I was being paranoid. "No problem," I said with a tight smile.

In my head, though, I was wondering if I had a problem.

* * *

Halfway into my first full week of work, I had to wonder exactly what my job was. So far, I had done nothing of real use.

Sam had sent me on a handful of errands, but anyone within the company could have done them. I was certain someone went to the post office on a nearly daily basis, but for whatever reason, Sam wanted me to personally take her handwritten correspondences out to mail.

With her money, I would imagine that any florist in town would be thrilled to deliver the fresh centerpieces she liked so well. But no. She sent me to pick them up. I went to the grocery store for her and to the corner drugstore to pick up a certain brand of cough drops she preferred. Instead of giving me a list of places to stop while I was already running errands, she strung the requests out during the day. If I hadn't known better, I would think she was just inventing things for me to do.

After just three days, the senseless errands had gotten old. I wanted to do something important. Something meaningful. I could only arrange and rearrange my desk so many times.

My desk was considerably smaller than Sam's and not nearly as cluttered. Since I hadn't been entrusted with any files or important papers, none littered my desktop. I did, however, have a fancy brass nameplate engraved with my name and the useless title of 'Personal Assistant.'

Were Rolodexes still a thing? I wondered. Because that would give me at least *something* that looked meaningful on my desk, other than the phone and the computer monitor.

I couldn't complain about my workspace. My office offered the same amazing vista as Sam's. The living room may have offered a great view of the ship channel and the bay beyond, but from my window, I could see over the city, all the way to the ocean. Our offices connected via a wide door in the middle of one wall, so the decor matched. Same light walls, same fixtures, same pale-green curtains.

And though the living room arrangement still made me uncomfortable, working in a penthouse wasn't exactly a hardship.

The kitchen and dining room were on the opposite side of the apartment from our offices. Simon said there was an ensuite guest room, as well as another hallway powder room. The huge living room yawned between the two ends. I wasn't sure of the square footage, but I assumed the apartment took up an entire floor. Something told me that Sam's private quarters were probably equal in size to the living room.

In my opinion, other than the views, the kitchen was the prettiest part of the entire apartment. The cabinets were painted a vivid blue and fitted with gold hardware. The light-colored granite made the space bright and airy.

The blue was repeated in the upholstered chairs in the dining room. Something about the color seemed familiar. Didn't Janine use this particular shade in many of her paintings? It was used in the large painting above the buffet, but I was almost positive I had seen it in several other pieces of her art. Had Sam commissioned the piece because of the chairs, or was it the other way around? Maybe she had liked the painting so well, she had used it as inspiration for the chairs in here and for her kitchen cabinets. Maybe one day, I'd ask her.

I learned that a maid came twice a week to clean the massive space. She cooked for both of us on those days and left easy-to-warm-up meals for when she wasn't there.

On that first day, I had gone to the dining room to eat, thinking my boss would join me there. But as I sat alone at a table that seated ten, it occurred to me that I had never seen Sam stand.

Could she? A woman of her size would surely have trouble walking, so did that mean she used a wheelchair? Maybe that was the reason all the doorways were so wide. Could that also be the reason I was instructed to *never*, under any circumstances, go into her bedroom?

Not that I would. A person's bedroom was their personal space. Hers was at the end of the hall, adjacent to her office. It would be a short walk — or roll, as the case may have been — to move between the two.

I had never seen Sam anywhere other than seated behind her desk. I originally thought the door between our offices was for ease of communication. She could call out a request or directive, and I would do it. Our desks were situated to face one another, making direct interaction possible when the door was opened. Yet whenever Sam needed me, she used the phone's intercom or sent me an email. The door between our offices had stood open exactly once.

Was it because she couldn't, or didn't, walk?

I had to wonder if, eventually, I would be expected to help Sam to and from her chair. I wasn't sure how I felt about that. During my interview with Simon, I made it plain that I wasn't a nurse, and he had assured me that Sam was perfectly capable of caring for herself. But now, after seeing her, I knew her size must present some unique challenges. I sympathized with her, but enough to take care of her personal needs? I wasn't so sure.

Did that make me a bad person? Possibly. But at least I was being honest with myself.

I liked Sam well enough, but the way she watched me sort of freaked me out. She was friendly and sometimes teased me, borderline laughing at my expense. She had an odd sense of humor, but then again, so did I. But sometimes, when she thought I wasn't looking, I saw her watching me. She reminded me of a lion, stalking its prey. Any minute, I expected her to pounce. Which was crazy, I knew, but it was still there, somewhere in the back of my mind.

That first day I met her, I had an eerie suspicion she was testing me. She had looked at me so strangely, her blue eyes boring into mine. I decided that was what was going on. It was a test, and she was judging how well I fared.

Maybe if I passed, she would give me more responsibility. Because, frankly, my job here was just as boring as sitting at home in my apartment. It definitely paid better, but I wasn't the kind to sit around and do nothing. It gave me too much time to think. Too much time to stress out.

Being here, in an apartment filled with so many things that reminded me of the man I wanted to forget, thinking wasn't a good thing. Knowing someone was keeping tabs on me made me all the more nervous. With so much time to think, I could come up with all sorts of scenarios, none of them good.

Even on that first week, I wished Sam had found me lacking and just fired me.

CHAPTER EIGHT

Galveston Memorial Hospital

The labor and delivery floor at Galveston Memorial was always a bustling place, and today was no exception.

Doctors moved from one delivery room to another, hidden behind masks and scrubs as they scurried to bring another life into the world.

Nurses bounced between rooms, carrying warm blankets on their way in and swaddled babies on their way out.

Nervous fathers paced the floor.

Impatient mothers waddled down the corridor with their rounded bellies and portable IV poles, frustrated with the stalled progression of their labor.

Call buttons tapped out a steady tune of need, keeping nurses and aides on their toes.

Proud grandparents huddled around the nursery window, pointing to which wrinkly, scrunched-up face belonged to them. Some of the family members held big brother or big sister up so they, too, could see the newest member of the clan.

Patient rooms were on the opposite end of the floor, where the sound of crying babies and the stale scent of dirty diapers reigned. Wreaths and door hangers marked the entrance to almost every room, touting the newborn's name, birth weight, and length. They even assumed the newborn's interests. Woven into the ribbons and bows were everything from teddy bears to horses, cheer megaphones to deer antlers, mini surfboards to ballerina tutus.

At the nurses' station, circus animals in checkered pastels tumbled across the cabinets and rode a train along the bottom of the waist-high counter.

A heavyset, gray-haired woman stood there now, smiling and chatting with the nurses behind the desk. Grandma Gail, as they called her, always brought them a treat when she came, and today's offering was a selection of cookies and scones from Galveston Gusto.

One of the nurses squealed in delight. "Ooh, a lemon and blueberry scone. That's my favorite!"

Grandma Gail chuckled. "I know it is, sugar. That's why I brought it." Her heavy Southern accent made the casual endearment sound like 'shugah.' After an appropriate pause, she switched to professional mode. "I hear we have a new mom?"

"Yes." Another nurse nodded. "Room 347. Her name is Veronica. She needs help getting the hang of nursing."

Grandma Gail smiled. "That's what I'm here for, sugar." With a wave of her fingers, she shuffled down the hallway.

Knocking on the door of 347, she waited for permission to enter. Hearing the invitation, she entered with a warm smile on her face.

"Hello, dear. My name is Gail Bickers, but everyone just calls me Grandma Gail. And you're Veronica, is that right?"

"Yes, ma'am. Veronica Hardy." A small woman, her eyes rimmed with worry, lay propped up in bed, holding a blue bundle. Frustration wrinkled her otherwise pretty face as the baby cried.

"And this little precious bundle of love?" Grandma asked, moving forward to peer at the baby's red, angry face.

51

"Donnie."

"Ah, a traditional name for a change." The older woman nodded in appreciation. "With all these new names floating around lately, it's good to hear a good, old-fashioned name. I always say they have more substance than the latest trend."

"He's named after my husband, Donald," the new mother explained.

"And where is Mr. Hardy?" Grandma Gail made a show of looking around the room.

"He went home to grab a shower and a change of clothes."

"Much needed, I'm sure."

Veronica looked at her in hope. "Are you the lactationist they told me about?"

"The official term is lactation consultant," Grandma Gail corrected. "Actually, I'm an international board-certified lactation consultant." She rolled her eyes. "I know, it's a mouthful and too long to put on my badge." She tapped the white nametag dangling from around her neck. It stated her name and the acronym IBCLC. Her eyes went back to the baby. "Now. Let's do something about this little guy's crying."

"I don't know what to do!" Veronica wailed, tears welling in her own eyes. "He just keeps crying!"

"First of all, you need to relax. Babies pick up on what you're feeling. If you're nervous, they're nervous."

"Of course I'm nervous. I don't have enough milk for my baby! Maybe I should just give up and use formula . . ."

"Don't give up without an honest try, sugar. You just have to give yourself time to get the knack of it."

"And let my baby starve in the meantime?"

Grandma Gail chuckled. "I don't mean to make light of the situation, but Donnie is far from starving. He just needs a little TLC and MTM."

Veronica frowned in confusion. There was so much she didn't know about being a mother! Over the past seven months, she had read dozens of books. Books about maternity. Books about labor. Books about newborns. Books about breastfeeding. Books about the first three months. Not a single one of them had mentioned anything about MTM, whatever that was.

"MTM?" she asked.

"It's the magic formula. Mom's Titty Milk."

The words sounded strange coming from the older woman's mouth. "Oh."

"There's nothing to be embarrassed about, sugar. It's what the good Lord intended. That's the sole purpose of a woman's breasts, no matter what fashion and men have to say on the subject. Now, let's get down to business. Let me see you feed little Donnie here."

"You mean . . . now? In front of you?"

"How else can I help you, dear Veronica? I have to see your technique, so I can give you tips and suggestions."

When the new mother hesitated, Grandma Gail encouraged her in a gentle voice. "Honestly, sugar, it's the most natural thing in the world. There's no reason to be ashamed." Without permission, she leaned over the bed and pushed the flap of Veronica's hospital gown open. "Can't keep the milk bottle capped and expect little Donnie to eat, now can you?"

"I-I guess not," Veronica agreed. Her cheeks were stained a deep red.

"I don't mean to make you uncomfortable, but you do realize he'll get hungry at random times, right? He doesn't care if you're in the middle of dinner or in the middle of the mall. He's going to expect his MTM, and you'll have to whip it out, same way you would whip out a bottle."

"In . . . public?" the new mother squeaked, looking aghast.

"Little Donnie won't know, and he won't care. He'll just want his titty."

Veronica started shaking her head. "Maybe this isn't the best idea, after all."

"That's up to you, of course. I would never dream of forcing this upon you, or making such an important decision for you," Grandma Gail assured her. The disappointed look in her eyes didn't match her words. "Just know that mother's milk is the best thing for your baby. It's economical, efficient, and best of all, it's all-natural. Studies suggest breast babies have the least number of allergies and food sensitivities. It's a truly healthy alternative to formula, and there's no fuss and muss of baby bottles and warmers. There's a slight inconvenience to mothers, of course, but it's the least we can do for our little angels, don't you agree?"

Veronica's reply was mumbled. "I guess so." It was obvious she wasn't quite convinced.

"You don't have to decide this moment. Let's see how this session goes, shall we?"

"I'll give it a try."

Grandma Gail presented her with a broad smile. "That's my little momma!"

CHAPTER NINE

Lexi

To my surprise, Sam had given me the morning off. She said she had business to attend downtown, so she wouldn't be in the office until afternoon. She told me to meet her back there around one, because she had a project she needed my help with.

After I left her office, I smirked and wondered what kind of 'project' she had come up with this time. Maybe she wanted me to select a new centerpiece based on her favorite stamp motif.

With the morning off, I took my time getting dressed. I put on a new pair of sandy-brown slacks, a simple blouse in the same shade, and topped it with one of my short-sleeved cardigans, this one a rich mocha color. The darker shade set off my blond hair and brought out the amber flecks in my eyes.

Before long, I would need to visit the hair stylist. My darker roots were just beginning to show. In my old life, I had dark, wavy hair that I wore short and sassy.

When I came to Galveston, I knew I wanted a completely different look. It had taken *forever* for my hair to grow past my shoulders. I had my hair professionally straightened, so without the curl, it reached my shoulder blades. And I had it dyed blonde. It was about as far from the old me as I could get.

In the ten years since I had left my father's world, I had gone through many different disguises. Different names, different cities, different hairstyles. I hated moving around, pretending to be someone I wasn't. I hated making a living under false pretenses. It felt like I was reverting to my formative years, those years when my father dragged me around on his latest scam. It felt like I was pulling a scam of my own.

But I knew my father well enough to know that he wouldn't allow me to just walk away. *No one* walked away from the mighty Leo Drakos. Certainly, no one who knew his secrets.

Dressed and with time to kill, I treated myself to a leisurely cup of coffee at Galveston Gusto. I found a table against the wall that faced the window, another trick I had learned from my father. It seemed that no matter how far and fast I ran, there were some habits I just couldn't outrun.

I reached into my purse and pulled out my sketchpad and pencil. That was one of the reasons I carried the big bag. It held all my stuff. It came in particularly handy when I worked for Janine. It not only carried all my stuff, but half of hers.

I wondered how she was getting along without me. I knew that sounded pompous. She had managed before I came along, and I'm sure she could manage once I left. Still, I did *everything* for the woman. Not just the business stuff, but I reminded her to eat, to take a break, to go to her nieces' birthday parties. The creative spirit in her overruled practicality.

Shaking thoughts of my former boss aside, I put pencil to paper. Once I was more established at Samson Shipping, I would ask Sam if I could add a few personal touches to my office. Plants seemed like a good jumping-off point. They weren't only aesthetic, but they added a bit of vitality to the space. I made a rough sketch of my office and added a couple of potted plants. New wall art would be nice, too.

Lost in thought, I jumped when someone appeared at my table.

"A sausage pastry for the lady," the young woman said. I had seen her behind the counter before, but I didn't know her name. Raven was the only one I had ever made a connection with, weak as it was.

"Oh, I didn't order anything," I said, correcting her mistake.

"Compliments of the handsome gentleman over there," she told me, tipping her head.

Following her direction, I saw him. The man I pegged as a lawman. Today, he was dressed in khakis and a navy shirt, but he wore the same hat and boots. When he caught my gaze, a small smile played around the corners of his mouth.

My eyes narrowed, trying to decide his game. My response made his smile widen.

I accepted the pastry grudgingly. It wasn't her fault that the man was laughing at me. I left it untouched as I finished my drawing.

"I hope you don't mind my token of apology." The deep voice beside me could only belong to one person. I reluctantly pulled my eyes up to his. Dang it! They were dark and chocolaty. Easily addictive.

I kept my voice cool, pretending not to understand his reference. "Apology?"

"For my rude behavior the other day." His eyes fell to the empty chair beside me. "May I?"

I wanted to say no. Nothing good would come from associating with this man. But he had bought me a pastry, and his apology seemed sincere. *Just this once*, I told myself.

It wasn't the friendliest of invitations, but I shrugged my shoulders and bumped the chair toward him with my foot.

He took the seat, taking a moment to arrange his own pastry and coffee in front of him. I noticed he had a sausage croissant like mine.

Noticing the direction of my gaze, it was his turn to shrug. "You seemed to enjoy it, so I thought I'd give it a try."

"You mentioned an apology?" I asked testily.

"Honestly, I wasn't laughing at you the other day. I was just . . . amused."

"Same thing."

"No, it wasn't like that. It was refreshing, actually, seeing someone take time to truly appreciate a meal. It seems everyone is in such a rush. We just gobble down our food, without really appreciating it. I was impressed with your thorough absorption in your meal."

I held in a snort. I had been absorbed all right, trying not to think of my troubles. It had been the only way I could keep from freaking out. Not that I would ever tell this man that.

I gave him a look. "Somehow, that doesn't sound like much of an apology. Are you calling me a pig?"

I have to admit. When his dark eyes flickered over my body, I felt a tiny thrill. Very tiny. He was a lawman, after all. I could never be attracted to his kind.

"Hardly a pig," he drawled.

What was it with Texans and their accent? It wasn't always so obvious, until they wanted to make a point. It slipped in on insults and compliments, especially when the compliments were spoken slow and sexy.

Whoa. What was I thinking! Sexy? No way.

"I could see you dissecting the different flavors," he continued. "What are you, a chef?"

Funny he should say that. I had pretended to be one in Ohio. I got busted when a patron requested beef Wellington and I had created a disaster, instead.

"No," I said. "Just someone who appreciates good food, even if it is served in a coffee shop."

"Don't let Betty hear you say that. She might take offense."

"Betty? Is she the one who brought this?" I hitched a thumb toward the untouched pastry.

"No. Betty is the owner and the one behind all the original recipes. She caters, you know, so it's not exactly run-of-the-mill frozen fare."

"Oh."

He nodded to my sausage croissant. "Aren't you hungry?"

I would have denied it, but my traitorous stomach chose that moment to let out a growl. Wordlessly, I reached for the plate.

We ate in silence for several minutes. I wasn't even offended when he closed his eyes and tried to decipher the flavors like I had done.

"Mmm. I like that kick of chorizo in there," he said.

"There's a little cumin, too," I volunteered.

"I see why you like these."

We finished eating, which presented a problem. Conversation. I nursed my coffee, finding it almost empty.

"Can I get that freshened up for you?"

I still don't know why I agreed.

He caught Raven's eye and motioned for refills. She was the sort of barista who remembered everyone's order.

"You have a talent," he said, nodding to my sketchpad.

"It's just a pastime." I shrugged off the compliment.

"Looks professional enough to me. Are you an interior decorator?"

I couldn't decide if he was making conversation or being nosy. I played it safe and asked, "Why do you ask?"

"It looks like you were trying to figure out where to hang artwork." He touched my sketchpad with a long finger, pointing to a half-drawn picture frame.

"Just trying to decide how to decorate my new office."

"Promotion?"

"New job."

"Oh yeah? Where do you work?"

I still couldn't decide if his questions went beyond friendly small talk, but I answered, "Samson Shipping."

It was subtle, but I saw the way his face tightened.

"You're familiar with them?" I asked.

"Everyone in Galveston is familiar with Samson Shipping."

His reply was cryptic. Other than a fleeting expression in his dark eyes, he gave no indication of what he was thinking.

"Is that good, or bad?" I asked. Somehow, I was the one asking questions now.

"Just a fact."

I didn't relish depending on this man for information, but there was no one I could ask. Anyone within the company, particularly Simon, wouldn't give a straight-forward answer out of loyalty to our boss. So, I asked this man.

"Then you know my boss, Sam?"

"Not personally," he said. "But I'm familiar with her name and her business acumen."

"She certainly seems to be successful if her offices are any indication. I think she owns the whole building." I was putting out feelers, as discreetly as possible.

My companion nodded. "She owns and operates one of the biggest shipping companies in the city." He leaned back as our coffees were delivered. "Thanks, Paula," he said, pressing a twenty into her hand. "Keep the change."

He had never had the sausage croissant before, but if he knew everyone by name, he had to be a regular. I kept the observation to myself. Other than information on Sam, I wasn't encouraging this conversation.

As if reading my thoughts, he asked, "What's she like? Your boss, I mean."

I thought about his question before answering. "It's hard to say. She's . . . different. There's an edge to her personality . . ."

"Well, she *is* a shrewd businesswoman," he pointed out.

"It's more than that." I was talking more to myself than to him. "Her words will be sharp, but then all of a sudden, she laughs. It's like she's playing with me. It's . . . weird."

"Sounds like it. What is it you do there? Do you interact with her much?"

I realized I had revealed more about myself to this man than intended. Not that I had said much, but I had planned to say nothing at all. I took a gulp of coffee, forgetting that it was hot. I all but spit it back out, along with a curse.

"Are you okay?" he asked, looking concerned.

"Fine," I croaked, my eyes watering. "Hot."

He sounded mildly amused. "No joke."

This man had laughed at me for the last time. I stuffed my sketchpad into my purse and straightened the clutter in front of me.

"You're leaving?" He sounded surprised.

I sounded pissed. Which I was. "Nothing escapes you, does it?" I snarked.

"I did it again, didn't I?"

"You mean because I burned my tongue off and you just laughed? No, of course not."

"Look. I didn't mean anything by it. It was just the look on your face and the way you tried to play it off."

"I'm glad my facial expressions amuse you so much. I accepted the croissant as your apology, so there's no reason to continue this conversation." I pushed back my chair and stood.

"Yet I offended you a second time."

"And you bought me coffee. All even."

I turned to leave.

"I'm Jack, by the way," he called to my retreating back.

I made no comment as I pushed through the door and into the humid Gulf air.

* * *

When I arrived back at the office, Sam was already behind her desk. I wondered if I would ever see her without the barrier between us.

"Enjoy your morning off?" she asked, watching me with those icy blue eyes again.

I wasn't sure my conversation with the man named Jack would count as enjoyment, so I offered a noncommittal answer. "I spent most of it drinking coffee."

She kept watching me. Had she driven by the coffee shop and seen me inside?

So what if she had?

"Have a seat, Lexi," she said. When she nodded to the chair opposite her, her multiple chins folded under one another. "Yesterday, I mentioned a special project I needed your help with."

"Yes, I remember. What did you have in mind?" I hoped it was finally something more meaningful than running silly errands for her.

"You may not know this, but I'm a big contributor to many important organizations throughout the city."

When she seemed to be waiting for a reply, I murmured, "That's very commendable of you."

"I do what I can." Which I took to mean: *I give a mere portion of what I can afford.* "One of my pet projects is the children's wing at the hospital."

Hearing this, I almost felt guilty for my uncharitable thoughts. "That's very nice of you. It sounds like a worthy cause."

"It's heartbreaking to think of those little children, scared and suffering without their parents there with them."

I cocked my head to one side. "Parents aren't allowed in their children's rooms?"

"They're allowed, of course, but they can't always be there. Which is why I'd like to volunteer my services."

Maybe I had misjudged this woman. "Wow," I said, duly impressed. "That's very generous of you."

"There's one problem."

Something in her tone made me a little less impressed. "A problem?"

"Obviously, I'm a very busy woman. I have a business to run. Phones to answer, appointments to keep, correspondence to return." She rolled her hand as if to keep the list rolling.

"I'd be happy to help you with those things," I was quick to say. "In fact, I assumed that was part of my job description." I went out on a limb and pressed. "As your assistant, I thought I would assist you in those duties."

"All in good time. You've just started, and I thought you should get the feel of the place before jumping in."

So far, I had a better feel for the post office and the florist than I did for Samson Shipping.

"This volunteer project is very important to me, Lexi, and I need you to be on board with this." I was being reprimanded, but I wasn't sure for what. It's not like I had objected. I had offered to pick up the slack — aka *DO MY JOB* — while she was out of the office.

I offered my best smile. "Of course I'm on board. I think you volunteering is a great show of support for your community, and a shining example to other CEOs." Maybe I was spreading it on a little thick, but I didn't understand the censure I had heard in her voice.

"Then you'll do this for me?"

Had I zoned out? Did I miss part of the conversation? Because I had no idea what she was talking about.

I knew I sounded confused when I repeated, "Do? Do what for you?"

"Take my place."

Hadn't I just sat here and said that very thing? I told her I assumed it was part of my duties. We didn't seem to be on the same page.

My frown must have been evident, because she barked out, "You don't like children?" Her voice was rougher than normal, which meant it sounded like a growling bulldog.

"I like children." I said the words too quickly. I didn't really know whether I liked them or not. I had never been around many, even back when I was one.

"Good. Then you should enjoy your time there."

This conversation kept getting stranger. "Where?"

"At the hospital. Volunteering on my behalf, of course." Sam acted like I should already know this. "I'm much too busy to squeeze it in, but I'll free up your schedule so you can go once or twice a week."

I just stared at her in disbelief. Of all the thoughts that were running through my head at the moment, one stood out.

If my schedule were any freer, I would be home in my pajamas right now.

CHAPTER TEN

Lexi

One week down, but it felt more like one month.

I opened the door to my apartment, threw my purse into the armchair, and flung my body across the couch.

"Oh. My. God." I spoke to the ceiling fan above me. "Could this job be any more boring? And now, she wants me to volunteer? At a children's hospital?" I pulled a throw pillow over my face and considered smothering myself.

I should look at my contract. Hadn't I seen something about a two-week trial period? Maybe if I made a really big mess of things like I had that time with the beef Wellington, she would fire me and get me out of my misery.

"That's a little hard to do, though," I said aloud, "since I literally have no responsibilities. Picking up the wrong flower arrangement doesn't constitute firing someone. So . . . what if she sends me to the post office again, and I lose an important-looking letter? Or change a zip code, so that it floats around in postal service la-la land for a few weeks?" I felt a spark of hope. "Maybe if I did all the above, it would be three strikes, and I'm out. Worth a try, huh, Lex?"

For the next hour or so, I plotted ways I could hasten my demise within Samson Shipping. It would leave me without a job again, but I was resourceful. When the delivery person came with the pizza I ordered, I could ask if they were hiring. Driving around town delivering pizzas would be a good way to learn about the area, right?

"Maybe I'm looking at this wrong," I told my ceiling after a while, once again sprawled across the couch. "Instead of trying to get fired, maybe I should be looking for ways to make myself useful. I could study up on the company over the weekend, and on Monday morning, dazzle Sam with my impressive knowledge. That sounds easier than convincing her to let me do something, just so I can purposely screw it up."

I ate my pizza at the computer as I pulled up every article I could find on Samson Shipping.

Like Sam said, she was a big contributor to local charities and organizations, but that didn't mean the company didn't have its share of negative publicity. It appeared that for all her philanthropy, Lillian Samson had equal amounts of controversy in her life.

Two years ago, there were allegations of bribing a public official.

"Hmph," I snorted. "Sounds like something my father would have done. Oh wait. Something he *did* do."

Just prior to the accusation against Sam, the shipping company's senior accountant had committed suicide. His widow insisted he would never do such a thing, and even though the coroner had his own doubts, the police called it an open-and-shut case. The man's widow left town soon after that.

More than once, warehouse workers threatened to walk off the job due to salary issues. The company was accused of coercing dock workers, intimidating their competition, and violating OSHA requirements, but one by one, all charges had been dropped.

Over the weekend, I studied more than news clippings.

I looked up public records. Financial postings, tax records, corporate holdings. I found that SS International, the parent company of the shipping giant, had several real estate holdings around town. They did, indeed, own the building where the business offices and Sam's residence were located. Along with other properties, they held the title to several apartment buildings, a prestigious restaurant location, and one address I was particularly familiar with. It was the building where Janine's studio was housed.

That could explain her connection to Sam, I mused, and why my new boss had some of my old boss' paintings.

I considered the rumors and accusations, and the fact that all were dismissed. I drew my own conclusions and set them aside. With that behind me, I concentrated on the operational side of the business. This would benefit me the most and possibly earn me a job more meaningful than running errands.

I belatedly remembered something in my employment packet about the company's background. I felt foolish for not having thought of this before. I thumbed through my new online account for Samson Shipping until I found multiple links with exactly the kind of things I needed.

"Duh, Lex," I berated myself. I was sure every other employee in the company had thought to do this the very first thing. Particularly if they hoped for any sort of promotion. I might not be looking for a promotion just yet, but I *was* the CEO's personal assistant. It would certainly be beneficial to have an in-depth understanding of the company. *How else can I assist Sam if I knew virtually nothing about the organization?*

Between the links and what I found on the web, I have to admit that I was impressed with my findings.

Samson Shipping was founded almost twelve years before, but it never flourished under George Samson. It wasn't until he died of a sudden heart attack that things changed. His estranged wife took the reins three years ago, and under her watch, the company grew to what it was today: imports, exports, and everything in between.

I gathered as much information about the company as I could and spent hours studying it. I memorized facts and figures, statistics, acquisitions, successful endeavors, and every bit of helpful information I found.

At one point, I came across an in-house report that made me pause. It gave a harrowing description of a violent storm at sea. The captain of the cargo ship was hailed a hero, able to bring the vessel into port without loss of life or load. It gave specific numbers on the weight, mass, and monetary value of the shipment safely delivered into port.

It wasn't the numbers or the prowess of the captain that caught my attention. It was the name of the vessel. *Bainbridge.* The name tickled the hairs at the back of my neck. I knew that name, but I couldn't quite place it. All I knew was that it had something to do with my past.

"You're being ridiculous, Lexi," I told the imaginary other me in the room. I pushed back from my chair, feeling the need to pace the room. "It's just a name. It's not even all that unusual. I'm sure there are dozens of Bainbridges, right here in Galveston. If not in the city of Galveston, here on Galveston Island. Or within the county of Galveston. It's not like only one person on earth has ever been named that. So what if a ship has that name? You're overreacting."

I wore a path in front of my sofa. Back and forth, back and forth. I ventured toward my bedroom, did an abrupt turnabout, and retraced my steps. I paced into the kitchen. I poured myself a glass of water, trying to delay the inevitable.

After pacing the apartment again, I gave in to the temptation. Walking into my bedroom, I opened my closet, turned on the light, and closed the door behind me. Then I parted the clothes to reveal what looked like an innocent stack of blankets. In truth, it was a mix of different colored and different textured towels, carefully folded to create the illusion of bulk and depth. I moved them out of the way to reach the safe they disguised.

To most apartment dwellers, a typical safe was a small box, often portable, with either an old-fashioned lock and key or a digital keypad. Most were lightweight and had little chance of surviving a fire.

Mine wasn't most safes, certainly not the kind found in apartments. Mine was made of heavy-duty, multi-layered steel. It was smaller than a two-drawer filing cabinet and about as heavy as a standard-sized refrigerator. It also had a mechanical combination lock, the kind not easily decoded. Per requirements in my lease agreement, I couldn't attach it to the floor. I had to depend on weight and camouflage to keep thieves from finding and removing my safe.

I sat on the floor to put in a combination that only I was privy to. My heart felt as heavy as the door I slowly tugged open. Visiting my past was always like this.

I pulled out several journals, all with a green cover. *Green for go.* These journals that chronicled what I considered our 'go years.' We were always on the go back then, traveling from one city to another. One scam to another.

The name Bainbridge brought those years to mind, so I methodically went through each entry, scanning the pages for the name.

I remembered the day I had gotten the first journal. My father and I were in a drugstore somewhere in Kansas, picking up cough medicine when I saw it. A slick green book with a bit of sparkle and shine. To a six-year-old, the trim looked like real gold. My father bought it for me, plus a pencil with pink and green pompoms dangling from its top. I had learned to write, but I hadn't yet mastered the art of spelling. The first several pages were filled with repetitive letters and silly gibberish.

Somewhere around the middle of the journal, real words appeared. To a stranger, they made no sense at all, but I knew exactly what they meant. The spelling was still hit or miss, but the message came through. *Michelle Brown, salesman, Chicago.* It was what I was supposed to tell people if they asked. I was Michelle Brown, my father was a car salesman, and we moved there from Chicago. The next few pages contained more pictures and scribbling, but later, there was an entry similar to the first. *Michelle Edwards, insurance appraiser* (the spelling was badly mangled), *Orlando*. This time, I added a crude drawing of the apartment we lived in, as seen through the eyes of a seven-year-old.

Over the next few years, I kept the journals up to date with details of our latest adventure. That's how I thought of them in the early years. They were adventures that took us to different cities and different surroundings, where we played make-believe, and I helped my daddy make money.

As some of the fun wore off, and as I learned to express myself better on paper, I kept more detailed accounts of our exploits. At first, I didn't keep the journals for anything other than for my own amusement. That, and because they served as good reminders of our current assumed lives. My father viewed my 'diaries' as something that kept me entertained and out of his way, so he made certain I had plenty. He bought green because it was my favorite color. It wasn't until later that I made the connotation in my own mind. *Green for go.*

As my artistic skills grew, my sketches became more realistic. I kept those in a blue sketchpad.

No one knew I had the journals. No one knew they contained more than a young girl's hopes and dreams. More importantly, no one knew I had the red journals. And certainly not the black one. The red held secrets. The black held horror.

But every time I felt eyes upon me, every time I felt the claustrophobia moving in, I feared my secret had been discovered. I feared someone knew about the journals, and that they were coming for them.

Pushing memories and paranoias aside, I concentrated on that name. I found it in the third journal. *Michelle Bainbridge, food critic, Des Moines*. I momentarily wondered how I could have forgotten all those fabulous meals we had eaten, many of them for free. By that time, I was in my adolescent years, and had already developed a taste for gourmet cooking.

"Focus, Lexi. No walking backward." I could never think of it as a stroll down memory lane. To me, that expression was equivalent to fond memories. Nope. I equated the words to falling into a deep, dark pit. I came to think of it as walking backward. "There was a point to looking through all these journals. You were right about the name. But what does that mean, really? Just that some company you work for that has *absolutely no ties* to your father" — I emphasized the words for my own piece of mind — "happened to name a ship the same thing. It's no big deal. Certainly not something to freak out about."

I kept telling myself that as I returned the journals to the safe, spun the dial to a random number, and painstakingly refolded my towels.

I returned to the living room and flipped on the television, determined to take my mind off Samson Shipping. I had spent the entire weekend doing research and studying. I deserved a break, preferably outside this apartment.

Yet, something kept me tethered to the space I had already been cooped up in for two days.

That something felt a lot like dread.

CHAPTER ELEVEN

Lexi

The dread followed me to the office the next morning. I rode the elevator up to the second floor, the only option available from the front vestibule.

As I had before, I wondered if there was a direct passage from Sam's penthouse apartment to the ground floor. It seemed improbable that she would ride a private elevator to the second floor, make her way along two corridors, and take a second, public elevator down to street level. I had never noticed another elevator in the apartment, but there had to be one.

I also wondered where she parked her car. The back of the building had loading docks with a few walk-through doors sprinkled between them. With the shipping channel practically in its back pocket, I figured Samson Shipping must store goods here before loading them onto ships and barges. There was a space for employee parking, but I somehow doubted Sam parked among us commoners. Perhaps the ground floor had a garage reserved just for her. I had seen an odd below-ground ramp, but I suspected any space down there was prone to flooding. Sea level, and all that.

I kept my mind busy with needless wonderings while I wound my way toward the elevator. It wasn't like I could stop and chat with co-workers I had developed a rapport with. I had no more friends since starting here than I had before. Which meant basically no friends at all. I was beginning to doubt whether Raven even qualified.

With nothing to delay my ascent, I stepped into the private car and pressed the button. I occupied my thoughts by going over the company stats in my mind. I carefully avoided all thoughts of a certain cargo carrier.

Ignoring the dread that grew stronger with every step, I gave a perfunctory knock on the French doors before letting myself in. Sam had assured me it wasn't necessary to announce my presence, but I had trouble just barging into someone's home. I suspected that security cameras alerted her to my arrival, even though I had yet to spot one. And believe me, I had looked for them.

I went to my office and deposited my things. With both doors to Sam's office closed, I assumed she didn't want to be disturbed. I turned on my computer, opened my email account, and sent her a message that I was there and ready to be of help.

I scrolled down for any messages that might require my attention, but of course, there were none. Other than brief messages from Sam, the only mail I had ever received was from HR and one welcome-type email from Cindy in reception. It provided a helpful diagram of the second floor, a few facts and tidbits I might find useful, and mentioned a bi-monthly newsletter that would be coming out soon. She included a link to the most current edition, should I be interested in reading it.

One day, I was so bored, I did just that. It didn't mean much to me, considering I had no clue about any of the people it mentioned. Ariana in Accounting had given birth to a baby girl. Henry, the night foreman in Warehouse 3, was a new father to a baby boy. Hermine in Shipping had been awarded Employee of the Month. There was a get-well card for someone named Paul, who was recovering from surgery — stop by the break room to sign it.

None of it applied to me, but reading it gave me something to do for five minutes.

The week before, I speculated that the walls around Sam's office were soundproofed. I never heard her talking on the phone, never heard her coughing, never heard her moving back and forth. If the door between us was closed, I never heard a thing. I supposed that was why she used the intercom or an email to contact me; I wouldn't be able to hear her if she called my name.

I was more convinced of the soundproof theory than ever when I heard Sam's office door open and, to my surprise, a man walked down the hall. I had a brief glimpse of his profile, but something about him looked oddly familiar. I couldn't place him, but the sense of familiarity made the dread in my stomach ramp up another notch.

Was I supposed to escort the man out? Then I saw Simon following behind, and I realized it wasn't necessary. Simon would take care of it, just as he took care of everything. Simon essentially did my job for me, so why had they even bothered hiring me?

I heard Sam's voice through the intercom. "Lexi," she said in her hoarse, raspy voice, "can you step into my office?"

"I'll be right there."

I grabbed a notepad and paper, hoping she finally had something for me to do.

Her ice-blue eyes were piercing, as always. "Nice weekend?" she asked.

"Not too bad," I said noncommittally. "And you?"

"Busy, as always." Her eyes zeroed in on the pad I held. "What's that?"

I felt a bit foolish, but I was determined to see my plan through. "A notepad. I thought maybe you called me in to have me take notes."

She looked genuinely confused. "About what?"

"Anything. I thought maybe you had some letters you wanted to dictate, or — or some ideas you wanted me to jot down, so that you didn't forget them."

"I have an excellent memory."

Hoping I hadn't offended her, I scrambled to cover my gaffe. "Without a doubt," I said quickly. "It's just that I know you have so much to do, so much to keep up with, and I thought I could be of assistance to you." I waved the pad in my hand. "To be honest, I don't think I do enough to justify the salary you've offered. I'd like to prove to you that I can be of value to the company."

"Value?"

Her tone was somewhere between a laugh and a challenge. I lifted my chin and met her assessing gaze. "That's right."

She eyed me speculatively. "Of value, you say."

"Yes, that's right," I repeated. "I spent the weekend doing my homework. I learned as much as I could about Samson Shipping, so that I could prove my worth to you. Go on. Ask me. Ask me something about your company."

In a weary tone, she relented. "Very well. Let's see. What are our most frequented ports?"

I easily touted off the top five.

"What is the average gross tonnage we handle in one year?"

I not only offered the average, but the highest and lowest amounts in the most recent three years.

She continued to quiz me, and I managed every answer correctly, except for one. And that was only because it was a trick question.

"I admit," she said with a satisfied gleam in her eyes, "that last wasn't a fair question. But I see your point, Lexi. You did, indeed, do your homework over the weekend."

"Voluntarily," I pointed out. "Do you think you could give me some responsibility now?"

"You have responsibilities."

"No disrespect, but I haven't done one constructive thing since I've been here. I'd like to have something meaningful to do for a change."

"Tomorrow, you'll be taking my place at the hospital. That, I can assure you, is very meaningful to those unfortunate children."

"I absolutely agree. But what about today, and Wednesday, and all the days I'm not volunteering at the hospital? I want to be useful on those days, as well."

"You're certainly persistent, aren't you?" For some reason, she seemed irritated that an employee wanted to actually do their job.

I answered distinctly, "When it's something I want, yes."

"And you honestly want more responsibility?"

I swallowed hard and put my neck out on the chopping block. I needed to get this over with, one way or another. Trying to convince this woman to trust me was as exhausting as plotting ways to get fired.

"Quite frankly, I need a job that challenges me. If not here, then somewhere else."

Lillian Samson looked at me with steely, calculating eyes. I realized then what a dangerous and powerful opponent she could be.

"You'd honestly walk away from the salary I'm paying you?" she demanded in her grating voice.

I met her gaze without flinching. "I would."

Her eyes bore into mine for another moment before she sat back in her chair and let out a deep, rumbling belly laugh. "You're all right, Lexi Graham!" she said between hoots. "You've got balls."

I wasn't about to correct her, not when I had just scored a major victory.

I didn't give her time to change her mind. "What's the first thing you'd like for me to do?"

My win was short-lived. "Bring me a Diet Coke," she said. Before my hopes dipped too low, she added, "while I pull myself together." She swiped a finger beneath an eye, indicating she had laughed so hard, she cried. I hadn't seen any tears, though. But my spirits lifted considerably when she said, "When you get back in here, I'll give you your first assignment."

Okay, so it didn't sound like the greatest of tasks, but it was a start.

As Sam had told me before, she believed in giving back to the community. She was currently looking for a worthy cause to contribute to. She had a few candidates in mind, but she wanted me to explore other options. She was particularly interested in the group homes for orphaned or abandoned children throughout the eastern coastal region of the state, whether public or private.

I was surprised that my boss seemed to have a soft spot for children. She was so gruff. Sometimes, her manner was brusque. Her tongue could be sharp, and her icy blue eyes glaring. The maid had come last week, and she made the girl cry with her cutting words. I wondered if there would be someone new this week, or if Sam's employees were accustomed to her ridicule. The thought of her caring about children seemed at odds with the personality I had seen so far.

"Find out how many long-term adoptees are in your top five most-worthy homes. Get me details."

"I'll see what I can do," I answered somewhat doubtfully, "but I'm sure there are privacy laws. They may not be at liberty to share that kind of information."

"If they know there's a hefty donation involved, they'll be willing to bend the rules." She sounded cynical. "There's a fine line between what's kosher and what's financially beneficial."

I tucked my lips into a seam, determined not to gasp. She sounded so much like my father, it was disconcerting. I supposed there was a common mentality between all moguls, no matter what kind of business they were in. I just hoped Sam's business was on the right side of the law, unlike my father's.

"I'm not asking for names," she continued. "I want gender and age, and how long they've been overlooked for

76

adoption. That's not too much to ask of you, now is it, Lexi."
It wasn't a question. When she stared at me with those cool
blue eyes, the look was condescending.

I swallowed hard and nodded. I had asked for responsibility, and she was offering me a chance to work on her pet
project. I should be grateful.

"I'll get right to work on it," I promised.

"If they're not willing to divulge such information, use
your creativity to get it."

My heart stalled in my throat. "Cre-creativity?"

"Your imagination," she fairly snapped. Her attention
had already gone to her computer screen. "I'm sure you have
some. Pretend to be a reporter. A social worker." She flicked
her hand, shooing me away. "I'm sure you'll come up with
something."

Her words left me shaken. I was glad her eyes were on the
screen and not my ashen face.

I couldn't get the strange encounter with Sam out of my
head. I finished the day out with as much concentration as I
could manage, but I admit, I was ready to go home and crash.

I stopped at the tiny postal box that came with the apartment and scooped out my mail. I hadn't checked it for a few
days and now had one bill and plenty of junk mail. Most
importantly, I had a letter from the Texas Department of
Transportation.

"Wow, that was fast. Color me impressed."

I held the mail in one hand, my deli order in the other,
and jogged up the narrow set of stairs. Once inside the apartment, I set everything on the coffee table and disappeared into
the bedroom to change out of my dress clothes. I came back
in pajama pants and a tee.

With my water bottle and sandwich combo in front of
me, I picked up the mail. The only thing of real interest was
my new driver's license. I ripped open the envelope eagerly.

"Okay, I appreciate the speed of their service," I grumbled to myself, "but they could have taken two seconds to include the standard form letter. Hello, thank you, keep in a safe place, yada, yada." The paper I held in my hand was unprinted, with only my new license folded inside. A single glue dot held it in place.

The card felt strange. When had they changed the paper? Cutting costs, I guess.

Grabbing my new wallet from my purse, I was about to slide the replacement into place when something else caught my eye. Where was the star? I thought all the new licenses had to have that REAL ID star or whatever it's called. The one so you can fly. What happened to mine?

I brought the card closer for inspection. Right picture. Right date of birth. Right . . . I gave a loud gasp. Maybe it was more of a sob.

No matter the sound, my reaction was to fling the card across the room as if it burned my fingers.

Everything else about my new driver's license may have been correct, but the name wasn't. Not anymore.

Michaela Drakos.

I shrank back against the couch, hands over my mouth. Who had done this? How had they known? What was happening?

I finally mustered enough courage to touch the envelope and bring it toward me. My hands trembled so badly, it took a moment to focus my eyes. Now that I was looking for it, I saw a tiny smudge of ink in the return address and logo.

Knowing the letter was forged did little to reassure me. If anything, it made matters worse.

I wasn't safe.

CHAPTER TWELVE

The Milkman

The night wasn't as dark as he liked, but it wasn't the kind of neighborhood with security alarms or scaredy-cat motion lights. It wasn't even the kind of neighborhood where people cared much about what their neighbors did. And if they noticed, they sure didn't report it. The last thing these people wanted on their streets was the police.

That was fine with the man. It made his job that much easier.

His target lived in a rundown house in the middle of the block. It was small and in bad need of maintenance. He hadn't been inside before, not like many of the houses he visited in the middle of the night, but he knew the layout of these old shotgun houses. Living room that opened into a bedroom that opened into the kitchen. The rickety add-ons in the back confirmed these particular houses were built before indoor plumbing, necessitating the need for the additions. An exterior door in the bathroom gave access to the so-called backyards. With all doors lined up in a row, it allowed a breeze to draw through the houses. The simplicity gave the design its iconic name. Supposedly, a shotgun could blast through the front door, peppering every room in the house before exiting through the back door.

The narrow houses were crammed close together, offering little space between them. There was no back alley and no driveways, so the street out front was lined with cars. That meant the man had to park at the cemetery and slap-toe his way in. But he didn't mind the walk. Anticipation fueled his way in, and euphoria would energize his way out.

Even in the middle of the night, he saw a drug deal taking place on the opposite side of the street. He kept his gaze straight ahead, ignoring the men who negotiated a price for the rock. They didn't bother with keeping their voices low. No one in this neighborhood cared.

He passed two men and a woman on their front porch, sitting on the steps and trading a joint between them. The porch light behind them illuminated their silhouettes and spilled weakly onto the sidewalk where he walked. Keeping his head down and his face obscured by the black hoodie, he lifted his index finger in casual acknowledgement and trudged on.

"Hey, honey," the woman called out in a sultry voice slurred by a high. "Wanna join us?"

"Got an appointment," he said over his shoulder, barely turning his head. He heard their laughter trail behind him.

Not everyone on the street lived on the outskirts of the law. For some, the shoddy houses were all they could afford. For others, they were family homes, passed down from one generation to another. Stuffed in here and there was a larger house, with gingerbread trim and shutters. But the house he headed for was small and cramped. Just big enough for a single mother and her infant.

He knew she had worked at the convenience store right up until her water broke. He knew her name was Helen, and that she couldn't afford to buy formula.

He knew the lock would be easy to jimmy open. He didn't bother going around to the back, not on a street like this.

He allowed his eyes to adjust to the darkness. The living room was sparsely furnished, just as he had suspected. It made crossing into the bedroom even easier.

The young woman slept on a full-sized mattress. It looked lumpy. His eyes narrowed when he didn't see a tiny bundle beside her. Had something happened to the baby? Had she decided life would be easier without the encumbrance of a child and handed it over to strangers?

The rage built inside him, until he heard the tiny whimper. It came from the far side of the room, which wasn't far at all. He tiptoed around the foot of the bed and saw the pallet arranged in the corner. Atop it was a small bundle of blankets.

Smiling, he knelt and gathered the sleeping child into his arms. He pulled the top blanket away. He may as well help wake the baby to move the process along.

The man stood and turned, taking the two steps toward the bed. He sat down on the sagging springs and whispered near the woman's ear.

"Helen. Wake up, Helen. It's time to feed your baby."

She stirred but didn't awaken. He spoke louder. "Helen. Don't neglect your son, Helen."

She woke with a stifled scream, her eyes wild. "Who-who are you?" she demanded. Her eyes went to the bundle in his arms. She let out a ragged gasp. "Why do you have my baby? Give him to me!"

She scrambled to her knees, frantically reaching for her son.

"He's fine, Helen. I would never harm him."

"What do you want?" she demanded. With the baby safely in her arms, she held him away from the man.

"I want you to be a good mother," he said calmly. "I want you to feed your son."

She whimpered, sinking back to huddle against the old iron bedframe. She drew her legs up in front of her, cocooning the baby the best she could. "Go away," she said. She tried sounding brave but failed.

"Not until you do as I say."

"Who are you?" she whispered in horror.

He didn't answer. He reached toward her, making her cringe and pull away even further. "N-no! I just gave birth!"

"I'm not here to rape you, Helen." His voice was oddly soft as he pushed her long, red curls over her shoulder, ignoring her whimpers. "I just want you to feed your son."

"I-I will. He's sleeping. I'll feed him when he wakes up."

"Then I'll wait here with you."

His calm statement made her tremble worse than she already did. She pulled away the other blankets the hospital had given her. Her small hands shook as she tried to rouse the sleeping baby.

"Take your top off," the man instructed.

She did so without turning loose of her baby. She shifted him from one arm to the other as she worked the T-shirt up and over her head. There was a small air-conditioning unit stuffed in the window, but no air blew from its rusty vents. The oscillating fan in the corner was off. Both pulled electricity, something she could barely afford to pay. It left the room hot, but still she shivered.

"Feed him," the man said.

After several attempts, the young woman finally woke the baby and pulled him to her breast. She was still trying to get the hang of this thing. It wasn't as easy as it looked. Sometimes, he didn't want to latch on. Sometimes, he cried and cried, leaving them both exhausted and angry.

The man leaned closer. She whimpered as he fondled her breast. She closed her eyes to the overwhelming disgust and willed herself not to vomit. "Make him take it," he said. When she opened her eyes, she saw that he was pushing her nipple to the baby's mouth.

The man sat back and watched as the baby latched on and began to nurse.

"Beautiful," he murmured. "Just beautiful." He hummed softly as he watched, a song she knew as 'Lullaby and Goodnight.'

When he left, he tossed two hundred-dollar bills onto the bed. "For the baby," he said.

He strolled leisurely out the way he had come. He stopped to lock the door behind him.

The woman lived in a dangerous neighborhood, and she had her son's safety to think about.

CHAPTER THIRTEEN

Lexi

I wasn't due at the hospital until noon, and Sam insisted that I didn't come into work at all that day. With the morning to do as I pleased, I had scheduled an appointment to have my hair done.

Because I knew that someone was watching me, and because I didn't want them to realize my straight, blond hair wasn't natural, I drove onto the mainland to see a hairstylist. Realistically, I knew that anyone following me could drive across the causeway as easily as I could, but it made me feel safer this way.

By the time I arrived back in Galveston, no roots were showing, and all hint of a curl was gone from my long tresses.

I checked in with the hospital and prepared for a long series of questions and verification. I was shocked when they only asked for my name and address.

"That's all?" I asked incredulously. "You aren't going to do a background check? Make sure I am who I say I am, or that I don't have a record?"

The man looked at me with a bored expression on his face. "Do you?"

"Of course not, but that's not the point!"

"What is your point?"

"I'm going to be around children. Shouldn't there be some sort of rigorous line of questioning I need to go through? What if I'm a pervert?"

"You just said you weren't."

I eyed him with disgust. *I* knew I was on the up and up, but *he* didn't. How would the parents of these children feel if they knew the hospital's lax standards when it came to allowing just anyone to volunteer? In today's world, it was risky to be so trusting.

"And you're just going to take my word for it," I said, disappointment in my voice.

"Not your word. Lillian Samson's word." He held up a clipboard. "She's already provided everything we need to know. She's given you her full endorsement, and that's good enough for us." He took a name badge, already printed with my name and picture — now where had he gotten *that*, my mind screamed — and handed it to me. It hung from a bright yellow lanyard.

I eventually pried my chin off the floor and followed him to the elevators. My boss clearly had more influence in the community than I gave her credit for.

"Several of the children have one of their parents or other family members with them," he explained as we wound down a corridor, "but many don't. You'll want to find one of the latter and keep them from feeling so scared and lonely."

"That's a shame their family isn't here with them."

"Yes, but most parents have a job or other children at home to care for. They don't always have a choice."

"I suppose not."

"I'll take you by the nurses' station, so that you can get acquainted. They can give you a feel for which rooms you should visit."

He relinquished me to a lively station decorated in a playground theme. It matched the graphics I saw along the corridors. The nurses were busy coming in and going out, but two sat at their computers. They both offered warm smiles when the man left me in their care.

"I'm Marsha," the younger nurse said. She looked just a few years older than me. "We're so happy to have you here with us. We don't have nearly enough volunteers."

"A lot of lonesome children?" I asked with empathy. I, too, had spent many lonely days as a child.

"Fortunately, the majority of them are more bored between visitors than they are actually lonesome. But there's a few long-term patients who don't get many visitors. They're the ones who are lonesome."

"It sounds like that's where I should start."

"Absolutely. Let me get those room numbers for you." She tapped the keys on her computer, sending the information to a printer behind her. She handed it to me with a brief background of each child.

"Tiffany Foreman in Room 3210. Both parents work two jobs, so it's hard for them to come. Sometimes, her elderly grandmother comes, but only on the days she's feeling up to it. Domingo Zapata in 3223. His family lives out of town, and his mother can't always afford the bus fare. We offer overnight accommodations, but she has other children at home. Anila Targe in 3227. Speaks limited English, and her parents come like clockwork. Seven thirty in the morning, and seven thirty at night. Stay for an hour and leave, meaning she has an entire day to get through without visitors. Tommy Dankworth in 3237. His mother is home with a new baby, and his father works all the time. There are a few more, but this should be enough for now."

Their stories touched my heart. "Am I allowed to bring small gifts when I visit?"

"Absolutely. Just no food or candy unless you run it by us first."

"Oh, yes, of course," I assured her. "I'm sure some of them have allergies and dietary restrictions. For now, I'll stick to non-edible treats."

"That's very generous of you, Miss Graham."

"Please, it's Lexi."

Marsha offered me a heartfelt smile. "We're going to get along just fine, Lexi. Just fine."

Walking away, I hoped it meant I could make a new friend.

I started at Tiffany's room and worked my way back. I found out that Tiffany liked anything frilly, especially the rumpled tutu she wore, hospital bed and all. She was recovering from a car accident and had casts on both legs and one arm. Her worst injuries were the ones I couldn't see, according to the nurse I encountered in the hallway. She couldn't divulge much, but I knew the little girl would be there for a while. Tiffany, I discovered, was also infatuated with the diamonds that bore her same name, so I made a mental note to buy a child's ring with an imitation rhinestone.

Domingo was a typical little boy. He was fascinated with trains and spaceships. I wasn't sure about the nature of his illness, but I suspected it had something to do with the IV drip and the scars on his face and arms. They looked like they came from a severe burn.

It was difficult conversing with Anila, but I found a universal language we could share. I pulled my sketchpad out and drew pictures of animals in playful positions. She giggled at the sillier ones. When I offered her the pencil and pad, I was surprised at her skill. She couldn't have been more than six or seven.

The last room I visited belonged to Tommy Dankworth. Judging from the pallor of his skin and the faint blue tint around his mouth and eyes, I would say he had a serious illness. My heart went out to him. No little kid should have to suffer.

Tommy liked dinosaurs, cars, and baseball. I knew very little about any of them, so I asked him to educate me. He was more than happy to do so, demonstrating a very impressive knowledge of all three. I supposed that when you were stuck in a hospital room all day, you didn't have anything better to do than study the things you liked.

Halfway into my visit with Tommy, someone knocked on his door. He called out a hello. I hoped it was his mother, even though I was enjoying our visit. For someone unsure of their feelings about kids in general, I had enjoyed all my visits today.

A middle-aged woman came in. The lanyard around her neck suggested she either worked or volunteered here.

"Hello, Tommy," she said. "I was hoping your mom was here."

"No, ma'am," he said politely, "but this is my new friend Lexi. I'm teaching her about dinosaurs and baseball."

"Don't forget cars," I reminded him with a smile.

Tommy put his hand up so that I couldn't see his mouth move, even though I could clearly hear his words. "To be as old as she is, she's sure not very smart about things."

The woman laughed, and the sound was deep and low. As she came forward, I did my habitual assessment. Fifty-ish, dirty-blond hair intermingled with gray, no memorable facial features. A rather masculine physique — *former athlete, perhaps?*

"I'm Sally Bevans, but everyone calls me Miss Sally." She offered her hand to shake. I wondered about the medical glove she wore. Was she sharing someone else's germs with me, or carrying mine to them?

"Lexi Graham." I didn't get a good look at her badge so I asked, "Are you a volunteer, too?"

"No, I'm a lactation consultant."

"A what?" She could have been speaking Yiddish for all I knew.

"A lactation consultant. I work with new mothers, helping them to breastfeed. It doesn't always come naturally, despite what some people say. I'm working with Tommy's mother, which is why I was looking for her."

I frowned as I looked at Tommy. Either he came from a cabbage patch, or she referred to his stepmother.

Seeing my frown, she laughed. The deep sound made me slightly uncomfortable. Was it because it reminded me of Sam's gravelly voice? Even though the day hadn't been so bad, I was still disgruntled about taking her place as a volunteer. Why offer your time if you aren't willing to give it?

"I should say mothers new to breastfeeding," she explained. "Tommy has a new baby brother, and Mrs. Dankworth is nursing this go around." The little boy was already playing with a dinosaur figure, so she lowered her voice and confided, "Poor Kim. She blames herself for Tommy's illness. Says she fed him formula instead of mother's milk, and she's determined to do things differently this go round."

I had no idea if mother's milk was healthier than baby formula, but I nodded as if I understood her meaning.

"What, uhm, do you teach them?"

She lifted her boxy shoulders in a shrug. "How to position the baby in their arms and their nipple in the baby's mouth. I help them massage their breasts to bring their milk down, and I keep them from being nervous, which is half the battle in being successful at breastfeeding. Babies can sense when their mothers are nervous, and it makes them nervous. They start crying, and then the mother starts crying." She spread her glove-covered hands. "It's all about trusting nature's process."

My eyes narrowed. I wouldn't want some strange woman massaging my breasts! Was she legit? "I thought you said it didn't always come naturally to some women."

"That's why I'm here, to nudge nature along." She said it with almost a smirk.

There was something about this woman I didn't like, but I couldn't put my finger on it. Maybe it was the whole breast-massaging thing. It just seemed weird to me. Plus, if I were nervous to begin with, I didn't think this woman could calm me down.

She eyed me for a moment with her dark gaze. She didn't quite sniff, but it was implied in the way she turned away and looked at Tommy.

"Tommy, dear, do you know when your mother will be back?"

He looked up from his dinosaur. "Not until my dad gets off work."

"I'll be gone by then, but tell her I stopped by, won't you?"

"Yes, ma'am."

Her eyes flicked over me. "Lexi, maybe we'll meet again."

"Maybe so."

As she left, I thought, *Maybe, but I hope not.*

* * *

I considered my first stab at volunteering a success, so I treated myself to an afternoon latte at Galveston Gusto.

"Look at you, girl," Raven said with a grin, "mixing it up a little. This isn't your normal."

I tried to act as if it were no big deal. Which, of course, it was. I didn't just change my order willy-nilly. Those self-help books stressed keeping a normal routine, and I took their advice to heart.

"It may be a one-time thing," I admitted sheepishly.

She went about measuring the coffee, steaming the milk, and whatever else was involved in creating such a heavenly smell. "Hey," she said, bumping her chin up, "your friend is here."

"J-Janine?" I squeaked, a little freaked at the thought of seeing her again.

"No. Your coffee date." Her eyes danced with mischief.

I followed her gaze and saw Jack By The Way. The lawman.

"Doesn't he have a home to go to?" I muttered. "Why is he always here?"

"Shall I remind you that you come in every day?"

"And get my order *to go*." I stressed the difference. "He just sits here." I glared at his back before whirling back around. "I did say make mine to go this time, too, right?" I knew very well I hadn't. I had planned to indulge myself in the slow, savory experience of cake and coffee.

"Too late. Already in a cup and a plate." She presented both with a shrug, as if she couldn't easily make both to go. This was one of those intimate little coffee shops that liked the personal touch of using real serving dishes when possible.

Less than graciously, I took my cake and coffee and looked around for a table. Preferably one as far from the lawman as possible.

The man must have had some sort of radar. His head popped up, and he swiveled around to catch my attention. I pretended to ignore him, but he was making a spectacle of himself, which meant he made a spectacle of me.

I inched forward with a hiss. "What do you want?"

"I thought you might like to join me." He pulled out a chair in invitation.

"You thought wrong."

"Come on," he cajoled. "Truce?"

Unwilling to give in so easily, I skirted around the table and came in from the opposite side. Partly, I was being obstinate. Partly, it kept my back from facing the door. When I stood by the table with full hands, he quickly stood and pulled the chair out for me. He would have pushed it back in like a true gentleman, but I was having none of it.

"Sit down," I snapped. "People are staring."

"So?"

"I don't like people staring at me."

"Shouldn't be so pretty," he quipped.

I wasn't falling for his fake flattery. "Are you homeless, Jack By The Way?"

Good. My words left him speechless, if only for a moment.

"I don't know which part to respond to first," he admitted. "Why Jack By The Way? What's that supposed to mean?"

"You told me that's what your name was. You said, 'I'm Jack, by the way.'"

A smile hovered around the edges of his mouth. "Let me correct that." He stood for a formal introduction. "Hello, my name is Jack Eastwood."

"You're doing it again!" I hissed under my breath. "Besides, I don't shake hands with homeless men I don't know."

"First of all, I just introduced myself, so between that and last week, you do know me. And second, what makes you think I'm homeless?" He looked down at his starched shirt and tie before taking his seat.

"I figured if you had a home, you wouldn't spend all day in here."

"First, I do have a home. Second, it's not like I'm here twenty-four seven."

"You have a real knack for counting, don't you?" I knew I was being a smart ass, but it was sort of fun. "Can you get past two?"

He was trying not to smile. The edges of his mouth quivered, but he kept an otherwise straight face. "First of all, how do I know you're not the one who's homeless? You seem to be in here a lot, too. Second, if anyone's a stranger, it's you. You haven't told me your name yet. And third, if I take my boots off, I can count all the way to nine."

This unexpected number got more of a response from me than I intended. So far, I had played all cool and blasé. There was genuine interest in my voice when I asked, "Why just nine?"

Dipping his head, I could see the grave expression in his face. He made a 'let's not talk about it' motion with his hands. "It's too graphic," he claimed.

I couldn't help it. I laughed out loud at his corny prank. "You, Jack By The Way Eastwood, are full of it!"

He still looked solemn. "Unlike my boot."

"Fine." I called him on his BS. "Prove it."

"Right here?"

"Right here."

"It's against the health code."

"That's for the workers."

"They won't serve me unless I'm wearing shoes."

I pointed to his coffee cup. "You've already been served."

"But I'm homeless, remember? You'd let them throw me out on the street, just to prove me wrong?"

I arched one brow in challenge.

He pushed his chair back enough to fold one long leg over his other knee. He pretended to go for his boot. "I'm warning you, the smell may ruin your appetite," he said with mock seriousness. "Not to mention the sight. Don't say I didn't warn you."

"On second thought, they may view me as an accomplice and throw me out, too." I put my hand on his arm to stop him.

BIG mistake. Touching him was like touching a live electrical wire. The current shot through me, making me snatch my hand away like it really burned.

He put his leg down and resumed his position at the table. After a moment of us both pretending the zing hadn't happened, he went on with his load of crap. "I would have done it, you know. I figured the least you could do for getting me thrown out was to tell me your name."

I gave a pointed look toward the floor. "I see why you wear those boots. Good for wading." He knew exactly what I meant. When he could no longer hold back a smile, I rolled my eyes and relented. "Lexi. My name is Lexi."

"You have a last name?"

"Just Lexi." *He's lucky to get that much.*

"Ah. So, Lexi is your surname." He nodded like he was sincere. "There's a lot of new names out there, but I've never heard of 'Just' for a first name. Is that short for Justine?"

"It's short for don't press your luck. If you insist on talking to me, call me Lexi. That's all you need to know. Lexi."

"Has anyone ever told you you're not very friendly, Lexi?"

"Only people I'm trying to ignore."

"Ouch. What have I ever done to you?"

I couldn't tell him, but it wasn't what he had done to me. It was what my father had done to me. My father had made me distrustful of men in general, and lawmen in particular.

And it wasn't just of men, but of *people*. He had said that the only person you could depend upon in life was yourself.

At least he hadn't lied and said I could depend on him.

"Look," I said, attempting to be civil. "It's been a rough couple of weeks. Let's just drink our coffee."

I had almost finished mine when he spoke again.

"The job? Is that what's been so rough?"

"I'd rather not talk about it."

"Fair enough. But sometimes, it helps to share the burden."

"Not this time," I assured him.

I left my cake half-eaten. I had been looking forward to it, but I lost my appetite. It sickened me, this tiny wish I had to share my burden with him, a lawman.

"Sorry. I'll keep quiet. Eat the rest of your cake."

I looked at him, perhaps to tell him it wasn't a problem, but the words never made it out of my mouth.

It was *her* again, with a coffee in hand and one foot out the door. The woman who seemed to show up everywhere I went.

I jumped up from the table so fast, I almost toppled it. Our dishes clattered. What was left of Jack's coffee sloshed over the edge and threatened to get his papers wet. He had turned them over so I couldn't see them when I sat down. Even I hadn't mastered X-ray vision yet, but from the look of worry on his face, I knew they were important.

I grabbed my purse, but it snagged on the chair, costing me precious seconds.

"Wait," Jack said. "I'm sorry. Don't go!" He thought I was leaving because of him.

I didn't have time to explain. I tugged my purse a second time, ignoring the crash of the chair.

By the time I reached the sidewalk, the woman was gone. Just like the purse snatcher, it was like she had vanished into thin air.

CHAPTER FOURTEEN

Lexi

Sam didn't bother saying hello when I arrived at work the next day. "Did you enjoy your time volunteering?"

"Actually, I did."

"You sound almost surprised."

"I'd never been around children very much, so I wasn't sure how it would work out."

"No younger brothers or sisters?" she asked.

"No."

"Older siblings?"

It was the first time she had expressed interest in my personal life, and I had no plans of encouraging her now. "Just me." Shifting the conversation away from myself, I said, "I was afraid I wouldn't like the kids, or they wouldn't like me. But I think it went well. They all asked when I would be back."

"That's up to you. You can go twice a week if you like. Your choice."

"In that case, I may go back again," I decided. The kids really had been pretty cool. "Would you prefer I was gone Thursday or Friday? In the morning or afternoon?"

"Take the full day off, whichever one you choose."

"Are you sure?"

She dismissed my worry with a toss of her hand. "You're on salary. You'll be paid the same no matter how many hours you work."

"I guess I'll go Friday."

"Starting the weekend early, are you?" She gave me an assessing look, and her raspy voice sounded sharp.

"If you'd rather I went Thursday—"

She interrupted me. "You need to learn how to take a joke, Lexi. I was just messing with you."

It hadn't sounded like a joke, just like this didn't sound like 'messing with me.' I needed a scorepad to keep track of this woman's moods and mixed signals. Thinking of a pad prompted me to say, "I think I may take the children some small gifts when I go back. No food, of course, but papers and colors, that kind of thing."

"Use the credit card I gave you. Don't buy cheap junk. Those neglected children deserve better." This time, her voice was bitter.

I didn't correct her on the neglect comment. I was certain she wouldn't appreciate me pointing out her misconception. The children I saw weren't neglected. Their parents just couldn't afford the luxury of spending the entire day with them. Like it or not, life outside the hospital went on.

"Oh, and that reminds me," I said instead. "I was wondering if I could put a couple of plants in my office. Not with the company card," I was quick to add, "but with my own money."

"Plants?"

"If you don't mind," I said hastily. "If you rather I didn't, that's perfectly fine."

"Why would I mind?"

It somehow felt like a trick question, so I simply said, "Thanks. I'll go shopping over the weekend."

"With that out of the way, are you ready to get to work?"

I was so shocked at the prospect of actual work, I could have easily missed the snarky tone in her voice. She made it sound as if I were slacking off.

I chose to ignore it and responded with a smile. "Of course! What do you need me to do?"

"One day, you'll need to sort these files," she snapped. Again, she sounded sharp, as if I had made the huge mess atop her desk. "But for now, I need you to help me plan a business dinner. Do you think you're up to the challenge?"

"Absolutely," I said with confidence.

"Very well. I'd like for you to come up with a menu and present it to me, along with samples of each dish."

The demand took me by surprise, but I tried to appear cool and composed. "Are there any dietary restrictions or allergies I should be aware of?"

"Have at least one vegan option, plus one gluten-free option."

"Do you mean a complete vegan menu, or a main course?"

"I believe in offering my guests options," she said with an air of superiority. "At least three main course varieties, with side dishes and a selection of desserts. I want to taste every dish that you're proposing."

"Is there a caterer you prefer to work with?"

"If you'll check your email, you'll see I've already sent you the list. Each will be willing to bring their samples here."

"When do you need this by?" I sounded professional, but inside, I was almost giddy. *An actual email. Woohoo! Score one for me!*

"The middle of next week will be fine."

If she thought the speedy timeline would frighten me, she was disappointed. My father sometimes gave me a day's notice to plan an elaborate dinner party. The parties were for the benefit of his 'associates' when they came to town.

I nodded. "That shouldn't be a problem. When is the dinner party, and how many will be in attendance?"

"Two weeks from Friday. Plan for fourteen." She saw the question in my eyes. "Yes, the table has an extension and additional chairs." She said it wearily.

As she so often did, she acted like I tried her patience. Like I should know these things. Like I had been with her all along, not in the office for less than two weeks.

"Is there anything else I should know when planning the menu?"

"We'll need a centerpiece. I want it to match the one in the front foyer. And smaller bouquets on the living room tables."

I jotted it all down on my pad. Luckily, I brought it with me when she buzzed. I glanced up and asked, "Do you have a color scheme in mind?"

"Something that complements the colors in the dining room."

"Speaking of that . . . I saw Janine's painting on the wall. Did the art inspire the color of the chairs?"

"I had them commissioned at the same time." She watched me closely. Was I supposed to be impressed? Because I sort of was. "Cerulean blue has always been my favorite color."

I sucked in my breath. Cerulean. Of course. That's why the color seemed so familiar. How could I have forgotten?

Because you've spent the last ten years trying to forget, my mind screamed. *It was your father's signature color, and you wanted no reminders of him.*

It seemed like I couldn't win. Like it or not, there were things that reminded me of the man everywhere I went. This entire apartment reminded me of him, and I was here every weekday. I wished I had asked to volunteer at the hospital three days a week. At least I could escape for another day.

"Is there anything else?" I hated the slight tremble in my voice.

"That will do for now."

I had been dismissed, so I turned to walk away. Just as I reached the door between our offices, Sam's scratchy voice stopped me. "And Lexi?"

I half-turned toward her. "Yes?"

"Make certain the menu includes beef Wellington."

I won't lie. My legs wobbled as I shut the door behind me, even without her asking.

It was just a coincidence, I assured myself. Plenty of people liked the dish. There was no way Sam could know about my botched impersonation of a chef. That was at least a year before I had my name legally changed. I had been going by Marissa Johnson at the time. I was working at a small bed and breakfast in Ohio, where the owners didn't ask many questions. If I could present an impressive breakfast buffet and a decent evening meal, that was all they needed to know. I doubted the couple had filed a complaint against me. They couldn't sweep the fiasco away quickly enough. All they were worried about was their reputation and that dreaded one-star rating.

Yes, a coincidence.

I repeated the mantra throughout the rest of that day.

* * *

That afternoon, I alternated between the two assignments Sam had tasked me with. I sent out inquiries to the caterers she provided. While I waited for responses, I switched to my orphanage research. I knew they were no longer called orphanages. They were now referred to as group homes or foster care facilities. I was just thankful for anything that kept my mind off the morning's weirdness, but in truth, both assignments were interesting.

I liked food, so that was no problem. I had some knowledge of what was expected at a business dinner. To grease pocketbooks, it helped to grease appetites. Simple homemade staples weren't good enough. These people liked gourmet dishes with fancy names. Unsmoked slab bacon didn't sound nearly as fancy as the new trend for 'pork belly.' It was all the rage among top chefs. And cornmeal mush didn't sound as sophisticated as polenta. It was all in a name, but I was good with names.

I jotted down some of my first thoughts. I would need to pair them with compatible tastes while keeping in mind different textures. Varied colors were important, too. Then there was selecting wines to complement each course. Planning a business dinner wasn't as easy as it may have seemed, but I had played many roles over my life. Surely, anyone able to pull off plots as a princess, a foreign movie star, and a chef could pull off plotting an impressive dinner for fourteen.

I would need to cross-reference my suggestions with previous menus. Unless it was an absolute hit with the guests, Sam wouldn't be pleased with serving the same dishes as before. I would start by finding out which caterers or restaurants had furnished her last several dinners and go from there. The request for information was included in the emails I sent.

My other project was more sobering, but also more fulfilling. Many of the places I had reached out to on Monday had responded. I was pleased to know that several had an excellent adoption record. They had no long-term residents within their homes. But there were a few who couldn't say the same, and those broke my heart. I asked for more information on the children left behind, but naturally, the prospective staff were reluctant to divulge the facts. It would take more greasing of the wheels, so to speak. It aggrieved me to know that in most cases, that grease would have to come in the form of money.

My last order of business for the day was to visit the florist. This time, the errand was all on me. Sam hadn't sent me. I wanted to discuss centerpieces for the business dinner, and I wanted to get a feel for my options. I suspected Sam would want to approve of my choices before ordering, so I sketched out a few ideas and went to her office door in the hall. It was closed, meaning she didn't want visitors. I returned to my office and sent them via email, telling her I planned to stop by the florist on my way home. She shot back a brief message that said she was on the phone, and that I could leave early.

I went by the flower shop, showing them my sketches and what I had in mind.

The florist let out a low whistle. "You have a real flair for drawing!"

"It's just a hobby."

"You're not a bad floral designer, either. If you ever get fed up with Sam's moodiness, keep me in mind. I could use your talents."

Finally, someone I could ask about my boss. Someone who might give me an honest answer.

"You know Sam, I take it?"

"Do I ever!" The woman didn't roll her eyes, but it was a technicality. I saw it written on her face and heard it in her exasperated tone. "She's a moody one, I'll say that."

"Tell me about it." I went for a casual complaining-about-my-boss mode, hoping to disguise my burning, need-to-know mentality. "Try working for her. One minute, nothing I do seems to please her. The next minute, she's laughing like I told the funniest joke ever."

"I can't even," the woman said. The embroidery on her shirt said her name was Joy. I pegged her as the owner since she had halfway offered me a job. Also, because the name of the shop was The Joy of Flowers. I didn't usually see her in here when I came, but maybe it was because it was near closing time, and most of her workers had left for the day. I saw someone in the back, putting flowers and arrangements back in the cooler.

"I'm new there, so I don't really know the dynamics of the place yet."

"Sam Samson is the dynamic," Joy said. "Everyone else is just there to do her bidding."

I kept fishing. "Have you known her for a long time? I think I heard someone say she and her husband were separated when he died. Did she ever come in while they were still a couple?"

"Are you kidding? No one on the island had ever seen the woman before. Most people didn't even realize George was married, and he had been working the docks long before he started the company. Years, and he never said a word! Everyone was shocked when she showed up at the funeral."

"Wow. That's sort of weird."

"Very weird," Joy agreed. "About as weird as the woman. But she's a huge customer of the shop — no pun intended — so I do what I gotta do to please her."

"I totally understand. Before she started sending me in, did she pick up the arrangements herself?"

"Not very often. I think it's hard for her to get in and out of a car."

"Because of a wheelchair?" I fished some more.

"Wheelchair? She's in a wheelchair now?" Joy looked shocked.

"I didn't say that!" I hastily backpedaled. "But it's headed that way, don't you think?" I injected a sense of sadness into my voice, before repeating my previous question. "Who did you say picked up the flowers before me?"

"She usually sent someone named Cindy, or that slicked-up Simon guy."

I dropped my voice to a conspiratorial tone. "Yeah, what's with him? He's a strange cookie, too. Is he her son or something?"

Joy looked startled at the suggestion. "No, I don't think so. I mean, I guess not. Like I said, no one knew she existed until she took over at Samson Shipping. But I suppose it's possible there was a child no one knew about, either." She paused to contemplate the thought. "Why do you ask?"

"I don't know. Simon just seems very secure in his job." Until I verbalized it, I didn't realize that was how I felt. But it was true. He seemed very comfortable at Samson Shipping, like he had nothing to worry about when he came to his continued role there.

"Well, now, that's something to think about." Joy clucked as she pointed to my sketches. "Can I keep these?"

"Sure. That's why I brought them in. Do you think you could have a sample of one of these smaller ones by Monday?"

"I'm sure I could do it by tomorrow."

"There's one other thing. Sam specifically wants to use cerulean blue in each arrangement. I know that's something you may not have on hand. It needs to match perfectly with her dining room decor, or she'll have my head. I won't be in the office on Friday, so Monday should give you enough time, right?"

"Leave it to me. I'll see that we get the color right, one way or another."

"Thanks, Joy. It was nice talking with you."

"You, too. See you on Monday."

I left feeling good about our conversation. Not only because I had ferreted out a few more pieces of information about my enigmatic boss, but because I had another name to put in the 'possible friend' column. Either I was getting better at this, or I was finally feeling secure enough here in Galveston to open up and risk friendship. Janine, I admitted, hadn't really counted. She had been my boss, after all, and when my employment with her ended, so had our friendship. I needed relationships outside of work, so that if something happened at my job, I still had someone to bond with.

I drove toward my apartment, pondering what it must be like to go out to eat with a friend. Or sharing a drink at one of the trendy little bars here in the city. Perhaps sunbathing on the beach, enjoying a conversation that flowed as effortlessly as the waves.

Lost in my musings, I almost missed my turn. I couldn't whip in at the last minute because of a pickup moving into the lane beside me. Rather than cut him off, I changed plans and went through the light. I moved into the turning lane, only to find that the side street was closed for construction.

Bad luck continued to travel with me. The next crossing was a one-way street going in the opposite direction. Pushed forward to yet another intersection, I put my blinker on. Glancing into my rearview mirror, I was surprised to see the same red pickup as before. Apparently, it hadn't turned because it was now behind me. So close, in fact, that if I had slowed down, it would have hit me.

I had no choice but to go through the light. I gently eased off the gas, hoping the truck would go around me or back off.

The truck stayed on my bumper.

A surge of panic washed through me. Was this the person who had been watching me? Had they followed me to the florist? I had been so sure my stalker was the woman with the frumpy wardrobe, but this wasn't a blue minivan. Naturally, she could be driving a different vehicle today, but she didn't seem the pickup truck sort. And she definitely didn't fit the fleeting image I had seen of my purse snatcher.

I tried to get a look at the driver in my mirror, but it was difficult to keep one eye on them and one eye on the road. I couldn't see anything other than a dark-colored hoodie. I couldn't tell whether it was a man or a woman.

The traffic was getting heavier as it turned five o'clock. People were getting off work and heading home. Maybe that would work in my favor. Surely, the person wouldn't try anything dangerous in public.

The truck stayed steadily behind me. It was ridiculous on my part, but I was reluctant to go home. If this was the same person who had been following me for weeks, they already knew where I lived. But on the off chance this was someone different, perhaps someone I had unintentionally made angry, I didn't want to blatantly lead them there.

Two more stoplights, and I pulled a trick I remembered seeing in a movie. The light was turning red, and I slowed as if to stop. Traffic from the other side was already beginning to move. Before I could second-guess myself, I put the pedal down and shot across the intersection. Horns protested, tires squealed, and I yelped as a car came within inches of hitting me. I knew I would probably get a traffic ticket, but I also knew it was worth it. The truck was stuck behind the light.

I turned right, stayed straight for two blocks, and made another right. I caught the next traffic light in time to get in the left lane and make a quick turn. After that, I went in a dizzying pattern that took me through an unwanted tour of the city. I had no idea where I was until I reached Broadway and saw the Old City Cemetery ahead. Going with the flow of traffic, I crossed the main avenue and into one of the historic neighborhoods. Unfortunately for me, this wasn't one of the streets undergoing restorations. It looked downright sketchy. I drove past skinny little houses that had seen better days. I wondered how people here ever found a place to park. Every inch of space along either side of the street was crammed full of vehicles. The few people I saw — some on the porches, some huddled around vehicles — looked unfriendly. Some looked downright scary. I was glad when the block ahead looked like its residents had at least *considered* renovations.

A few streets more, and I saw definite signs of improvement. I reached Seawall Boulevard and turned left.

And when I reached the block where my apartment was located, I found a parking space out on the street, rather than heading into a darkened, sometimes secluded alley.

CHAPTER FIFTEEN

Lexi

The next morning, it was all about search, assess, and react. SAR before stepping onto the sidewalk. SAR when leaving Galveston Gusto. (Thankfully, no sign of the lawman, the red truck, or the gray-haired woman.) SAR before getting into my car. Just to be safe, SAR before getting out of the car at the warehouse. I bustled inside the Samson Shipping building, for once eager to go upstairs.

I stepped into my office and froze. A lemon tree stood near the window. A *lemon* tree. My very favorite kind of tree as a child.

Another coincidence. She couldn't know that about me. No one could know that about me. That had been a lifetime ago. It was just a coincidence.

I approached her door and found it open. Sam looked up, saw me, and motioned me forward.

"Did you like it?" she asked, actually smiling.

"The tree? Yes, very much. Thank you."

"Thought you might be partial to lemon trees."

"Uhm, why would you think that?"

She spread her hands. "Doesn't everyone? They brighten any room, can live indoors in a pot, and they produce fruit. Hard to go wrong with a lemon tree."

See, Lexi? I silently chastised the other me. *I knew there was a plausible reason. She can't possibly know anything about my distant past. Nothing prior to Lexi Graham's existence.*

"Well, it's perfect. Exactly what I wanted."

She reached down beside her, her intentions hidden behind the massive desk. "You said you wanted to give your office a personal touch, so I thought you might like this."

She pulled out a large frame, not turning it toward me until the last moment. "For you," she said.

I gasped when I saw it. "This — this is an original! It's one of Janine's early pieces." I took the framed canvas in my hands, admiring it. I had never seen it in person. It had long since been gone by the time I started working for her. But it was part of her catalog, and I had seen images. I held it back toward Sam. "But I couldn't possibly take this."

"Why not?"

I hesitated, not wanting to make a fool of myself and have her laugh at me again. Was she giving the piece to me or simply letting me borrow it? I wasn't sure, so I stumbled through an excuse. "Well, uh, what if it got damaged? It's far too valuable to fall to the floor and risk getting messed up."

"Use a sturdy nail," she suggested dryly.

"What, uh, what if there's a water leak, and water comes out of the ceiling and runs down the wall?"

"It's insured."

"That's good, but—"

Sam stiffened. "Are you refusing my gift?" she barked in her too-gruff voice.

Had she said gift? Either way, I couldn't accept.

"It's far too extravagant for a gift."

"I should be the one to decide that, don't you think?"

"Yes, of course. And I appreciate it, I do. But . . ." One look at the glare in her eyes, and I pulled the frame to me in a hug. "Thank you. I love it."

"Good. Because I was about to second-guess giving this to you." She reached behind her desk of tricks and pulled something else out.

"It's amazing what gets shipped through Samson Shipping lines," she said. "When things go through customs or quality control, I'm sometimes able to make a deal with the customer and snag a few of the treasures for myself. I saw you eying my cigar box on the desk, and I thought you might like this." She pushed a satin bag toward me. I could tell its contents were bulky.

With hands that took on a tremble, I eased the bag open. I already knew what was inside. The breath stalled in my chest, but she didn't notice. "It's smaller, of course, but of similar quality. Hand-crafted in Havana," she boasted, "like the cigars I favor. It's lovely, don't you think?"

I wasn't concerned about the way her sharp eyes now watched me. I was concerned about getting through the next few minutes without air in my lungs. My legs weren't too steady, either.

"Y-yes," I managed to whisper.

Luckily for me, her telephone rang. Sam let it go to the second ring before picking it up, her eyes still watching my reaction.

I didn't wait to be dismissed. I took the coward's way out.

I managed a shaky breath, clutched both gifts to me, and mumbled, "Thank you so much!" and fled to my office. In my haste, I all but slammed the door.

I found a nail in the wall between my office and Sam's. Its metal base was already neatly driven firmly into a stud. It looked sturdy enough, so I tested the frame's weight on it. It looked as if it were destined to hang in that very spot.

I sank into my chair and propped my chin on my palm, staring at my newly acquired Janine Morrow original. Even though Janine had offered me a generous employee discount and a generous paycheck, I could never afford one of her art pieces. She had given me a few reproduced prints (which were valuable in their own right) and one very small painting, but none compared to this piece.

It was a riot of color and motion, and it livened any space with its vibrant energy. I loved it.

I gazed at it for a long time, admiring her talents.

And that's when I spotted it.

With a tiny gasp, I peered at my new painting more closely.

The piece had been tampered with. The new version definitely sported more cerulean blue than its original rendition. It was so artfully integrated that I had to wonder if Janine, herself, had made the modifications.

I dropped my head into my hands, wondering if I were going crazy.

"She's taunting me," I murmured aloud. "I don't understand why, but somehow, she knows. And she wants me to know that she knows."

There were too many coincidences. Too many seemingly 'innocent' reminders of my father.

There were those remarks about using my 'creativity,' even if it meant pretending to be someone else. I had felt her gaze on my back when I left. It was like she was gauging my reaction to the casually dropped words. Had my father told her about all the roles I had played in the past?

What about the lemon tree? Only my father knew it was my favorite. We had at least a dozen of them when I was little. Every time someone caught onto our scam, and we had to leave in the middle of the night, we left my tree behind. It was easier to just get a new one for our new location. Did he tell Sam that little tidbit about my past?

And what about the request for beef Wellington? I asked myself. She had that look in her eyes. My father must have told her about that. I was using a different name then, but I knew he always had a way of finding me. Her comment was a reminder that he had tracked my every move. For whatever reason, my father had told her about me, and she was taunting me with the knowledge.

Then, there was the color. Cerulean blue. Easily explained, except for the retouched painting. As improbable as it was, Sam could have tampered with the original so that it incorporated her favorite color. It *didn't* explain why she would give it away. And to *me*, a new employee. Giving me the painting was a deliberate act. It was meant to be a daily reminder of my father.

The biggest tip-off of all was the cigar box. The boxes were my father's signature gift. He kept several on hand, presenting them to new associates and investors with his flair for theatrics. He filled the boxes with expensive cigars from Havana to create the illusion of great wealth. They were all carved with an intricate design I had never seen on other boxes. Not until Sam presented me with her gift. I knew it had come from my father.

It was a maddening circle, bringing me back to *why*. Why would Sam play my father's game?

Unbidden, I heard my father's voice in my head. *Every single one of us has something someone else wants, Michaela. If the other person wants it badly enough, that gives us bargaining power.*

What was it Sam wanted from my father? Prison bars hadn't stopped him from conducting business on the outside. Did she need his connections? Was this what the games were all about?

My father had always been a crook. With enough scams and enough 'business associates,' he became a legitimate businessman.

'Legitimate' presented another thin line, one with a lot of angles, a lot of definitions. It could be defined as accepted. Recognized. Genuine. Lawful. Scoring three out of four ain't bad, so in that sense, my father was a 'legitimate' businessman. It was the business he was in that wasn't legitimate, and certainly not lawful. My father twisted every situation to his advantage, and he was never shy about breaking the law. He didn't just break it, he splintered it, just like he splintered me.

I wasn't fooled by his sudden rise to wealth. It hadn't been the result of his own prowess. It was obvious that he had gotten mixed up in organized crime. He had connections.

Had he made some sort of bargain with Sam, offering those connections if she carried out this game of his? Or was it the other way around?

I closed my eyes as a wave of terror washed over me. I swore I wouldn't run again, but the thought of my father and Lillian Samson scheming together stoked a fire beneath my heels.

"The real question," I said aloud, "is where do I fit into all of this? Am I his bargaining chip, or hers?"

CHAPTER SIXTEEN

The Milkman

The sky was cloudy. The small sliver of moon was obscured, leaving the night dark.

The perfect cover, he thought with a smile.

Engaging the signal jammer, the man proceeded silently on his mission. He came in through the laundry room door. It was on the east side of the house, and his car was parked one street over to the west.

It took an agonizingly long time to make his way through the house. He knew the husband was home, so there would be two pairs of ears to hear him should he make a sound.

He didn't.

The man proceeded through the laundry room, which opened ingeniously into both the master closet and the kitchen. He should have thought of this clever design for his own home.

The Dankworths lived in a new build, so they had employed all the latest trends and conveniences into their home. *All except a state-of-the-art alarm system*, he mused. The one they had wasn't nearly sophisticated enough to keep out determined guests such as himself.

The master closet spilled into the bath, which was attached to the master bedroom. It made his getaway so much more convenient.

He listened intently before opening the closet door. It wouldn't do to have one of the new parents tinkling in the commode when he came in. Satisfied that he heard no sounds of movement, he cautiously stepped over the threshold. He paused again to make sure both parents slept. Hearing the harmony of deep, steady breathing paired with a rattling snore, the man smiled. It was almost showtime.

He pulled a slender case from his pocket, opened it, and removed the syringe from within. It was pre-filled and ready to go.

He silently crept into the bedroom and approached the husband's side of the bed. It was almost too easy. Dad was dead asleep, oblivious to the prick of the needle.

The intruder was patient. He could wait until the sedative took effect. It sweetened his anticipation.

He hovered a few feet away, ready to pounce if need be.

It wasn't. Dad was fully out. He never knew when the man nudged him, or when he slipped across the bedroom toward the nursery.

The man turned off the baby monitor. He didn't want Mom waking up and stealing his thunder. *He* was the one to use the element of surprise. It gave him power over them.

He stopped to admire the infant for a moment. Oh, the innocence of babies! So trusting. So sure their mothers would forever love them and keep them safe. So ignorant.

Lifting the baby into his arms, the man retraced his steps. He woke the baby as he walked. By the time he stood at Mom's bedside, the baby was gearing up to bawl.

Kim Dankworth mumbled something like "not again" and tried to rouse. It had been a rough night. Trey had a tummy ache, meaning she spent the first half of the night pacing with the baby in her arms. Like the trouper he was, Tom kept his wife supplied with the warm towels she held to the infant's tiny tummy. After an hour, she insisted he go back to bed. She heard him snoring long before Trey quietened enough to put him in his crib. Two failed attempts later, she put the baby down and fell into her own bed. She swore that couldn't have been but two minutes ago.

"Kim," the man said softly. "Wake up, Kim."

She mumbled something and slid a hand toward her husband, thinking he was the one calling her name.

"Kim." The man's voice grew more insistent.

Eyes still closed, the exhausted mother mumbled a sleepy, "Huh?"

"Your baby, Kim. Did you forget about your baby?"

She came awake with a start. "Trey?" she asked frantically. She wasn't sure why, but she thought he was in danger. Ever since Tommy was diagnosed with leukemia, she had been paranoid. When Trey was born, she questioned every sniffle, every cry.

She swung her legs over the side of the bed. "Momma's coming, baby," she promised. She was surprised when she met resistance. Had Tom already gotten up and brought the baby to her? He had to work the next day. He should be asleep.

"Tom? Give me the baby and go back to bed." With her panic waning, exhaustion took over again. Sleep deprivation slurred her words.

"Tom's already in bed."

Her mind still half-asleep, Kim's first instinct was to whip around and confirm the words. Sure enough, Tom was there on his side of the bed, deep in slumber. Her brain was slow to compute. If Tom was beside her, who was . . .

Her scream was shrill as she came fully awake. There was a stranger in their bedroom! And he held Trey in his arms.

"Tom! Tom, wake up!" she cried. She reached backward to shake her husband's arm, but her eyes never left the man dressed all in black. "Who — who are you? Why do you have my baby? Give me my baby! Tom! Tom, wake up!"

"Shh," the man cautioned. "Tom's asleep. But little Trey is awake, and he's ready to eat. You need to feed your son, Kim."

"How — how do you know my name? And why . . ."
None of it mattered, not as much as Trey's safety. "Give him
to me! Give me my baby!" She tried to stand, but the man
nudged her back with his knee.

Her frantic screams made Trey cry in earnest. Beside her,
Tom never stirred.

"Don't worry. I'll give him to you as soon as you're ready."

"I'm ready now! Please give him to me." She was grove-
ling now. "Please, please. Please give me my baby."

"Is that a nursing gown?" the man asked.

Thrown by the question, Kim looked down at the cotton
gown with its convenient slit. "Y-yes."

"Then pull out your milk jug and feed your baby."

"My . . . ? Who are y—? What is happening?" She could
hardly complete a coherent thought, much less a sentence.

"You're going to feed your son, Kim," he instructed firmly.
As the baby's wails grew louder, he raised his voice to be heard.
"You're going to sit back against the bed, get situated, and pull
your gown aside. When you're ready, I'll give you your baby,
and you can feed him."

Her frantic movements were clumsy as she scrambled to
do as he said. It felt strange to expose herself to this stranger,
but everything about this moment was strange. It felt surreal.
Was she having a nightmare? Yes, that had to be it. It was
another nightmare, the kind she had before Trey was born.
Worries about delivering a healthy baby had haunted her sleep
during her pregnancy. She had failed her precious Tommy;
what if she cursed this new baby, too? That's why she insisted
on nursing this time. Mother's milk was best.

"Hurry up!" the man snapped. "Don't you hear your
baby crying? He needs you. He needs his mother."

"Yes. Yes." Kim arranged herself better and reached her
arms out. "I'm ready. Please. Give me my baby."

"And you'll feed him?" the man asked. He sounded
suspicious.

"Of — of course." Her voice wavered. She couldn't admit
to this madman that she was having trouble breastfeeding.

Nerves, the lactation consultant had assured her. She needed to calm down and relax. If she was nervous, Miss Sally told her, her milk wouldn't come down.

But how could she *not* be nervous with a stranger in her house, standing beside her bed and holding her baby? She was scared to death. One whimper away from hysterical. And why wouldn't Tom wake up?

The nightlight gave off a dim glow, enough for Kim to see wariness in the man's face. He didn't believe her.

"Give him to me, and I'll prove it to you!" Her bravado wasn't entirely sincere, but her demand was.

The man lowered the wailing baby into his mother's waiting arms. She held little Trey close, trying to console him with kisses and tears and a too-tight hug.

"You said you would feed him," the man barked.

Her head jerked up and down like a bobble-head doll. She pulled the baby to her breast and willed him to take it. "Please, Trey." She breathed the plea into his sweet-smelling hair. "Please nurse."

For once, his tiny mouth found her nipple and tugged. Relief swept over the desperate mother.

"Ah, that's more like it," the man said, pleased.

"Will you go now?" she whispered.

"Not yet."

She looked over at her husband, still in the same position. "Wh-what did you do to him?" She dared not wonder if he was dead.

"Don't worry," the man assured her. "The sedative will wear off in about an hour."

She closed her eyes and said a thankful prayer. Now, to pray this man didn't hurt them.

Slightly less frantic than before, Kim asked, "What do you want?"

"This," he answered, nodding to the baby nursing at her breast. "Just this."

"You — you just want to watch me feed my baby?"

"Yes. That's all. I'm not here to harm you, Kim. I swear. I just want to see this perfect sight."

"How — how do you know my name? Who are you?"

"It doesn't matter. All that matters is that you take care of your baby."

He wore a serene expression on his face as he watched the infant nurse. He even hummed softly.

"Who are you?" she whispered again.

The nightlight cast a shadow, distorting his slight smile into an eerie twist. "You can call me the Milkman."

Kim held her baby closer and trembled.

This man was insane.

CHAPTER SEVENTEEN

Lexi

The children were thrilled with their surprises. None of the gifts were expensive, but the look on the children's faces when they saw them was priceless.

I took Tiffany a puzzle of sorts, a chunky cut-out image of a girl. A half-dozen magnetic princess outfits came with it for hours of mix-and-match fun. I included a pink, plastic tiara for Tiffany to wear with her tutu, and a huge fake diamond ring.

For Domingo, I had picked up a dainty little train that could circle his hospital tray. It came with a track, front engine, one cargo car, and a caboose. The boy was more than ecstatic with his present.

Anila loved her sketchpad and colored pencils. She drew flowers and trees, and what I assumed must be the stick version of her family. She was still busy drawing when I left.

I presented Tommy with a book about baseball (he said he didn't have that one) and a pack of mini cars. While happy with the gifts, I noticed he kept watching the door, waiting for his mother to show up. He said she usually came in the morning and stayed until lunchtime. So far that morning, she hadn't come.

After I left the children's wing, I stopped at the nurses' station. Marsha was there, and we struck up a casual conversation. We were cut short by the ding of multiple call buttons.

"I understand," I said, pushing away from the counter. "Have a good day."

"It was nice talking to you, Lexi. Maybe I'll be on shift the next time you come."

Her sincere smile warmed me. *Definitely friend possibility*, I thought.

"Oh, I forgot to tell you," she called after me. "The elevator on this side is down for maintenance. You'll need to use the one on the maternity wing."

"What way is that?"

"Take a left at the vending machines."

I passed the nursery as I started down the long corridor. I gave the glass windows a cursory glance. I was just getting comfortable around children. I wasn't ready to see babies.

I headed for the elevators up ahead. A woman came from one of the rooms, her back to me. But I recognized the ugly blouse and the gray head. My steps quickened.

I easily caught up with her. Keeping a few steps behind, I called, "Ma'am! Excuse me. Ma'am."

She turned with a question in her eyes. "What can I do for you, shugah?" she asked. "You looking for directions?"

Now that we were face to face, I wasn't sure how to proceed. Even in my own head, my questions sounded crazy.

"I, uhm, recognized you. I, uh, just wanted to say hello," I stammered.

"Oh, that's sweet of you, shugah. Forgive me for asking, but I'm afraid I don't recognize you. How do you know me? Are you one of my former titty mamas?"

Her words shocked me. "Ex-excuse me?"

"My titty mamas. The ones who breastfeed," she said without hesitation. "That's what I call them. My titty mamas."

I glanced down at the lanyard around her neck, realizing it was a hospital badge she wore. I was vaguely familiar with the letters IBCLC. I had seen them on Miss Sally's badge. "Are — are you one of those lactation specialists?"

"Yes, indeed," she said proudly.

"That's not how I know you," I was quick to correct. "I, uhm, have seen you several times around town." I could see the slight frown forming on her face and the question in her eyes. "Your blouse," I said, glancing down at the jungle of patterns. "I was there in the store when you bought it."

Recognition dawned in her face. "Oh yes, now I remember! You helped me decide on the blouse." I cringed, not wanting to take the blame for such an atrocity. Her smile wrinkled her too-thick makeup. "You can't imagine how many compliments I've gotten on this blouse."

It had to be the understatement of the decade. I couldn't imagine anyone liking that blouse.

I was starting to feel foolish. I began to doubt my theory about this woman following me. She seemed like a perfectly nice older woman. But I had gone this far, so I pushed on. "I've seen you other places, too. Hahn's Deli. And, uh, Galveston Gusto."

"I frequent them both. I just love the roast beef sandwich at Hahn's." She used hand gestures to express her admiration. "And the coffee and raspberry tortes at Galveston Gusto are to die for!"

She raved about her favorites and all but salivated, adding something about her good fortune to live near her favorite eating establishments. I mumbled through a polite, "Oh. Really? That's convenient."

See, she isn't following you! She's practically your neighbor!

I forced a smile I didn't feel. For some reason, the neighbor thing didn't exactly comfort me. "Well, uh, I won't keep you any longer. I-I just wanted to say hello."

"That's so sweet of you, shugah. Oh, and by the way. They call me Grandma Gail."

I felt a headache forming. I didn't offer my own name. I just hurried to the elevator and left.

* * *

No real surprise, but I wound up at my favorite coffee shop. Structure and caffeine were exactly what I needed.

I ordered coffee and the last sausage croissant left in the case. It was long past breakfast, and I wondered if the croissant was stale. Just in case, I added an orange-cranberry scone. That was the story I was going with, anyway.

I turned from the counter and saw him. Jack By The Way, also known as Jack Eastwood, was sitting at a table along the wall, facing the window. It was the same one I had seen him at before, so I figured it was his favorite.

I had to admire his choice. Discreet, away from main traffic, with a clear view of the shop and the street outside.

Not stopping to question my motives, I asked Raven which sweet treat was his favorite.

With a sly grin, she answered, "Without a doubt, the triple layer cake."

Figures, I thought. *Chocolate, like his eyes.*

"Add it to my order, please. And a refill of whatever he's drinking."

"My pleasure!" Her tone was playful.

I carried a filled tray to the table and stopped beside him. He still hadn't seemed to notice me.

"It's my turn for a peace offering," I said, feeling foolish. *Wow. Twice in one day. Not a trend I care for.*

He didn't look up from his papers, but a smile played around his mouth. "I wondered if you had the gumption to apologize."

"Gumption?" I considered smearing the decadent cake over his smirking face and down his crisp, pressed shirt. "Gumption!"

He pretended to look furtively around the room and used my own words against me. "Shh. You're making a scene."

I huffed and plopped down at his table, uninvited. I took the chair beside him because it offered nearly the same vantage point he enjoyed.

"I owe you a coffee," I said, almost sloshing this one over the edge as I handed it to him.

"I suppose the cake is for making such a racket when you ran out of here the other day?" His chocolaty-brown eyes held a tease. "I had to perform CPR on the woman behind us."

"You are such a liar. Do you want the cake or not?"

"I can never resist chocolate."

Don't, I told the other me. *Don't even go there. We're talking about cake, not eyes.*

Settling the treats in front of us, I took a deep breath and sheepishly admitted, "I guess I did leave rather abruptly." I didn't do sheepish well.

"You think? Did you see a fire I somehow missed?"

"I . . . saw someone."

With a deadpan expression, he drawled, "Is that like a phobia or something?"

A lawman who thinks he's a comedian. That's just great.

He went back to the paper he was working on. I didn't see anything of importance there. From my limited view, it looked a lot like gibberish.

I ate my croissant in silence and started on the scone.

"Hungry again today?" he asked, again not looking up.

I ignored the barb about our first encounter. "Yep."

Jack paused to take a bite of his cake. "Ever had this? It's Betty's finest."

"I don't care for chocolate," I lied.

He took another bite and said in singsong, "You don't know what you're missing."

When he picked up his pencil again, I couldn't resist. "You said you weren't homeless, but are you office-less? Is this where you do your work?"

"Not always," he answered smoothly.

I studied him as he went back to his paper, seemingly engrossed in his work. After a moment, I asked in a flat voice, "Who are you watching?"

His head jerked up. His face held no expression. "Watching?"

"Yeah. You're watching someone." I casually propped crossed arms on the table and leaned across them. I kept my voice low so that no one else could hear our exchange. "You're slick about it; I'll give you that. But you're definitely watching someone."

He was obstinate. "Don't know what you're talking about."

I ignored his denial. "If you're undercover, you're going about it all wrong."

He looked at me with calculating eyes. "Why would I be undercover?"

"You're a lawman, right?" My expression dared him to deny it.

After a long moment, he gave a single nod. "I am."

"Is this a sting? Is that why you're always here?"

I finally saw an expression cross his face. Irritation.

"You watch too much TV," he scoffed.

"Not really."

He looked back at his paper, signaling he was through with the topic. "What do you know about stings, anyway?" he grunted. It wasn't a question. It was an insult.

I snorted. "You'd be surprised."

With an exasperated sigh, he put his pencil down, closed the notebook he had been scribbling in, and gave me his full attention. That is to say, he kept one eye on me, one eye on the door. It was almost the same thing.

"I would be," he agreed, referring to my surprised statement. "Want to explain?"

"Not particularly."

He twisted his lips. "How did you peg me for the law?"

"I know the look."

He didn't pretend not to know what I meant.

"Which side do you know it from?" Jack asked.

I didn't pretend not to know what he was asking. "Does there have to be a side?"

"There always is."

This conversation had gone downhill fast. I should have never started it. I tried now to salvage it. "You didn't answer. Are you pulling a sting?"

"Just observing," he replied in a calm voice.

"Good seating choice," I commented. "Good view of the street, good view of the door, good view of the register."

"You know," Jack said, scrutinizing me with a gaze that made me squirm, "to have been so reluctant to give me the time of day last week, you sure are talkative today. What gives?"

I had asked myself the same thing. I could only attribute it to nerves. No matter how much logic I applied, no matter how many pep talks I gave myself, I was still reeling. I knew something was very wrong, but I couldn't figure out *how*. How did all these coincidences keep happening? Coincidences that weren't truly coincidences at all, I suspected. I was unnerved, to say the least, waiting for the next shoe to fall.

I lifted one shoulder. "Bored?" I suggested.

He shook his head. His voice was certain. "There's more to it than that."

Within seconds, our roles were reversed. This time, it was Jack who jumped up from the table. "Stay here!" he more or less ordered.

His exit was much more graceful than mine had been. I was momentarily distracted with thoughts of last week. I was ashamed of myself. I was definitely losing my touch. I knew how to skip out without sloshing coffee and knocking over chairs. Once upon a time, I was as agile as Jack. As agile as the assailant who bailed with my purse. For a split second, I wondered if they were one and the same. That was ridiculous, of course. Jack was much taller and more athletic than that person had been.

Jack was across the room and out the door before I blinked. I saw him run out onto the street, and a streak of red as someone darted ahead of him. They both disappeared from view.

I sat there for a good fifteen minutes, wondering when he would be back. I had finished my meal and drained my coffee. I allowed Paula to take our dishes. Jack hadn't emptied either of his, but the coffee was cold, and I had a feeling he had lost his appetite for cake. So, I sat there alone, just me and his notebook, as I waited for his return.

Another fifteen minutes, and I was growing restless. I had pulled my sketchpad from my purse and started random drawings, but I couldn't concentrate. It wasn't like I *wanted* Jack's company. It was more that I didn't want to be alone right now. Without the children at the hospital to distract me, too many thoughts swirled in my head.

Yet here I was alone, and there was no sign of the lawman. How long did he expect me to wait? And what about his papers? What was I supposed to do about them?

There was a leather satchel propped against the leg of the table. After a moment of hesitation, I stuffed his notebook into it, grabbed the satchel and my own things, and went to the counter. The coffee shop would be closing soon, and who knew how long Jack would be.

"If he comes back," I told Raven, handing her a piece of paper with my number scrawled across it, "tell him I have his satchel. He may need it before you reopen."

"You mean Jack? Sure thing," she said.

As I turned away, I saw a teasing smirk on her face.

CHAPTER EIGHTEEN

Lexi

SAR. I swept the street with my gaze, part of me looking for Jack. I didn't see him. I didn't see anyone suspicious for that matter, but the feeling was back. The sensation of someone's eyes upon me.

With hurried steps, I crossed the street and went up to my apartment. Sometimes, the space felt cramped, but right now, it felt safe.

When my phone rang, I literally jumped. I thought I was alone here in my apartment, my thoughts safe within its small confines. It took a few seconds for me to realize the intrusion was the unfamiliar sound of my cell phone. The temporary one.

I couldn't say why, but I had instinctively given Jack the number to my other phone. The no-frills one. The one no one could track.

He was the only person who knew the number, but still my voice wavered. "Hello?"

He sounded irritated. "What happened to you? Where did you go?"

"Home."

"I told you to wait. I was coming back."

I glanced at my watch, my voice sarcastic. "An hour later."

"It took me longer than expected," he said in a tight voice. "Do you have my briefcase?"

"Yes."

"Tell me where you live, and I'll come get it."

Geez. I had done the man a favor, and here he was barking orders at me.

I started to say I was busy. Instead, I gave him directions.

Within minutes, I heard his knock on the door.

"I wasn't stealing your case, you know." I made that much clear the moment he stepped through the door.

"I never said you did."

"You weren't happy I brought it home with me. But I didn't know how long you'd be, and the coffee shop was closing soon." I don't know why I defended myself to the ungrateful man.

"In that case, thank you. There are some files that I need to work on tonight." His tone was still stiff.

"It's a Friday night. Sounds like you really like to party."

I swear. I wasn't fishing for information on his personal life. The statement was meant to be flippant, not flirty.

"In my line of work, weekends don't matter."

It was an excellent reminder that he was an officer of the law, and that I had invited him in. *Desperate times,* I assured myself.

His eyes zeroed in on the bottled water I had left on the coffee table near his satchel. His thirsty swallow spoke for itself.

Without a word, I went to the kitchen and pulled a cold bottle from the refrigerator. I handed it to him with a warning. "Try not to drool on the furniture."

Jack mistook my smart aleck reply as an invitation. He took a seat on the couch. I chose the armchair.

"Did you catch your suspect?" I asked.

"Person of interest," he corrected. He twisted the cap off the bottle and drank half of it in one swig.

"Thirsty, much?"

"It's hot out there, chasing down would-be criminals."

"It's hot out there, period," I snorted.

"Where are you from?"

"Why do you ask?" I hedged.

"You have the accent." It was his take on my 'you have the look' observation.

I shrugged, but he persisted. "I detect one of the northern states."

"I lived in Ohio once," I offered. I left out all the other places I had lived, particularly New York.

He tipped the water bottle up to his mouth. "I see you're back to not giving me the time of day," he muttered.

My reply was snippy. "I invited you in, you know."

"That you did." Jack drained the water and scooted forward to stand.

I believed in giving credit where credit was due. *At least he knows when he's outstayed his welcome.*

"Thanks for getting my briefcase for me." Formality slipped into his voice.

"No problem."

We reached for the case at the same time, which *was* a problem. As our hands bumped, we knocked the leather case to the floor. It was one of those upright styles, and I hadn't bothered securing the top. The contents scattered, spilling under and around my coffee table.

Jack bent to scoop up the files and papers nearest him, as I went for those fanning out on the opposite side.

I wasn't being nosy. I was making sure all the file folders were facing the same direction, so that I wouldn't upend one and make a bigger mess. My eyes just happened to snag on one tab in particular.

I swear, my knees literally buckled. The air left my lungs, and I'm sure the color in my face disappeared.

"What — what are you doing with this?" I meant to demand an answer, but my words were little more than a whisper.

On his feet in a flash, Jack snatched the files from my hands. "Give me those!" he snapped.

I let him take all but one. The file in my hand trembled as I repeated, "What are you doing with this?" It finally sounded like the demand it was.

"Give that to me, Lexi," he growled.

I held it behind my back. "Answer me!"

"I. Said. Give. It. Back."

"Not until you answer me. Why do you have this file, Jack?" I hated the way my voice started to tremble, especially when his was as unyielding as stone.

"Because I am an officer of the law," he reminded me coldly. "Don't make me arrest you for tampering with an investigation."

It wasn't the thought of being arrested that made me relinquish the folder. It was the thought of an investigation.

"In . . . invest . . . investigation?" I had trouble getting the word out as I sank back into my chair.

"That's right, an investigation." His eyes narrowed as he looked at me. "What's wrong with you? Are you all right?"

I shook my head slowly. I was anything but all right.

"Are you sick?" he asked, his voice turning to one of concern.

Of course, I was sick — sick at heart, and sick to my stomach — but I didn't tell him that. "Why do you have that file?" I asked again.

He wavered between concern and condemnation. "I'm not at liberty to say."

"I need to know." I wasn't above begging. "That — that case was closed five years ago."

His dark eyes flickered with surprise. "You're familiar with the Milkman case?"

I closed my eyes at the name. At the horror.

"Some," I whispered.

Jack forgot that he was leaving. He sat back down and leaned forward over his knees. His voice wasn't as rigid now, but I could hear the urgency there. "What do you know about the case, Lexi?"

"It was all over the news." It was a statement, not an answer. "They caught the guy." I couldn't help but gasp when I saw the look on his face. "Right, Jack? They caught the right man. Right?" I had a sick feeling that three rights could prove one wrong.

"Yeah," he said, but he looked less than certain. I saw the way he rubbed a hand along his leg. He was either nervous or lying. Possibly both.

"What aren't you saying?"

"I told you. I'm not at liberty to discuss an ongoing investigation with you."

"Why is there an investigation?" My voice was unusually high.

"Lexi—"

I grabbed his arm, gripping it so hard, my fingers dug into his flesh. "Tell me the truth!"

Indecision crept across his face. I tightened my grip. "The truth, Jack."

He eased my hand off his arm, prying away one finger at a time. "This stays between us." His tone was clear: his demand was not up for debate.

"I swear."

When he hesitated, I made a move to grab his arm again. The impression of my fingers was still there. He sighed and finally spoke. "We haven't released this to the press." His voice was low. I had to lean close to catch his words. "The case could be re-opened. Right now, the files are being closely re-evaluated."

He took far too long with his answer. I all but screamed, "Jack!"

"There's been another incident."

With those words, the world fell from beneath my feet.

To be clear, I did not faint. I may have swooned just a little. I definitely fell back against my chair, my body limp. But I did not faint. I had never fainted before in my life, and I wasn't about to start then.

"Lexi? Lexi, talk to me!"

Jack was on his knees in front of me, clutching my hands. I saw one move toward my cheek.

Summoning all my strength, I muttered from between my teeth, "I swear, if you slap my face, I will punch you in the balls."

To my surprise, he grinned. "On second thought, don't talk to me. Not if you're going to threaten an officer of the law with bodily harm."

"Then don't hover."

He held his hands up in surrender and moved away. "Not hovering."

Still flung against the back of my chair, I pressed my hands to both sides of my head. It was the only way to keep it from exploding.

"What just happened?" he asked quietly, watching me closely for my reply. Most likely to detect whatever lie I would concoct.

"I was surprised. I felt lightheaded."

"You fainted."

"I *did not* faint!"

"Matter of opinion."

"But I didn't faint." It was important to stress that fact.

"Fine. Why did you do whatever it is you did or didn't do?"

"I told you. I was surprised."

"That was a very strong reaction to a surprise."

I rephrased my answer. "I was *very* surprised."

"Look," he said in reprimand. "I broke protocol and told you more than I should have. Now, it's your turn to tell me why you're so '*very* surprised.'"

"I, uh, I told you. The press led everyone to believe it was over. The Milkman killed himself. Now you're telling me he's back?"

"I didn't say that," Jack was quick to say. "I said there was an incident. Something that had enough similarities to warrant looking into the old files again."

My head was pounding too hard to think straight. "That's . . . That's all?" I asked.

He spread his palms wide. "I'm just looking at the files."

I pretended not to notice, but we both knew he hadn't given me a straight answer.

CHAPTER NINETEEN

Lexi

Jack couldn't leave quickly enough to suit either of us. His reasons were probably along the lines of botched protocol and making certain I hadn't withheld some important paper from the file. My reasons were along the lines of panic, followed by determination. I was now on a mission.

It was a good thing I had gotten my first paycheck from Sam. Booking a flight on such short notice cost me a fortune.

Early the next morning, I drove into Houston and boarded an airplane headed to New York. The traffic along Interstate 45 wasn't bad on a Saturday, so I made good time. The downside was that the added wait at the airport, plus the three and a half hours in the air, left entirely too much time to think. I had sworn I would never speak to my father again. I was done with his lies, done with his excuses, done with his no-remorse mentality. Done with whatever game this was he shared with Sam. Thoughts of facing him again, even through bars and glass, left me nauseous.

Yet, here I was, on a flight to hell. I had to go to that prison to see with my own eyes. To assure myself that Leo

Drakos was still where he belonged: securely locked away with the other criminals. He wasn't eligible for parole for another ten-plus years, but I knew my father had a way of smudging lines. Any line. If possible, he would bargain for less time behind bars, or for a new trial based on just-discovered 'evidence' his sleazy lawyers supposedly unearthed. Never mind that the evidence was bought and paid for. If it changed the boundary lines and pushed them in his favor, he would stop at nothing to make it happen.

Despite the early hour, I ordered a Bloody Mary. I reasoned that tomato juice could be considered a breakfast drink.

I had paid for in-flight internet service, so I spent most of the time pulling up article after article concerning the Milkman. The earlier ones followed his sordid trail of horror up and down the East Coast. Citing an ongoing investigation, the reports didn't offer specific details, but it didn't take much for readers to imagine what his victims had gone through. To ponder the psychological effects that would forever haunt them.

It was the latter articles I devoured. The Milkman had been caught. A handyman named Doyle Roland had come forward and confessed to the crimes. Before he could stand trial, he had taken his own life inside his jail cell. The case was closed, and the country could sleep easier now, knowing the sporadic attacks were over.

A second Bloody Mary took the edge off my nerves. I managed a fifteen-minute nap before the flight attendant came over the intercom, educating us on how to prepare for landing.

I called for a rideshare the moment I stepped off the plane. Without as much as a carry-on bag to slow me down, I went straight to ground transportation. And then I was off to the prison, torn between wanting to get this over with and wanting to prolong it for as long as possible.

I thought I might hyperventilate as I walked through those prison gates. I was designated as a pre-approved visitor, even though I had used the entitlement exactly once. But I knew I took the risk of not being allowed in, showing up today unannounced. I would cite a family emergency, claiming dire news that needed to be delivered in person.

As I went through a rigorous security check, I questioned the wisdom of coming. I could think of a dozen reasons I shouldn't be there. I could think of only one that made today necessary.

I wasn't surprised when my request to see him was initially turned down. I had expected as much. What I hadn't expected was to be redirected to the assistant warden's office.

"Please, Miss Drakos, have a seat." The older man motioned to a straight-backed chair, and we both took our places. For convenience, I had used my true credentials as Michaela Drakos to register with the prison. Novel concept, I know, but in this case, it was necessary.

"I know I didn't request this visit," I hurried to say. "But this is an emergency. I hope you understand." I put just enough urgency in my voice, accompanied by a bit of a whimper.

"I'm afraid it's you who doesn't understand, Miss Drakos." He looked uncomfortable, and unsure of how to proceed.

I sensed trouble. What had my father done now? As long as he hadn't been released, I didn't care how many fights he had been in or how severe his punishment. Solitary confinement seemed like a good fit to me, no matter the offense.

"Is there a problem?" I asked, my back stiffening.

"I don't know how to tell you this, Miss Drakos," he said in a kind voice, "but your father, Leonardo Drakos, died over three years ago."

Completely stunned, I stared at the warden. Of all the ways I had imagined today's meeting might go, of all the scenarios I had conjured up in my head and all the outcomes I had braced for, death wasn't one of them. Certainly not a death that occurred three years prior.

"How?" I asked.

"Prison fight." This in itself wasn't a huge surprise. "He suffered significant injuries," he went on. "Infection set in, and the doctors were unable to save him. I'm so sorry, Miss Drakos."

He mistook my silence for grief. "I do apologize for blurting it out this way. I know it must come as quite a shock." His belated realization seemed less than sincere. "I should have called for clergy to be here with you. I can do so now if you like?"

I shook my head. "That's not necessary."

"We have his last effects in storage. If you'd like to leave a forwarding address, we'll be happy to send them to you."

"No need." I wanted no physical reminders of the man. The mental and emotional ones were more than enough.

After a moment of silence — I suppose intended for me to compose myself — the warden cleared his throat. "If you have any questions, I'd be happy to address them."

"Just one. Why am I just now hearing about this?"

"We tried reaching you, but the number you had listed with us had been disconnected. Our letters came back with no forwarding address. I'm sorry, Miss Drakos, but we had no way of getting in touch with you."

And they wouldn't have, now, would they? I realized. I had given them my birth name, Michaela Drakos, but that person no longer existed. There was no trace of her in Lexi Graham's life.

I took less than a minute to digest all that he had told me. I nodded, picked up my purse, and stood. "Thank you, Warden Gables, for taking time to speak with me today."

There was little else he could say. "I truly am sorry, Miss Drakos," he said to my departing back.

I didn't bother dropping my voice. "I'm not," I said.

With head held high, I walked from his office. Only one thought kept running through my head. This time, I was free of Leonardo Drakos for good.

* * *

The full impact of the warden's words sank in as I flew back to Houston, crossed the bridge onto Galveston Island, and drove toward my apartment. On a whim, I wound up at the wharfs, treating myself to a decadent meal of fresh seafood.

I know it sounds cold, but I didn't feel sadness over my father's death. I can't even say I felt regret. The meal wasn't a celebration of life, nor was it a celebration of death. I was celebrating this incredible sense of freedom I felt. My father's chains no longer bound me.

For the first time since taking the job at Samson Shipping, I felt a stir of excitement on Monday morning as I rode the private elevator to the top floor. I had used the trope expression many times in the past, but this time, I meant it. I was truly starting over, freed from my past.

Ready to tackle whatever project Sam gave me, I entered the apartment with an optimistic smile on my face.

Some of my optimism slipped when I saw Simon coming from Sam's office.

Nothing like Simon the Slippery Snake to dampen a girl's enthusiasm, I grumbled inwardly.

I had come to think of him by the non-affectionate nickname over the last couple of weeks. With his slicked-back hair and his dark, beady eyes, it was an easy comparison. Something about the guy still made me feel icky.

"Good morning, Lexi," he greeted me. There was that smile again, the one that was never reflected in said beady eyes.

"Good morning."

"Have a nice weekend?"

The question, which could have been innocent enough, pushed my confidence down another notch.

I shrugged as casually as I could. "Not bad. Yours?"

"Mine was rather interesting. Thank you for asking."

If he expected me to make further inquiry, he was sadly disappointed. Moving past him in the hallway, I injected enthusiasm into my smile. "I hope your week will be the same."

"I'm sure it will be," he said enigmatically. I had almost reached my office when he reminded me, "Don't forget. We have that lunch on Wednesday."

I gave him a thumbs up without turning around. It wouldn't do for him to see the queasy look of dread on my face. How would I stomach an entire meal stuck between Simon and Sam? The caterers were bringing their samples, and Sam insisted we make a meal of it.

"On my calendar," I assured him.

I put my purse away and powered on the computer. I refused to allow Simon Brewster to ruin my day.

The cigar box on my desk caught my eye. By the time I raised my gaze to the altered painting, the last of my optimism leaked away.

How could I have forgotten about all this over the weekend?

True, a lot had happened over the past seventy-two hours. I visited the hospital, took gifts to the children, and met Grandma Gail, the woman I could have sworn was following me. I saw Jack at the coffee shop again and actually *invited* a lawman into my home. I found the folder. I flew to and from New York in a matter of ten hours. I discovered that my father had been dead for three years. By anyone's standards, it was seventy-two hours on a rollercoaster of emotion.

Discovering that my father was no longer a threat had made me almost delirious with relief. But enough to forget all that happened last week? To forget all the coincidences, and the conclusions I had drawn?

Last week, I had been so certain that Sam and my father were working together.

This week, I realized it was impossible. My father was dead.

Why, then, did I still have this sinking feeling in the pit of my stomach?

Plus, how could all these weird happenings be explained? One or two coincidences were plausible. Three or more were possible. But the cigar box? The painting? Those moved firmly into the Highly Suspicious column.

Before I could ponder their meaning, Sam buzzed me through the intercom, summoning me into her office.

Like Simon, her first question was: "Nice weekend?"

Like Simon, it could have been an idle greeting.

And like Simon, she waited for my answer with an odd gleam in her eyes. It was that lion-ready-to-pounce look.

"To be honest, I spent yesterday on my couch, binging on movies and popcorn." That much was true. I didn't mention all that came before.

"It's good you were able to rest." She somehow made my day of recuperation sound slovenly. "We have a busy week ahead. You've checked in with the caterers, right? Everything is on schedule for Wednesday?"

"As far as I know."

"Find out. Be certain," she snapped.

Agreeably, I managed a smile. "Of course."

"And the flowers?"

"I'm picking up a sample arrangement today. If you approve, I'll order them for delivery next Friday morning."

"We'll need to send out invitations."

"Do I need to take care of those, or will you?"

Her sniff was a reprimand within itself. "I'll handwrite them, of course. You'll see to it that they're mailed. Promptly."

Again, I agreed with a forced smile.

"Leave time on your schedule tomorrow to interview serving staff for the dinner party."

"Tomorrow? Oh. I planned to visit the hospital tomorrow." I was surprised at the pang of disappointment I felt at the thought of missing a visit.

"I can only spare you one day this week. Thursday will have to do."

None of the assignments she had mentioned so far would require a full day's attention. But she paid my salary and paid it well. I couldn't very well object.

"Yes, ma'am."

"You'll need to carry my business suit to the dry cleaners. I want it back no later than next Wednesday."

I scribbled it under my *To Do List* heading.

After two more mundane task requests, Sam switched topics. "Do you have your list of prospective candidates ready for me to review? My accountants are asking for an update on this year's donations."

I felt good about my answer. "Given your generous nature with children, I've selected three worthy group homes as possible recipients."

"I'd like to think I'm generous with *all* worthy causes."

Leave Sam to spoil that feeling for me. I was beginning to think nothing I did would ever suit the woman. She had clearly taken offense to what I had meant as a compliment.

Her tone was stiff, and so was my reply. "I'm sorry. I didn't mean to imply otherwise. If you'd like me to include candidates outside foster care—"

She promptly cut me off. "No, that would severely derail contribution deadlines." It was unclear whether the deadlines were imposed by her or by the establishments. It was an odd time to start a fiscal year, but I supposed planning a budget was always a timely subject. Bottom line: no matter who imposed the schedule, she seemed to blame me for messing it up. Her sigh was long-suffering. "Just email me the list, and I'll take care of it myself."

"Of course." This time, I didn't bother faking a smile.

CHAPTER TWENTY

Lexi

Sam actually approved of my floral selections. The next morning, I personally visited The Joy of Flowers and requested to see the owner.

"Come on back!" Joy called from somewhere in the back.

The front of the flower shop was bright and airy. A variety of bouquets and colorful arrangements were artfully displayed on glass shelves and modern fixtures. Not so in the workroom. A massive cooler lined one wall, filled with flowers and bulbs. The opposite wall held vases and baskets ready to be filled. In the middle, there was a long worktable, its surface scarred and nicked. I found Joy there, snipping stems with her clippers before placing them into a cut glass vase.

"Good morning!" she greeted me with a warm smile.

"Good morning to you."

"So? Don't keep me in suspense! Did Sam like the arrangement?"

Her eager expression made me smile. "Believe it or not, she did."

"You mean we actually pulled this off?"

"Yes!" By now, I was laughing, suddenly feeling as giddy as her. "We did it! For once, I was able to please her. You did an amazing job with the flowers, Joy."

"Don't sell yourself short. You're the one who designed it. You and your talented sketch."

"I sketched, you created."

"See?" She wore a big grin. "We make a great pair. You really should consider coming to work here."

"You have no idea how tempting that thought is," I confided. There would be no more reminders of my father, no more wondering where the painting and the cigar box fit in. "But I have zero knowledge of flowers."

"Can you operate a cash register?"

"Some are more complicated than others, but I've managed to do okay."

"See? When you aren't sketching designs, you could work the counter."

"Are you serious about a job?" I asked Joy.

"I never joke about offering someone a job."

I took a solid thirty seconds to reply. "Can I think about it? It's tempting, but . . ."

"But I can't pay anything near what she's paying you," Joy said on a sigh. "I get it."

"It's not that. I have a couple of projects I'd really like to see through." I thought mostly of the long-term children in the group homes. The ones who no one wanted to foster. I wanted to help them, and Sam offered the means.

"I can appreciate that. Just let me know. I have a girl who's going out on medical leave in a few weeks."

"I'll definitely think about it." I pulled my notepad from my purse. "But first, I need to order these flowers. Sam said to spare no expense."

Back at my office, I helped Simon interview prospective servers. Again, he did most of the work. I didn't understand why I had to be there for the process. Most of his questions centered around confidentiality and prior high-profile clientele. He stressed the non-disclosure form they would be required to sign. His questions made me uneasy. I had to wonder about Sam's business associates.

For my part in the process, I focused more on etiquette. Did they know which side to serve from? Did they understand the difference between attentive and hovering? No water glass should ever be less than half-full. Dirty dishes should be whisked away immediately. Dessert shouldn't be offered until every guest had finished eating. Attention to detail was important.

When the last candidate was gone, Simon turned to me with a rare compliment. "You did well, Lexi. It's obvious you've done this before."

"Thank you."

"This dinner is important to Sam. It needs to be perfect."

"I'll do everything I can to make sure that it is," I assured him.

Flashing me his fake smile, he said, "I knew Sam made a good choice when hiring you."

* * *

I had to tolerate that smile all through lunch on Wednesday.

To my surprise, Sam walked to the dining room for our meal. She stopped twice to catch her breath. I avoided looking at her massive thighs or the way they jiggled during her slow journey. She wore a pair of shapeless pants and a blue blouse. Cerulean, of course. Like most of her tops, it had long sleeves with elastic at the wrists.

Four chefs vied for the chance to cater Sam's business party. I ate no more than a bite or two of each dish. Between four chefs presenting samples of an entire meal, it was a staggering amount of food.

For such a slim man, Simon ate like a bottomless pit. He and Sam eagerly awaited every last dish. I didn't think I could take another bite of anything, but Sam insisted that I try everything. We had to sample the wines, too. By the time we left the table, I was feeling a little tipsy.

The only bright spot of our meal was the markedly improved spirits of my companions. While I sipped the wines offered, Simon gulped them. With each glass, his stiff demeanor softened, and occasionally, his smile looked sincere. And fine food and wine made Sam happy. She was actually a pleasant dinner companion. She even complimented me on the menu I had chosen.

I was feeling optimistic about the dinner party next week. The flowers were ordered. The serving staff was arranged. Sam made an immediate choice on which caterer she preferred, so now, the food was ordered. Things were falling into place.

It hadn't escaped my attention how quickly Sam had decided on the caterer. I had to wonder if she had known all along who her choice would be. Having the others here could have been a test for me or could have been a way to score free food from the city's finest chefs. Doing so wouldn't have been a matter of money. It would have been a matter of flexing her power. To test the boundary lines.

I once knew someone else who would have done the same thing.

I left the office early, allowing me enough time to make the post office and buy stamps. Personally, I thought it was short notice for a formal business dinner. Something told me that Sam's invitations were more of a summons. Guests had only one week to rearrange their calendars and prepare for the meeting. But maybe, I reasoned, the handwritten invitation was a formality. Maybe the date had been reserved in advance, and the note penned on expensive stationery served as a reminder.

I collected the envelopes from Sam and listened to her instructions. "Ask to see all the stamps available for first class mail. Find one that complements the stationery, as long as it shows some semblance of dignity. No comical characters."

"I'll ask to see their full tray," I promised. The last time I had done so, the postal worker looked at me like I had lost my mind. I resisted telling him it wasn't me who had lost her mind, but my employer.

"Very well. I'll see you on Friday."

I carried the letters to the post office and dutifully asked to see their entire offering of stamps. The woman started to object, until she saw some of the names written on the envelopes. After that, she was happy to accommodate my odd request.

When she offered to stamp them for me and put them in the post, I thanked her for the kind gesture but turned it down. Since I knew virtually no one in Galveston, I hadn't paid attention to the guests' names. However, the woman's reaction made me curious. I wanted to see them for myself.

I moved to one of the counters provided for customers. I applied the first two stamps to the envelopes, but neither name meant anything to me. The name on the third note was vaguely familiar. A local politician, maybe? The sixth name I saw tickled a memory. I remembered the man I had seen coming from Sam's office, and the name clicked with the face. Dean Henry. Seeing a glimpse of his face that day had been enough to make me apprehensive, and now I knew why. He had been an associate of my father's.

Sick to my stomach, I flipped through the remaining invitations. I was familiar with four more of the names. Eduardo Diaz. Juan Arenas. Milton Sawyer. Luca Pesci.

At the risk of sounding like Jack Eastwood, I counted the reasons I was confused.

First, I couldn't understand why Sam would invite these men to her dinner party. Diaz lived in Mexico. Arenas in Cuba. Sawyer in Washington, DC. And I knew very well that Pesci was from New Jersey. Were they all flying in for a convention or something? Surely, it wasn't just to attend a business dinner with my boss.

Second, at least a third of these letters wouldn't reach their recipients in time for the party. Especially not the ones outside the United States. Why had she waited so long to mail their invitations?

Third, I didn't understand why or how Sam knew these men. These men had been 'associates' of my father's. None, I suspected, were honorable businessmen.

Fourth, and most importantly, did this mean my suspicions from last week were confirmed? Before his death, had Sam been connected to my father in some way?

My hands felt tainted, having simply touched the men's names. I felt as if every set of eyes in the post office were upon me. I felt a headache coming on. I felt nausea. I felt panic.

Some rational part of my brain thought to use my burner phone to snap pictures of the men's names and addresses. They might prove to be useful. I might add them to the red notebooks.

Pictures taken, I scooped up the letters and slid them into the out-going mail slot. I glanced around, but no one paid me attention. Relieved, I hurried out the door and back to my car. I went straight to my apartment and didn't come out until it was time to visit the hospital the next morning.

* * *

When Marsha stopped me to say Tommy Dankworth was no longer there, my heart stalled in my chest. I know my face paled.

"Did he . . . ?" I left the question hanging, unable to voice the terrible thought.

"Oh. No, no, nothing like that. But his parents checked him out. There was some sort of family emergency."

"Oh. I hope nothing too serious?"

"They didn't say, but from the look on the father's face, I think so."

"That's too bad," I murmured. "I'll miss seeing Tommy. Is there anyone else I should stop by and visit?"

"I thought you might ask. There's a little girl in 3212, Traci, who might enjoy a visit. I'm afraid her story isn't good. She came in from foster care with unexplained bruising and a broken leg. The only people who've come to see her are the social worker and the reverend. She doesn't talk much, but sometimes just seeing a friendly face or hearing a kind voice is enough to lift a child's spirits."

"Of course. I'll visit her first."

Seeing a girl no more than eight or nine years old with so many bruises and cuts tore at my heart. I felt angry at her foster parents and for the system that placed her there.

I couldn't let Traci see my anger. It would frighten her, and the last thing this child needed was to be frightened. So, I smiled as brightly as I could and introduced myself to her. When she didn't respond to most of my questions, I asked her if I could read her a book. It was a used copy I had picked up in the gift shop's bargain bin. It was intended for children younger than she was, but it was fun and uplifting and had a picture of a comical pig on the cover.

Traci listened but made no comment. She didn't laugh at my dramatic reading or at the silliest parts in the story. When I closed the book, however, I noticed how her eyes looked sad. She had enjoyed it more than she had shown.

"I have an idea," I told the little girl. I reached into my purse and pulled out my sketchpad. "How about if I draw my version of Clotilda the Pig? I might even draw you riding her!"

Interest flared in Traci's eyes, but she said nothing.

I drew a caricature of her riding the pig. I saw a hint of a smile when I showed it to her.

Encouraged, I added to my drawing. This time, they both wore huge cowboy hats. This earned a definite smile from the child.

On a roll, I drew high-heeled shoes and jewelry on both of them.

I scored big with a giggle.

I continued to draw, adding silly backgrounds and pigs flying in the sky. When the page was full, I started on another.

By the time I finally left her room, Traci was smiling, and she said a shy, "Thank you."

"You're more than welcome, Traci. You keep the drawings, and whenever you see them, I hope they'll make you smile."

I didn't go by the coffee shop that day. I was afraid I would see Jack, and I wasn't ready for that. Instead, I went to Stewart Beach and walked along the shoreline. I went outside my comfort zone and tried a different sandwich shop along the seawall. I couldn't resist ordering the same kind of sandwich as usual, but at least the atmosphere was different.

As I was leaving the deli, my phone rang. Trying to juggle the door and my to-go cup with one hand while pulling my phone out with the other, I failed to notice it was from an unknown number.

"Hello?"

The line was silent. "Hello?" I asked again. Cell service could sometimes be contrary.

The person on the other end of the line started breathing heavily. Not enough to be suggestive. Just enough to let me know someone was there. Just enough to be threatening.

I went home, took a shower, and turned on a movie. I needed to rest my mind and calm my nerves.

CHAPTER TWENTY-ONE

The Milkman

Betty Ann Finke had told the pediatrician she wasn't ready to be released from the hospital yet. She needed more time to get this breastfeeding thing down. But her insurance said it was time to go, so go she did. She was home now, doing her best to nurse a baby who didn't seem interested in eating.

At his one-week checkup, the doctor said little Dylan wasn't gaining the way he should. He suggested she re-enlist the hospital's lactation consultant for help.

With Betty Ann's husband back at work, her mother picked up the slack. She came during the day to help her daughter adjust to life with a newborn. Mrs. Clemons did the laundry, swept, ran errands, and gave Betty Ann time for a much-needed nap most afternoons.

At the moment, she was at the grocery store. Mrs. Clemons had planned out the menus for the week, and when she returned, she would help Betty Ann prep and precook what they could.

She left her daughter resting on the couch, but Dylan had other plans for his mother. Knowing Miss Sally would be here at any moment, Betty Ann unlocked the front door and went to answer her son's wails. The baby would need changing before she settled on the couch to nurse him. By then, the consultant should be there. The timing couldn't be more perfect.

Busy cooing to her son, Betty Ann's back was to the opened nursery door. She never heard the man when he crept across the carpeted floor. Before she knew he was there, he had a blindfold over her eyes and had it tied in a hard knot.

She yelped and would have reached for the blindfold, but he grabbed her arms and held them behind her back.

"Ouch! Who are you? What do you want?" she demanded.

"I'm not here to harm you, Betty Ann," the man said.

"You — you know my name? How?"

"That's not important. What's important is that your son is crying. You need to pick him up, Betty Ann."

"I can't. You — you have my arms."

"That I do." He almost chuckled. "So, here's what we're going to do. I'm going to slowly turn your arms loose, and you're going to pick up your son from his crib. You aren't going to try anything smart." There was no laughter in his voice now. "I'm right here behind you."

Betty Ann bent forward but discovered a problem. "I can't see to pick him up," she whimpered. "Please, untie the blindfold."

"I can't do that. But I can guide you." He reached his arm around her. His body was close to hers, reminding her that she had no place to run. Not that she would ever leave her baby behind.

"Here," he said. "This is his left side. Use your other hand to feel your way to his right. Like you do in the middle of the night. In the dark."

She would have protested, telling him she used a nightlight, but her words were trapped in her throat. She couldn't even scream. She was too afraid to do anything but follow his orders.

"Easy does it," the man coached. His tone was almost gentle. "There you go. You've got him. Very good, Betty Ann."

She finally found her voice. It was weak and held a decided waver. "Who are you? What do you want?"

"Just do as I say, and everything will be fine."

"You-you should know. I'm expecting company at any moment. And my mother is due back here soon."

"About that . . ."

"What? What did you do? Did you do something to my mother?" Her voice rose with hysteria.

"Not at all. Unfortunately, when she comes out of the grocery store, she'll discover she has a flat. That should detain her for a while."

"My — my company—"

"Is running late," he told her. "A minor emergency came up at the hospital."

"How do you know all this? Wait. Where are we going? Why are you pushing me?"

"I'm not pushing you. I'm guiding you. To the living room."

"I'll fall. I'll hurt my baby. Please, undo my blindfold so I can see where I'm going!"

"Just trust me, and you won't fall. You'll do fine."

She didn't trust him, not at all, but Betty Ann had no choice but to let him guide her out the door and down the hall.

The man took the lead at some point, leading her through doors and around pieces of furniture. When they reached the couch, he took the baby from her arms.

"No! Give him back to me! Give me Dylan!"

"I will, Betty Ann, just as soon as you get settled on the couch. See? You can feel my knee against yours. I'm not going anywhere. Sit down, get situated, and I'll give you the baby."

Betty Ann quickly sat down. "He's crying. Give him to me."

"Don't you need a pillow to rest your arm on? Or a nursing pillow? Don't you have one?" There was a hint of disapproval in his voice.

"It's in the nursery. You can get it for me. Give me Dylan, and you can bring it to us."

"Nice try. That pillow beside you will do just fine."

She arranged it the way Miss Sally had taught her. "Okay, I'm ready."

"Not yet you aren't. You need to take your top off."

"No!"

"How else will you feed him? Take your bra and your top off."

"My bra is designed for nursing," she protested.

"Not good enough. Take them both off and toss them behind you. I'll hold Dylan until you do."

Whimpering again, Betty Ann shed her clothes and sat shivering on the couch. "N-now give him to me." Between her nerves and the cold, her teeth chattered.

"Of course." The man placed the crying baby in her arms.

Unable to see him, the mother ran one hand over her small son while holding him with the other. Then she held him close, kissing his head and whispering into his ears.

"He's crying because he's hungry, Betty Ann. Be a good little mommy and feed your son."

"I just want to make sure he's safe."

"He's safe. He's just hungry!" the man snapped.

Nervously, Betty Ann pulled the baby to her breast. Tears escaped the blindfold and ran down her face. She was a terrible mother. She had left the door unlocked and now, a madman was inside her house. Even if she found a way to escape him, she wouldn't be able to see where she ran. He would stop her, and there was no telling what he might do to them then. And to make everything worse, she couldn't even feed her son!

"You need to relax, Betty Ann. Think pleasant thoughts. Let your milk flow."

"I'm trying," she whispered. "I'm trying."

She cringed when he touched her. To her amazement, the baby began to nurse.

"Yes," the man said in satisfaction. "That's right, Betty Ann. You're doing exactly right. Yes. Beautiful."

Betty Ann cried the whole time she nursed her son. She stopped to change sides, burping him in between. Occasionally the man murmured his approval, but otherwise, he softly hummed Brahms' 'Lullaby.'

When she was done nursing, and Dylan had fallen asleep in her arms, Betty Ann waited for more instructions. The man didn't speak. After a while, she wondered if he was even there, but she was afraid to ask. She sat there with her baby, crying softly, content for the moment to hold him in her arms.

As terrified as she was, she fell asleep on the couch, until a woman's voice startled her awake. "Betty Ann! What is going on? What is on your eyes?"

"Miss Sally? Is that you?" Her voice was thick from tears and sleep.

"What happened?"

"A-a man. He was here, and he put a blindfold on me, and he made me walk to the couch. He made me take off my top and feed Dylan."

"Where is he now? Is he still in the house?"

"I don't know."

Miss Sally untied the blindfold and ran her eyes over the young mother in assessment. "Did he hurt you?"

"No. He just . . . watched."

"We need to call the police."

"No! I-I don't want anyone to know. My husband would worry, and my mom would blame herself for leaving. It was my fault I left the door unlocked."

"I don't know . . ." Miss Sally said with a frown.

"Please. Don't say anything."

Betty Ann was adamant. With a sigh, her companion agreed.

CHAPTER TWENTY-TWO

Lexi

Once at work the next morning, I concentrated on Sam's philanthropy project. Like I told Joy, I wanted to see this project through.

Sam had instructed me to find the long termers, as I had come to think of them, in my top five recommendations for her donation. I was pleased to find that two of the homes had no children residing there for over five years. Between the other three, however, there was a heartbreaking fifteen. Who knew how many others there were like them in other homes?

I knew if I dwelled on the subject too long, I would be pulled back into thoughts of my father. As a child who grew up in the system, he always used foster care as a bribe of sorts to keep me in line. If I told anyone what we were doing, he warned, they would take him away, and they would stick me in foster care. He made it sound as if it were the worst fate ever.

As if life with him had been much better.

Early in the afternoon, my phone rang. My attention was on the computer. I absently picked up the receiver to the desk phone.

The ring continued, and I realized it was my cell phone. But the ringtone was different, meaning it was my other phone. My burner, so to speak. Meaning the caller had to be the man I was avoiding.

I considered ignoring it, but curiosity got the better of me. "Hello?"

"We need to talk." No hello, no how are you doing. Just those four tersely spoken words.

"Why?"

"Not over the phone."

"Good, because I'm at work."

"I'll come to your apartment. Tell me a time."

"Never?" I suggested sardonically.

"This isn't funny, Lexi. We need to talk."

After a long silence and an even longer sigh, I huffed, "Fine. Let's just get it over with."

"When?"

"I'll get off around five. Give me time to eat." I had a feeling this wasn't a conversation to have on an empty stomach.

"I'll bring pizza. I'll be there at five thirty."

He didn't bother with goodbye. He just hung up.

"Rude," I complained into the silent line.

I tossed the phone in my purse and went back to work. When I had all my information together, I sent Sam an email, asking if I could speak with her.

I know. It was a weird way to communicate when our offices were connected, but it was the method she preferred. The intercom was used only for summoning me.

She emailed me back with permission to come to her office.

"You needed something?" she asked. She sounded irritated that I dared to disturb her.

"Yes. You asked me to gather information on long-term residents at the group homes. I concentrated on five homes and found fifteen children who have been there for over five years, overlooked for adoption or foster care. I have their ages, interests, genders, and clothes sizes."

She looked surprised. "You found time to work on the project this week?"

"I feel like this is a worthy project that deserves prompt attention." I handed her the pages I held. "With your permission, I would like to buy each child something special. I was thinking of a backpack, filled with things that fit their needs and interests."

Sam studied me for a moment, narrowing her eyes and giving me that assessing look I had come to hate. But for once, I met her approval. She nodded and said, "Make it a suitcase. You have an allowance of fifteen hundred dollars for each child."

Her generosity left me speechless. This woman never ceased to surprise me. Cold and hard at times. Giving and kindhearted at others. She was a study in contradictions.

"Wow," I finally managed. "That's very generous of you."

"It's no less than they deserve." Her manner turned brusque again. "Was there anything else?"

"Nothing. Thank you. I'll get to work on this immediately."

"Close the door behind you."

* * *

I had just enough time to go home, take a shower, and change into something comfortable before my unwanted guest arrived. I wasn't trying to impress Jack By The Way Eastwood. I put on exercise pants and a simple T-shirt and twisted my hair into a messy top bun.

Promptly at five thirty, he knocked at my door. I could already smell the pizza on the other side, its delicious aroma wafting in through the cracks and crevices.

I swear, the man must have had an aversion to standard greetings. When he came through the door, his first words were, "I didn't know what you liked, so I bought a medium meat lovers and a small cheese pizza. Where do you want them?"

I motioned toward the coffee table. I had a small dinette set, but that seemed a little too formal for pizza. It also seemed too much like I had invited him for dinner, which I hadn't.

"What do you want to drink?" I asked, going to the kitchen for napkins and paper towels.

"I didn't know if you had any, so I brought beer." He pulled a six pack from the plastic bag he carried.

"Good enough for me."

I joined him in the living room, reluctantly taking a seat beside him on the couch. It gave us both easy access to the pizza. We devoured our first slice of meat lovers before bothering with conversation.

"I guess you're wondering why I'm here," Jack said.

I was getting good at this Texas drawl thing. "It may have crossed my mind."

"You had a *very*" — he stressed the word — "strong reaction last week to mention of the Milkman."

"At which time I *did not* faint," I pointed out. "I may have sagged, but I did not faint."

"Either way, it wasn't a normal reaction."

"It wasn't a normal statement."

"You seemed to know a lot about the case."

I shrugged as I reached for a second slice of pizza. "It was all over the news."

His dark eyes watched me intently. I tried hard not to squirm. He finally asked the dreaded question, "Who are you, Lexi Graham?"

My mouth went dry. I had never told him my last name. Then again, he was an officer of the law.

I answered with a question of my own. "Who are you? Professionally, I mean. You never said what division of the law you were with."

"I'm a special agent liaison between Homeland Security and the United States Marshal Service." He shifted so that he could pull a badge from his jeans pocket. He held the badge toward me for inspection, but I didn't bother. It was enough just knowing he carried a badge. It made me queasy in the stomach, but in some weird way, it made me feel safe.

"Why are you here, Special Agent Eastwood?" I knew my voice sounded resigned. It reflected the way I felt. Resigned, wary, and weary.

"Here in Galveston, or here in your apartment?"

"Both."

"I serve the region. I'm renting a house here for a case I've been assigned to."

"And in my apartment? Why did you call me this afternoon and insist on seeing me?"

"Would you believe that I missed seeing you around the coffee shop this week?"

I made a point to look down at his boots. "I see you're wearing your boots again, so you can wade through all your own crap."

"Fair enough." He took a long draw of the bottled beer. I wasn't familiar with the local brand, but I had to admit it was good.

"Isn't there some rule about drinking while on duty?" I asked.

"I'm not on duty. This is an unofficial visit."

I took a sip of my own beer, delaying the inevitable.

"I told you who I was," Jack said. "Now, it's your turn."

"You already know my name. Lexi Graham."

"I know the name. I don't know the story, or why there's nothing in your background until six years ago. It's like you popped up out of nowhere." His chocolate eyes watched me carefully. "Who are you, really?"

My back stiffened. I'm sure my voice reflected the same rigidity. "Am I under investigation, Agent Eastwood?"

"I never said that." His answer wasn't a denial.

"Have I broken any laws?" I posed the question as Lexi Graham, not as Michaela Drakos.

"Not that I'm aware of."

"Then, what does it matter if you can only poke around in the last six years of my life?"

"Let's just say that your lack of any personal background piques my interest."

"Let's just say it's none of your business," I shot back.

Jack pulled the good ol' boy routine and tipped his beer slightly forward, his manner a little too casual for my liking. "You see," he said with a laid-back drawl, "that's where you just might be wrong. As an officer of the law, particularly when it comes to Homeland Security, it's my job to check out anything or anyone who looks suspicious. Popping up out of nowhere six years ago definitely looks suspicious, don't you think?"

"Not particularly," I lied. "Some people lead more private lives than others. Believe me, I'm hardly one to post my every move on social media."

He gave a slow, interested nod. "I did notice that." His words sounded like a sincere observation, but I knew otherwise. He had been snooping around in my life.

"In that case," I pointed out in a snippy voice, "it should be obvious that I value my privacy."

"I can understand that," he said amicably. "At the same time, though, you can see why it does make me curious. It's almost like you have something to hide." Good ol' boy or not, his eyes keenly watched for my response.

"I don't know what you're talking about." I aimed for a flippant tone, but even to my ears, it sounded defensive.

"Are you sure about that?"

"I'm sure I don't know where this line of questioning is going. Either you have a reason to poke around in my private life, or you don't!" There. I sounded indignant now, just the effect I was going for.

"Actually, I do have a reason."

"Which is?"

He seemed to contemplate his reply. "Not only is your past a big void, but you have a . . . connection" — he finally decided upon the word — "to the case I'm working on."

My heart skipped a beat, possibly two, but I forced myself to sound nonchalant. "What case do I supposedly have a connection to?" I asked, cocking my head to one side.

Jack leaned back against the couch, propped his booted foot on the edge of my coffee table, and took a long sip of his second beer. "What would you say," he said in his deep drawl, "if I told you Samson Shipping was my assignment here in Galveston? That I'm investigating the company you work for?"

"You are? But . . . what about the Milkman file?"

"That happened after I was here. I originally came to dig up dirt on SS International."

I considered his words for a few seconds before nodding. "I guess it shouldn't surprise me. The day I told you who I worked for, your face tightened, making your lip curl just a little bit in the corner." I touched my own in correlation. "You really should work on your tell."

Jack squinted his eyes and studied me. "Are you working undercover? Is that why I can't find anything on Lexi Graham?"

I hooted with laughter. "Me? A cop?" I didn't tell him I knew more about running from the law than I did about enforcing it. Instead, I conveniently changed the subject. "What are you investigating Sam for?"

"Off the record?"

I countered with: "Isn't this entire conversation?"

A nod, and then an answer. "Illegal trading practices, smuggling stolen and prohibited goods in and out of the country, corruption, and racketeering."

I ingested his words with a slow nod.

"That's not the reaction I was expecting," Jack noted.

"I guess I should be shocked, but . . . I'm not." I had to be honest with him. "Ever since I took this job, I've had my suspicions. There's something weird going on in that place."

"Weird? Can you be more specific?"

I withheld a key issue, while volunteering another. "Other than the fact that Sam is paying me a ridiculous salary for doing practically nothing? Or other than the fact that I think she may be stalking me?"

"Stalking you?" His voice was sharp. "When did this happen?"

I frowned when I thought about the timeline and how it would sound to him. He would think I was overreacting. "Before I took the job there, actually. But I know she's involved."

"Describe stalking."

I rolled my eyes. "Knowing that someone is watching me, even though I can't see them. Having a truck ride my bumper, making every move that I do. Having my purse stolen, only to have someone mail me a fake driver's license with a different name on it. Someone calling and hanging up." I shrugged. "You know, the usual stalker behavior."

"Someone stole your purse? Did you report it to the police?"

"No."

"Why not?" Jack demanded.

Once again, my answer was only a part of the truth. "There was nothing of value in it. You've seen the hobo bag I normally carry, but that day, I was carrying a tiny handbag. The only thing in there I needed was my driver's license."

"You still should have reported a purse-snatching to the police."

"So, sue me."

His eyes narrowed. I didn't think he was buying everything I was saying. "If this started before you were hired at SSI, why are you so certain your boss is behind it?"

This was what I hadn't said before, but what I had to say now. "Sam . . . knows things," I offered slowly. "Things from my past. Things she has no way of knowing yet does. Things that no one could possibly know."

"Not even your family?"

"I have no family. My mother took one look at me and high-tailed it out of the hospital." I said it as if it still didn't hurt after twenty-eight years. It did. "My father died three years ago." That fact didn't hurt at all.

"No siblings?"

"Just me."

"Why don't you confront Sam? Come out and ask how she knows these things?"

"Because it's some kind of game to her. She's . . . baiting me." I searched for a suitable word. "She drops little hints. Leaves clues. Gives me gifts that represent another time in my life. She's slick about it, but I know what she's doing. She's letting me know that she knows. She watches me like a lion about to pounce on its prey. She's playing me, but I don't know her game. It's just a matter of time before she leaps."

I didn't like how his chocolaty eyes probed my face, searching for the things I didn't say. He finally commented, "She really has you spooked, doesn't she?"

I nodded. If I spoke right then, I would have said more than I wanted.

"How long have you suspected the company might not be strictly legit?"

"When I heard the starting pay they were offering and saw the benefit package. If I was a lawyer in a top firm, yeah. But a personal assistant?"

"You took the job." It was a statement of fact, not judgment.

"I saw no reason to turn down the money until I knew for sure." I released a sigh. "I guess now I know."

"There's still a chance I could be wrong."

I looked over at Special Agent Jack Eastwood. He didn't seem to be the kind of guy who was wrong very often. "Two questions." I held up the same number of fingers. "One, you said I have a connection. Are you accusing me of being involved in whatever illegal activities are going on there?"

He turned the question back on me. "Are you?"

I met his gaze without flinching. "No."

"Didn't think so." His tone was casually dismissive. "Second question?"

"Would you be open to a proposition? I think we'll both find it beneficial."

Jack let his dark eyes roam over me. I saw a flicker of interest. Felt the betrayal of a tiny spark deep in my belly.

He extinguished any potential flame between us with a drawled response. "If you're suggesting what I think you're suggesting, I don't take bribes."

My cheeks burned in embarrassment. A dash of a guilty conscience could have been partially responsible, but I'd stab myself in the eyes before I ever told him that.

"As if!" My tone suggested disgust. My eyes raked over his long, toned body, determined not to like what I saw. "Don't flatter yourself, cowboy."

Jack was neither flattered nor insulted. His face was unreadable. "What are you proposing?"

"Lillian Samson is hiding something. You need to know what that is to prove she's breaking the law. I need to know what that is before she breaks me. I propose that we pool our resources. I'll tell you what I know if you'll tell me what you know."

"My reasons relate to criminal acts and breaking the law."

"Because stalking someone isn't," I said sardonically.

"Because I won't allow this case to be used as some bargaining chip."

Ice was no match for my words. "I'm very familiar with bargaining chips, Jack."

"So, now, you're saying you're a professional gambler? Is that how you know about tells and bargaining chips?"

"Maybe I am taking a gamble," I admitted. "But I have something that you don't. I have information, and the only way you're going to get it is to make a deal with me."

God, I hated how much I sounded like my father. I told myself that some things were worth the sacrifice. Stubbornly, I crossed my arms over my chest. "Take it or leave it."

CHAPTER TWENTY-THREE

Lexi

"What do you have on Lillian Samson?" Jack demanded.

"Not until we have an agreement. My information, in exchange for your intel."

"My intel?" Jack suddenly looked even more suspicious than he already had. "You say you aren't a cop. What about a PI?"

"What about it?"

"I'm asking you. Are you a private investigator, Lexi Graham? Is that how you know to cover your tracks so well?"

"If you think leaving a six-year-old-trail is covering my tracks, what kind of private investigator would that make me?" I scoffed.

"I'm referring to the — what? eighteen years? — before that."

His flattery didn't work on me. I pointed to the boots still propped on my table. "I see why those boots come in so handy, cowboy. That would only make me twenty-four." Pursing my lips, I said, "No, I'm not a PI. Nor was I born last night. I'm not making your job any easier for you. Not until we have an agreement."

"You may be getting the short end of the stick," he warned. "Before we make a deal, you need to be aware of that."

"Duly noted."

"Fine." Jack stuck out his hand. "I'll tell you what I have on Sam. You'll do the same."

"Agreed."

We shook on the agreement, and I beat him to the punch. "You start."

"The thing is, I seriously don't have much. Lillian Samson's past is filled with as many holes as Lexi Graham's."

I ignored the barb. "How so?"

"From what I understand, George Samson was BOI. H—"

"He was *what*?" I interrupted.

"Born on island. What's more, he never once mentioned having a wife. By all accounts, he was a quiet man, worked hard, never made a fuss about anything. He was completely dedicated to his job. No one remembered him leaving town very often. They couldn't imagine when he had time to get married."

"Maybe it was in his youth," I speculated. "An impulsive marriage they never bothered to get annulled."

"Maybe. But everyone was shocked when Lillian Samson showed up at his funeral, claiming to be his wife."

"Not even his family knew?"

"No family to speak of. A nephew in Arkansas he hadn't seen in years, and a few cousins he hadn't kept in touch with. They all came to the funeral, of course, hoping to claim whatever share of the company they might have."

"I thought the company wasn't successful until Sam took over."

"It was successful, just not the multi-million-dollar enterprise she turned it into."

I had heard this before, but it made even less sense now than ever. "In less than three years? That's . . . fast."

"Go on and say it. It's highly suspicious, which is where I come in. To be such a brilliant businesswoman, Lillian

Samson has no business experience. No work experience. No college education. Not much of anything. Until she came to Galveston and took over Samson Shipping, she was practically a ghost."

Unease crept into my stomach. It was a scenario I knew all too well. "You suspect organized crime."

Jack tipped the long neck of his bottle toward me again. "See? That right there is the reason I pegged you as the law."

"I watch enough TV to know that's the usual culprit," I claimed.

"Somehow I doubt that."

When he offered nothing more, I just stared at him. "Surely, you have something more than that!"

"I warned you I didn't have much."

"I already knew most of what you told me!" I protested. "That was zero help."

"You took the deal anyway."

"Fine." I crossed my arms again and lifted my chin in defiance. "I'll tell you as much as you told me. In other words, practically *noth-ing*." I said the last word with attitude and volume.

"Then I'll make you a new proposition."

"We already made a deal," I snapped.

"I hear this one pays better."

"What are you suggesting, Special Agent Eastwood?" Hearing the hint of humor in his voice made my eyes narrow. There was no way I would ever work for the feds, reward or no reward.

"You just said Sam pays you a generous salary," Jack pointed out. "Why not continue taking it while you can? Because if I find what I'm looking for, you won't have your job forever."

"You want me to spy on my own boss."

"Don't sound so indignant. You already said you don't trust her."

"I don't."

"Then helping me shouldn't be a problem. You work there. You have an inside advantage I don't have."

"Unless you want to know about picking up postage stamps and floral arrangements, I doubt it. She doesn't trust me with anything remotely sensitive."

Jack looked around the apartment, but I knew it wasn't to admire my decorating style. He was formulating a rebuttal. "Look. You say someone is stalking you, and you think it's your boss. You say she knows things she shouldn't. That means she must be someone from your past. Help us both figure this out. You help me get something on her, and I'll promise to watch your back. I may not have access inside the building, but the minute you step out that door, I'll protect you."

I refused to admit how good those words made me feel. How safe.

I willed the feeling away. "The problem is that being inside the building is where most of the danger is," I told him.

"It sounds to me like that's where she plays her psychological games. Lions, on the other hand, like to roam the plains. They like a physical challenge. Lions like to stalk their prey in their natural habitat, and strike when they least expect it."

My voice dripped with sarcasm. "No, Jack, that doesn't make me nervous at all."

"I told you that I'll be here to protect you."

I weighed all he had told me. For confirmation's sake, I asked, "You plan to take her down?"

"All the way to hell."

My nod was one of approval, but also one of acknowledgment. "I'll be putting myself in danger. If she ever found out what I was doing . . ."

"She won't. We'll be careful."

Making a decision I prayed I wouldn't regret, I told him quietly, "In a show of good faith, I'll give you more than the few paltry facts you gave me. I'll give you proof that she has connections to the Italian mafia, a known smuggler in Cuba, a drug cartel in Mexico, and to one of the biggest criminals in DC."

His surprise turned skeptical. "And you know this, how?"

I went to the bedroom and retrieved my hobo-style purse. Rummaging through it at the coffee table, I pulled out a half-dozen things before finding what I was after. Sketchpad. iPhone. The tattered children's book. Two ballpoint pens. Wallet. A small case protecting my art pencils. Finally, I pulled out the no-frills phone that contained only Jack's number and a few incriminating photos.

"You have a burner?" he asked in surprise.

"Not a burner, per se. A couple of weeks ago, I lost my phone and had to get a temporary replacement." I opened it and thumbed over to the photos app.

"Sam's hosting an important business dinner next Friday. We've been preparing for it all week. She had me mail the invitations, and I recognized some of the names. I, uh, took a couple of quick pictures."

"What prompted you to do that?"

"Instinct."

Jack looked at the names and addresses in the photographs. With a low whistle, he said, "Those are some pretty heavy names. Big-time criminals."

"Yes," I agreed.

"Mind if I send these to my phone?"

"I guess not."

He made quick work of the transfer. Handing my phone back, he asked, "Why did you take these pictures? And be honest with me this time."

This was the hard part. Where once I crossed that line, there was no going back. Not even my father's thin-line philosophy could change this one.

"They're, uh, names from my past." I let the last sip of my beer trickle down my throat.

The special agent sitting beside me said nothing. His feet came down from their perch, and he leaned forward, so that he could see my face. "Explain."

"My father was a criminal."

"Then it was his past, not yours." I think he was telling himself that. His tone sounded relieved.

My voice was sharp. "Don't be so sure about that." Like I often did when uncomfortable, I resorted to snarky humor. "Don't let this cute little face fool you, cowboy. I'm not as innocent as you may think."

"Anything you care to share?" Sensing I might need it, Jack opened another bottle of beer and handed it to me.

"I'm beyond caring anymore." It was a lie I told myself. After a long draw from my bottle, I spoke the truth. "Before he became a full-blown criminal, my father was more of a con man. And I helped him. Even though I never got a pink elephant, I was his accomplice."

Understandably, Jack's forehead crinkled in confusion. "Pink elephant?"

My short laugh held no humor. "Whenever he picked a pocket or stole a purse, my job was to distract the person. My father told me we were playing a game. He said there was a pink elephant in one of them, and when he found it, I could have it." I tucked my leg beneath me. The casual pose belied my matter-of-fact tone. "Never got it."

"You were just a little kid. You didn't know any better."

"Don't make excuses for me. As I got older, I knew what I was doing was wrong. I won't bore you with the details but believe me when I say I was as guilty as my father. I watched, and I learned. He even let me plot and run my own scam one time. I was weirdly proud of myself."

Jack remained quiet while I bared my sins. "I developed a conscience about the time my father got mixed up with some really bad people. People like Diaz and Pesci. We had moved up in the world by then, all the way up to a penthouse in New York City. And still, I helped him. I played hostess at his dinner parties. I helped him impress fake friends and questionable *associates*. Pretended not to hear when they talked about their shady business dealings right there in front of me. I laughed at their crude jokes and flirted just enough to serve them another drink and another round of my father's lies. I never stooped low enough to sleep with any of them, even though my father would have approved, had it benefited him. But after every dinner party and after every time those men visited, I took a shower and tried to scrub away the feel of their eyes on me."

When he spoke again, it was a question. "When did you finally leave?"

I didn't sugarcoat the truth. "When I was able to steal enough money to make a clean break. All those times I played hostess, I didn't just take their coats. I took their cash and anything of value I found. Once, I even helped one of the wives look for a very expensive necklace, knowing fully well it was in my pocket. I'm not proud of what I did, but after some of the things I overheard — some of the things I knew they were doing — I couldn't stay. I was afraid of them, but my biggest fear was becoming one of them. Of becoming my father."

Jack's dark eyes looked thoughtful. Perhaps doubtful. Did he think I was making this all up?

"If you knew so much," he said, "I'm surprised he let you leave."

"He didn't. Like I said, over the years, I watched and learned. I knew how to skip town without getting caught. Like all those times in my childhood, I had to leave everything behind. My phone, my identity, all my favorite things. I had a duffel bag full of clothes and books" — I didn't say what kind — "and ran as fast and as far as I could. I used different aliases and different looks, and every time I thought my father's goons were on my trail, I ran again."

"Are you still running?"

I set my half-empty beer on the table. I didn't look at him when I admitted, "With a past like mine, I doubt I'll ever stop running. Even if it's only from myself."

"So, the name Lexi Graham . . . Are you in WITSEC?"

I knew being in the Witness Security program could explain the holes in my background. It would explain how I had gotten a new social security number. But I wouldn't lie. Not now.

"No. After I left home, my father was convicted of tax evasion and some other white-collar crimes. He was sent to prison, but I knew he still had connections on the outside. I knew he would never stop looking for me." I was leaving out huge hunks of the story, but that would come out later. "I had my name legally changed. And though it still meant never staying in any one place for too long, I could finally sleep at night."

"How'd you wind up in Galveston?"

"Would you believe Facebook? I saw an artist was advertising for a new assistant, and it sounded like fun. I did a Zoom interview and got the job. And here I am."

"In the same town where your father's former associates show up." I heard the skepticism in his voice.

"This isn't another scam, Jack. I'm telling you the truth."

"Explain to me again why you would confess all your crimes to a federal agent if there wasn't something in it for you."

I took offense. "Did I ask you for anything, Jack? Did I ask you to keep my name out of it, or to go easy on my sentencing? Did I, Jack?" I demanded.

That muscle worked along his jaw again. "No. You did not."

"Nor will I. I told you. I don't care anymore. I deserve whatever punishment I get." Casual pose and all, my voice was obstinate.

"So, why tell me all that?"

"Because I need to prove to my father — to myself — that I'm nothing like him."

His chocolate eyes narrowed, thinking he had caught me in a lie. "I thought you said your father was dead."

"He is. But he's probably somewhere in hell watching me, just waiting for me to mess up and join him there." My voice was bitter. "My father wouldn't confess to breathing if it didn't benefit him. He always had an angle. Always tried to twist the line between right and wrong, good and evil. I have to prove that I'm better than him. That I didn't inherit his . . . faults."

"If your father was involved with the likes of Diaz and Pesci, he must have transformed from lowly conman to big-time heavyweight."

"He did," I confirmed needlessly.

"Was he anyone I might be familiar with?"

My eyes held his. "Ever heard of Leonardo Drakos?"

Jack's mouth fell open. "Leo Drakos was your *father*?"

I lifted one shoulder in a lopsided shrug. "You know what they say. You can't choose your relatives."

"Leo Drakos." He still sounded stunned.

"Yes. Leo Drakos."

"I never saw that one coming," he admitted. "And you think Sam knows?"

"Without a doubt. The clues and the taunts are spot-on. I thought I had covered my tracks this time, but somehow, she knows. That fake driver's license I mentioned? It was in the name of Michaela Drakos. My birth name."

"How would she have come by this information? Are you certain you don't remember her from a former association with your father?"

"I'm positive."

He considered my words. "They must have met after you left home. They must have made some sort of business agreement."

"Actually, I have another theory." I rubbed sweaty palms along my sweatpants. The thought had been eating at me, and it still made me slightly nauseous. "My father grew up in an orphanage. He never talked about his family, presumably because he didn't have one. But Sam . . ." I swallowed hard and forged on. "Sam has a lot of similarities to my father. Same tastes, same phrases, same taunting look in her eyes. She has a soft spot for children and a surprising desire to help kids stuck in foster care. I-I have no proof, but I think . . ." My voice dropped with the admission. "I think Sam may be my aunt."

Jack did his best to keep his jaw from dropping. Again. "Wow," he finally said. "You're just full of surprises."

"Not the good kind, I'm afraid."

Jack pushed up from the sofa to pace my small living room. "Maybe you shouldn't stay there after all," he said. "It would be too dangerous. I'll find another way to bring her down."

"No. I need to do this."

"You've already given me more than I had. You've already proved you're not like your father."

"I want to see this through, Jack. I want to be part of it. If she's anything like him, she needs to be stopped."

He ran a hand over his short hair. "I need to think about this."

"What's there to think about? I can get you the inside information you want. I can get you proof."

"How do you plan to do that? You said she didn't trust you with anything sensitive."

"She doesn't. But that's the thing about rich people. They're suspicious of their own, but they forget to be suspicious of mere underlings."

"What are you talking about?" Jack looked slightly irritated at my cryptic words.

"The help, Jack. She's having a dinner party, and I plan to be there. Not as a guest, but as the hired help."

"You're there every day as the hired help. She hasn't let a thing slip yet."

"I'm talking about waitstaff. Believe me, when the wine and the conversation start to flow, no one remembers that the servers are still in the room. They give up all sorts of secrets in front of the help."

He looked at me with something akin to horror. "You can't possibly think you can—"

I didn't let him finish. "I can, and I do. I helped Simon interview the servers. He grilled each of them over their understanding of privacy and discretion. He even made them sign

NDAs. Sam and her guests won't think twice about speaking freely in front of the help."

"You'll never get away with it. They'll recognize you."

"I told you, Jack." My voice was hard. "I know how to fly under the radar."

He stared at me, still horrified at my suggestion. "Do you have any idea how dangerous that would be? It would take a seasoned professional to pull that off!"

I rolled my hands in a silent gesture of *ta-dum*. "I rest my case."

"Y— But . . . You aren't a professional!" Jack sputtered.

"Didn't you hear my resume? I've been playing make-believe my entire life. I *am* a professional, Jack."

He was having none of it. "No. I refuse to let you do this."

I came off the couch and pushed my way into his face. Granted, I had to tilt my head back to do so, but the fierceness of my sudden move commanded his attention.

"No man," I swore darkly, "will *ever* tell me what I can or cannot do. I lived under my father's rule for eighteen years, but never again. Do you hear me, Jack Eastwood? You *will not* tell me what I can and cannot do."

He was angry at my outburst. I saw it in the way his nostrils flared, and the way his jawline twitched. But he didn't say a word. Nor did he back away.

When I realized how close we were standing, I took a tiny step in retreat, but my words were as strong as ever. "I'm doing this, with or without your help."

"You must have some sort of death wish," he muttered.

"Is that why you became a lawman? Because you had some sort of death wish?"

"I became a lawman for the sake of justice. I wanted to make the world a better place."

"That's what I want, too. Justice. And a world without people like Leo Drakos and Lillian Samson and Eduardo Diaz would definitely be a better place."

"They'll recognize you."

I shook my head in disagreement. "It's been a long time since any of those men have seen me. I look completely different now."

"What about Sam? And Simon? They see you every day."

"As I said, I helped Simon interview the servers. There was one woman I can easily pass as. I need a disguise kit, but I know I can pull this off. No one will ever know it's me."

"You'd better pray they don't, or else they'll kill you!"

"Scare tactics don't work with me, Jack. Not on this. I know exactly the kind of people I'm dealing with, and I know exactly what they're capable of. Get me a pair of earrings with a camera and mic, and leave the rest to me. I'll get you the information you need."

"Lexi . . ."

I held my ground. "Jack."

After a lengthy moment, he released a weary breath. "Let me see what I can do. We'll need more than just earrings. I'll have to arrange logistics. We need a way to intercept the original server, slip you into her place, set up a surveillance area, plus dozens of other details." He eyed the leftover pizza on the coffee table. "Mind if I take some with me? I have a feeling it's going to be a long night."

"Take it all," I told him. I no longer had an appetite.

With his hands once again full, I opened the door for him to leave. Jack paused in the doorway. "And, Lexi?"

"Yeah?"

"I'm glad you weren't offering something else earlier. Because, frankly, I might have taken the bribe."

He was gone and down the stairs before I realized he hadn't been wearing that playful little smile at the corners of his mouth.

I think he may have actually been serious.

CHAPTER TWENTY-FOUR

Lexi

"We have a problem."

Jack. *Did the man not understand the concept of hello?*

"I don't have time for problems," I told him. "I have enough already."

Sam had sent me on a half-dozen errands as her big dinner party drew closer. I had just stepped out of my car, one hand already full of bags and reaching for more when he called.

"Now you have more. The names on Sam's guest list? Some of them aren't viable."

"And this is a problem, how?"

"Juan Arenas is serving time in prison. Luca Pesci has been on the no-fly list for eighteen months. Robert Slaughter has been dead for two years. The address on Milton Sawyer's invitation doesn't exist. Phil Phillips took two bullets in the head earlier this year. None of those men would be able to attend a business dinner, and I think she's very aware of that fact. Samson Shipping sent a floral arrangement to Slaughter's funeral."

"Why would she invite people who obviously can't come? That doesn't make any sense."

"It does if she's just playing with you."

"Hmm." I nibbled on my lip. "I did think that was terribly late notice to send out invitations."

"Apparently, they weren't actual invitations. She just wanted you to see the names."

"If there's not an actual dinner party taking place, she is spending a medium-sized fortune just to toy with me."

"I'm sure there's a party. Diaz and Garrido are already in the country."

"I don't know who Garrido is."

"Consider yourself lucky."

"Look, I've got to go. Sam was expecting me back a half hour ago."

"Meet me tomorrow at the coffee shop. If you think you're being followed, sit at the table next to mine. Three o'clock." He hung up without saying goodbye.

"Typical," I grumbled, throwing my secondary phone into the bottom of my bag. I still had trouble calling it a burner.

I wrangled all seven or eight bags in my arms, butt-closed the car door, and got lucky when another person exited the building at the same time I entered. The woman held the door open for me with an amused look in her eyes.

"Thank you," I panted. I wasn't sure I could have pulled the door open on my own, and I certainly didn't relish the idea of picking the bags up again after they sagged against the sidewalk. I had a vision of me chasing their runaway contents. "You're a lifesaver," I told her.

"Now, wouldn't that be nice," the woman replied. She raised her eyebrows just enough to make the hairs on my neck do the same. I detected something in her voice as she said, "Have a good day," and left me to manage the elevator on my own.

Which was fine by me. I was busy trying to decide what that 'something' in her voice had been. A warning? A threat? An observation of my overloaded arms? Had she been amused that I crammed it all into one trip, rather than making separate, more manageable trips? Something told me it had nothing to do with my state of disarray, and everything to do with my statement. *You're a lifesaver.*

As the elevator stopped on the second floor, I realized what that 'something' in her voice had been. Her entire response had been more than polite conversation.

It had been a bad omen.

The afternoon passed in a blur of activity, prepping for the party. Today was only Monday. I shuddered to think what the next four days would be like.

Sam was more critical than ever, questioning my every move and my every decision. She sent me on a last-minute trip to the florist, where she instructed me to buy arrangements that would be similar in size to the ones I had designed and ordered. She said color didn't matter, but I knew her well enough to know that if I returned with a hodgepodge of colors and styles, she would find a way to retaliate. I had no idea what other secrets she might know from my past and how she would use them to taunt me, so I took the safe route. I asked Joy to create a cohesive theme among the arrangements and have them delivered as quickly as possible. I even offered to help make the spur-of-the-moment order.

"You won't get in trouble for staying to help?" Joy asked.

"With Sam, there's a fifty-fifty chance no matter what I do. Either way, if I bring back something she approves of, she'll be less likely to have my head."

Joy's eyes lit with a smile. "Then put this apron on, and let's get busy!"

I was no match for her quick and nimble fingers, but I soon got the hang of it. We had settled on a very simplistic theme. We snipped, shaped, and stacked bunches of greenery into the rough dimensions needed. Then, Joy expertly added white tea roses at random.

"You have a true gift!" I beamed at my new friend. "These are perfect. I don't think even Sam can find fault with them. They're simple, yet sophisticated. Thank you so much for creating them at such late notice!"

"Thank you for helping." I knew she was as pleased as I was about the arrangements. "Plus, I thought it was a good way to get you initiated into the world of flowers." She winked slyly before asking, "Have you given any more thought to my offer?"

"Actually, I have," I told her. "I have one more special project I'd like to see through, and then I'd love to come to work for you."

"Really? That's perfect!" Joy squealed.

I stopped her before she broke into a happy dance. "There's one problem, though. I don't know how long this project will last."

If you don't live through the party, it really won't matter, now, will it? I heard my inner Lexi smirk.

Joy brushed away my concerns. "Doesn't matter. I can make do until you come on board." We walked back to the front as she chattered about future plans with me as the designer and her as the creator. Her enthusiasm was contagious. By the time I crawled into the car, I was smiling.

* * *

When I met Jack for coffee the next day, my smile was gone.

SAR didn't detect anyone suspicious about, but it still seemed prudent to fake-search for an empty table.

"Here," Jack offered, barely looking up from his paper. "Have a seat."

I tumbled into the seat next to his, landing harder than I intended.

"Trouble with the dream job?" he mused.

"You mean the nightmare." I slurped my still-steaming coffee, welcoming the scalding heat. "I should have asked for a triple shot of espresso," I muttered. "Better yet, whiskey."

"That bad?"

"I swear that woman's panties are in a wad!" I huffed. I gave him a brief rundown of the past two days, concluding with: "She's been like a grizzly bear. I think we'll all need a tranquilizer by Friday."

"There must be a lot riding on this meeting," he murmured thoughtfully.

"I think that's an understatement. You saw the guest list. Even if it were all a ruse, at least two of those men will probably be there. There's no telling who else she has waiting in the wings." I reached into my purse and pulled out several rolls of candy. "Here. Have a Lifesaver or five."

That quirky smile lifted the corners of his mouth. "Is this some sort of addiction I should be aware of?"

"Actually, it's more like a trial test. These may or may not be poisoned, so I thought you might like to be my guinea pig."

He choked on a sip of his coffee. "Did you say poisoned? Why would you think that?"

"Maybe poisoned is an exaggeration, but I definitely think they're suspicious. I found an entire box of them on my desk this morning."

"Another of Sam's mind games?"

My sigh was heavy. "I'm not sure." I told him about my strange encounter with the woman holding the door for me yesterday.

"What did this woman look like?"

"Five foot six, slender, shoulder-length brown hair, gray eyes, between sixty and sixty-five years old, manicured nails and eyebrows."

"Wow," Jack said. "That's . . . very specific."

"A trait I picked up early in life." My tone was nonchalant, but my words were telling.

He tapped something into his phone before turning the screen toward me. "Was this her?"

"Yes. Who is she?"

"Vivian Mann. Her late husband was CEO of MannLife Pharmaceuticals. After his death last year, she took over the helm and turned the company's nosedive into bankruptcy around. It's now on a rocket ship headed to the moon. Sound familiar?"

I snorted. "What is this, some sort of a weird widow's club? Maybe their tagline is 'Profit from your husband's death and become a millionaire.'"

"Or maybe 'How to kill your husband and get rich quick,'" he suggested.

I'm not sure why, but I gasped. Sam was a lot of things, but I had never quite pictured her as a murderer. "You think that's what's happened?"

Jack lifted his shoulders in a shrug. "It's a theory I'm tossing around. Sam's estranged husband dies of an apparent heart attack. No one close to him was aware that he had a heart condition, *or* a wife. She swoops in at his funeral, takes over the company, and gets insanely rich. Vivian's husband dies in a one-car accident, she takes over the company, and is raking money in faster than a dozen bunnies can reproduce."

"Thanks for the visual," I muttered.

"It's either a very exclusive widow's club or one hell of a racket."

"Do you think this Vivian is invited to the dinner party on Friday?"

"I'd bet my other nine toes on it."

I rolled my eyes at his lame joke. I'd never known a lawman who had a sense of humor, and certainly not one with such astute observation skills. Jack might like to joke around, but behind those chocolate-colored eyes, I often saw the gears churning in his brain. I instinctively knew he was a good and dedicated lawman, which made our strange partnership all the more unlikely.

I resented having such an epiphany, so I changed the topic. "You do realize I had to face the dragon's roar to make it here by three. Now's not the time for you to play This Little Piggy."

"That's what I like about you, Graham. You're all business." When he said it in that tone, it hardly sounded like a compliment. "Besides, I thought she was a lion, not a dragon."

"Same difference."

"Not true. Lions like to stalk their prey before they pounce. Dragons skip the foreplay and go straight for the flame." He used his hand to emulate flames coming from his mouth.

"Fine. She's a lion. A lion who's stalking me and feasting upon every last one of my nerves." I glared at him with more than a little flame of my own. "Which you are getting on, by the way. Just tell me why we're here, Jack."

"I wanted to tell you that your earrings will be ready tomorrow. We'll need to do a test run, so we're having dinner at Miller's."

"We are?" My tone was indignant. "When did we decide this?"

"I've made all the arrangements. All you have to do is show up."

I knew I could sputter and complain all I wanted, but nothing would change. The truth was, we did need to do a test run. What better place than in a noisy, crowded restaurant?

"Wear something nice. Not nice like what you're wearing now, but date nice."

"*Date* nice?" I asked incredulously.

"How's it going to look if a guy gives his girlfriend a nice pair of sparkly earrings, and she looks like she's dressed for a funeral?" Before I could launch into a very verbal protest, he held up his palm. "Not that this is a date or that you're my girlfriend. And not that you look like you're dressed for a funeral, but the look isn't exactly island wear. Don't you have something more . . . feminine?" He made another hand motion toward my slacks and jacket.

Up until that moment, I had been pleased with the professional air my outfit evoked. Not so much after his statement.

"I'll do my best to find something date appropriate," I assured him dryly. "But I do agree with you on the island wear thing. This will definitely be too dressy for my new job."

"You have a new job?" he asked in surprise.

"Yes. Like you said, if we're successful, I won't have my current job much longer. I've accepted a job offer with a florist in town."

"You know flowers?" This surprised him even more, but I couldn't take offense.

"No," I admitted, "but I'm a fast learner."

"Good for you. I'm glad you're planning for after."

I had to admit, it did feel good. Especially knowing this was the second job I had gotten on my own merits.

A terrible truth dawned on me, and I was crushed.

I hadn't really gotten my job with Samson Shipping on my own!

Why had it taken me so long to see it? The signs were all there: Janine had fired me without warning; Sam owned the building that housed her studio. Janine promised me a letter of recommendation; Sam's job offer magically appeared. My credentials weren't questioned; Sam already knew who I was.

What a fool I had been. I thought I had been hired without bargaining my soul to the devil, but all along, the devil had been playing me.

"Lexi?"

I waved off the concern in Jack's voice. This was no time to get tangled in the remnants of a burst bubble.

"In case you're wondering," I told him, "I've already covered my bases for Friday night." My voice was matter of fact, revealing none of the heartbreak I felt. "On the very off chance that Sam invited me to the dinner party — which she wouldn't, of course, but still — I asked for Monday off. I told her I'm a bridesmaid in an old college friend's wedding on Sunday. The rehearsal is supposedly on Saturday, so I said I had a flight scheduled for Friday evening. I pretended to worry about letting her down, but she was — no surprise here — very supportive of me going."

"That's good," Jack said, nodding his head. "Very good. Even if someone thinks their server bears a striking resemblance to you, you've already established your alibi."

"And thanks to the very generous salary Sam pays me, I went so far as to literally buy a plane ticket."

"You thought of everything, didn't you?"

He meant it as a compliment, but I was less than impressed. My voice was flat. "I told you, Jack. When it comes to taking on an alternate persona, I *am* a professional."

183

CHAPTER TWENTY-FIVE

Lexi

After a whirlwind day at the office, I left early enough to stop by the hospital for a quick visit. I knew the children were disappointed I couldn't stay longer, and so was I. I promised to come twice the next week and to bring a special surprise for each of them.

I also vowed to myself that I would continue to volunteer, even when my stint at Samson Shipping ended.

Rushing home from the hospital, I thumbed through my closet for a *feminine* dress to wear for dinner. It still irked me that Jack had dared to make such a dig about my wardrobe.

"We'll show him, won't we, Lex?" I said to the inner me. I pulled out a sky-blue dress with thin, flirty straps and a decidedly *feminine* neckline. Without the thin sweater, it showed off my very *feminine* features. I left my hair long and straight and fastened a simple necklace around my neck. The infinity charm hung an inch above the dress' sweetheart plunge. I slipped into my best pair of sandals, which just happened to have a very *feminine* sparkle to them, and critiqued myself in the mirror. With a spritz of a heady perfume, it was as feminine as I could get.

I texted Jack as I pulled into the parking lot. He met me at the door, dressed in his own version of island date attire. The jeans, boots, and hat were a given, but he had swapped the starched white shirt for a short-sleeved version in light, mossy green. I supposed this was one of those pearl-snap western shirts Texans were known to wear. In spite of myself, I had to admit the color looked great on him and brought out the rich chocolate of his eyes.

Those eyes moved over me with obvious appreciation. Stepping up to take my elbow, he spoke near my ear. "Damn, woman. For someone who doesn't like to make a scene, you're bound to be the center of attention tonight."

I pretended not to be affected by his response. "Is this *feminine* enough for you?"

"Oh, yeah," he said in his low, sexy drawl.

Okay, yes. I said it. Jack Eastwood was sexy. But tonight wasn't a date. I would never, *ever* date a cop. This was retribution for just some of my father's evil ways. I still hadn't figured out his connection to Sam, but shutting her down felt like I was somehow standing up to my old man and proving that I was nothing like him.

We had about a ten-minute wait, so that meant ten minutes to make small talk. There were several people around us in the small vestibule leading into the restaurant. Anything we said could be easily overheard.

Jack cleared his throat and pulled a small box from his front shirt pocket. I guess this was what he meant about the boyfriend giving his girl a present thing.

"I know we've only been seeing each other for a few weeks, but I saw these and thought of you." The lie fell from his lips so smoothly, I realized we were *both* professionals. I wondered if he had ever been undercover.

"Jack! That's so sweet of you!" I cooed, taking the box from him. I untied the red satin ribbon and lifted out a pair of sparkling stud earrings. With the crystals fashioned into different cuts and odd angles, it was impossible to see the camera lens cleverly hidden within. "These are perfect! Can you help me put them in?"

We went through the motions of fastening the flashy studs to my pierced ears, and me asking him how they looked.

"Beautiful," he said. His dark eyes looked sincere when he added, "Just like you."

Knowing it was expected of me, I kissed him on the cheek. His cologne was an entirely different level of heady.

"I love them, Jack. Thank you." I pretended to beam up at him.

When our pager buzzed, Jack steered me to our table with a hand on my lower back. It was just low enough to make a convincing statement. For all outward appearances, this was a date.

The hostess led us to the requested back booth, where our dinner was definitely *not* a date. We were taking my earrings out for a test run.

"I'm texting my tech guy right now," Jack spoke quietly so no one else could hear. "I want you to look around the building slowly, as if you're checking out the building and its decor."

"Actually, it is pretty cool," I said. "That looks like the woodwork from an old bank or something. And those chandeliers are gorgeous. Antique, by the looks of them."

"They are. They're from the state capitol in Austin, acquired after one of its many remodels. These were from the early thirties, I think." He tapped something else into his phone and waited for a reply. "Okay, Randy says to move a little slower. Be natural, but make slow, graceful moves."

"I can do graceful," I assured him with a serene smile. "I've played the part of a princess, a movie star, and the daughter of a business mogul. Oh yeah," I said as an afterthought, "that last scenario was actually true."

"Randy says you're doing great. He also said you look very hot tonight." After reading an incoming message, he looked at me apologetically. "Oops. I wasn't supposed to read that last part out loud. But, hey, that means the mic is working, right?"

"Right."

"For the record, I happen to agree with him."

I forgot all about being graceful. My head whipped back so I could see if he was teasing me again.

He wasn't.

"Randy says enough flirting and to get back to work." In a loud stage whisper, Jack leaned across the table and said, "I think he's jealous. And I know the dude over there in the red shirt is. Three o'clock, round table."

As gracefully as possible, I turned my head a quarter round. I caught the eye of the man in question and offered a wan smile. He quickly dropped his gaze and tuned into what his female companion was saying.

"Very smooth, Randy said. Again, I agree. You really do know what you're doing."

"Am I supposed to be flattered that you think so, or irritated that you doubted me?"

"Just making an observation."

The server came to take our order before we had even opened our menus. Jack already knew what he wanted, so I followed suit. "Make that two," I said, hoping I liked shrimp and grits.

"Are you feeling confident about Friday night? It's not too late to back out, you know," Jack said once our orders were placed. "I want you to be sure."

"I am very sure. I did my homework on the woman I'm posing as. Ask me anything at all."

"Name?"

"Fiona Jackson."

"Agency?"

"White Table."

"Experience?"

"Three years at the Waldorf Astoria in Orlando. Two years in private service to Victor and Amarillo Lopez of Dallas. After his death, Amarillo moved back to her native Mexico. She secured a position for me at the prestigious Adyson House

Hotel in Houston. I worked my way from server to hostess to manager. After three years of managing two of the hotel's restaurants, I moved to the coast. I enjoy the slower pace of working for a specialized service such as White Table." Quite without knowing it, I had slipped into first person.

"Very nice," Jack said with approval.

I wasn't through. "Fiona Jackson is close enough to my size and height for us to share a wardrobe. She's one of two servers from White Table chosen for the night, and her co-worker is a man she's only met once. Keeping my cover with Raul won't be a problem. She's never worked with any of the other servers, so no worries there. I'll have the same tiny mole as her on my lower right jaw. I'll wear a darker wig to match her hair and pin it into a tastefully braided bun. Nothing too flashy, but neat and demure. I'll speak with a tiny lisp that makes my S's sound like a hiss. And I'll move my head slowly and gracefully, just as I'm doing now."

After a demonstration, I looked at Jack with a cool smile. "Any questions?"

"Just one. Randy wants to know if you have a boyfriend."

"Tell Randy I'm single, and I plan to stay that way."

"It's just as well," Jack said dismissively. "Randy has a wife and three kids at home." When his phone buzzed again, Jack read the text and laughed. "Randy said to tell you I'm single." Again, he leaned in with a conspiratorial admission. "But what with the nine-toe thing, I think it's best I stay that way."

Mirroring his pose, I leaned in, too. "I think so," I said in like manner. "I also think our dinner is here. So shut up, eat, and let's get back to business."

Even though his phone didn't buzz, Jack laughed and reported, "Randy says he's filing for divorce and plans to woo you out of your single status."

"With all my baggage?" I scoffed. "I would never be so cruel. I'm afraid my status is set in stone."

And sorrow, but I couldn't tell Jack that. Not when the mysterious Randy was listening, and certainly not when Jack would ask what I meant by that.

We didn't say much as we ate, only an occasional comment now and then so that Randy knew the mic was still working.

We finished our meal, and I did another gracefully visual sweep of the restaurant. Randy reported the camera was working well, and that the mic had an impressive range, picking up voices from several tables away. I allowed Jack to pay for our meal before he escorted me back to my car.

"I'll follow you home," he said. "And don't bother arguing. It was part of our deal. You get the information I need, I provide the protection you need."

Without protest, I crawled into my car. Before shutting the door for me, Jack asked, "I forgot to ask. Nice visit at the hospital this afternoon?"

I was impressed. "I didn't notice you following me."

He offered a smug smile. "If you had, I wouldn't be very good at my job, would I?"

"Shut the door, Jack. I'll try not to notice you following me home, either."

I expected Jack to wait at the curb in front of my apartment until I opened the door to the building. Instead, he pulled in behind me, escorted me from the shadowed alleyway, and up the stairs to my apartment door.

"You don't have to come in," I told him.

"I need to show you how to charge the earrings. I thought pulling a charger out of my pocket in the restaurant might kill the look I was going for."

"Good point."

Jack helped me take the earrings out and showed me how to place them into the charger. I rubbed my earlobes as he went over the simple instructions; the jeweled cameras were surprisingly heavy.

"Just pop them back on the charger before Friday to make sure they're fully charged," he told me.

"Got it."

"I don't think we should risk being seen together for the next couple of days. Of course, if you have any questions or feel uneasy about something, don't hesitate to call or text. I'll come over if you need me."

"I'm sure I'll be fine."

"I'm sure you will be, too," he said, his smile sincere. "Don't forget. Call me if you need me. Even if you don't see me, I'll be nearby."

"Thank you."

"I think it's the other way around. Thank *you*. You're the one taking all the risks."

It hardly sounded like something I would say, but I heard the words coming from my mouth. "Anything for justice."

CHAPTER TWENTY-SIX

The Milkman

The Milkman preferred to make his visits during the darkest hours of the night. There had been that one daytime visit a few days ago, even though he had been taking a huge risk. He couldn't afford to be so reckless again. Not now.

Even this visit was pushing the envelope, but some addictions had to be fed. For him, these visits were as habit-forming as cocaine. He needed his fix. Needed the high they provided, and the glow that lasted for days.

After the week he had gone through and the week yet to come, he couldn't resist.

It was almost four in the morning. Anyone with an early-morning job could be stirring. The roads would be waking for the day. There was a greater risk someone would see him.

He was doing it anyway.

Today, he was visiting Cherise Cahill, the proud mother of a perfect little boy. As owners of a bakery near The Strand, the Cahills' daily routine started early. Lashawn's missing pickup from the driveway was proof.

The gate opened with a tiny squeak. The wind was awake and sweeping across the backyard, rustling the neatly trimmed hedges and teasing the wooden swing built for two. Its chains made more noise than the gate did.

He knew where the couple kept their 'hidden' key. He used it to let himself in the kitchen door.

The small Victorian had been redone on one of those televised makeover shows. The construction crew had done him a favor by removing unneeded walls to create a better traffic flow. It made moving about in the dark so much easier.

There was no time to admire the meticulously restored staircase with its sweeping curve and hand-carved railing. His attention was set on creeping up the steps undetected. Surprise was half of the fun.

He definitely had a surprise in store for Cherise.

His first stop was the nursery. Keeping a low profile, he unplugged the baby monitor before lifting the baby from his bed. He paused for a moment to breathe in the essence of the infant. Why wasn't there a candle that mimicked this scent? An air freshener? It should be called Innocence.

Maybe, he mused, he should create it himself.

He carried the baby with him into the master bedroom. Walls had been removed here on the second floor, as well, giving the master plenty of room. It even had a convenient chair for him to sit in.

He was already humming Brahms' 'Lullaby' when he lowered himself onto the cushions. He proceeded to unwrap the baby's tidy bundling, eliciting a small mewl of protest from the sleeping infant. As another layer was removed, little Trevon's protest grew louder.

Cherise stirred. Between the man's humming and the baby's whimpers, her sleep cycle had been interrupted.

When she heard a genuine cry, the new mother came fully awake. Her first act was to glance at the baby monitor on the nightstand. When it glowed blank, she reached out to pull it closer.

"Huh?" she mumbled. She sat up and shuffled her feet into fuzzy slippers, still trying to come awake enough. Her sluggish brain couldn't quite compute why the monitor was blank.

"No rush," the man said quietly. "I have Trevon."

Cherise's head swiveled to the sound of the voice. It was hard to see in the semi-darkness. "Lashawn?" she asked uncertainly. "Why does your voice sound funny?" She glanced back at the alarm clock's glowing numbers. "Why aren't you at the bakery?"

"Don't worry. Your husband's not late. He's already left for work."

"Who — who are you?" she demanded.

"Think of me as your well-meaning friend. I've been keeping Trevon company while you grabbed a few more minutes of sleep."

With a cry of alarm, Cherise hit the remote to light up the room. Seeing her baby in a stranger's arms, she shrieked.

The shrill sound startled Trevon. His wails matched hers. "Give me my baby! Who are you? Give him to me!" She flew across the room, trying desperately to free the baby from his arms.

"Stop it, Cherise!" His voice was harsh. "You're scaring the baby. What kind of mother does that to her child?"

"Please," she pleaded in a softer voice. "Give me Trevon."

"All in due time," the stranger assured her. "You need to feed him."

"Give him to me, and I'll get his bottle."

"Bottle?" Surprised, the man pulled back, cradling the baby against his chest protectively. "You aren't nursing him?"

"I-I use a pump. It's easier that way. Just give him to me!"

His voice turned cold. "No. You will nurse him, the way good mothers should."

"I *am* a good mother! Give me my baby, and I'll prove it."

"Fine. Let's do just that." The man started to stand. Instinctively, Cherise put a step between herself and the vile stranger. When she would have reached for her son, the man held him away. "Nuh, uh, uh," he said in a patronizing manner. "Not until you get back in bed."

"B-But—" she started to protest.

"But nothing. If you want your baby, you're going to get back in that bed, and you're going to nurse him."

"I can't! He — he won't take it. Not for me. Grandma Gail makes it seem so easy, but it's not. It's not easy. Please," Cherise begged. "Give me my baby and leave us alone!"

"I'm not here to hurt you, Cherise. And I'll prove that to you, if you just do as I say. Get in the bed and put a pillow under your arm. I'm sure your grandmother showed you how to do it."

"She's not — oh, never mind." Cherise didn't have time to explain who Grandma Gail was. She just wanted her baby, and if she had to follow the man's orders, that's exactly what she would do.

She sprinted back to bed, threw back the covers, propped herself on one pillow, and pulled another beneath her arm. "Now give him to me," she said, holding out her arms.

"You'll need to take your top off."

Nodding in compliance, she pushed her sleep shirt upward, just beneath her nursing bra.

"Take it all the way off."

Warily, Cherise did as instructed.

"Now, take off the bra."

She swallowed hard. "It has a flap."

"Take off the bra," the man repeated.

With a whimper, Cherise took off her bra. Naked from the waist up, she again reached for her baby. He was still crying, but the man had a way about him. He gently bounced the baby in his arms, all the while humming a lullaby. But he was walking toward the bed, and that was all Cherise cared about.

"Ready to go to mama, little man?" he said to the baby. "Ready to get some of mama's special milk?" Oh so carefully, he lowered the baby into the waiting woman's arms.

Her first instinct was to clutch the baby to her chest. The frantic move startled him into crying again.

"Do I have to take him back?" the man asked sharply.

"No! No, please, no!"

"Then take care of your baby. Feed him. Make him happy."

"I-I need his bottle."

"No. Nurse him."

Cherise's hands trembled as she lowered the baby and positioned him in her arm. She was thankful for the pillow beneath her elbow, giving it support, lest she drop him. By now, she was shaking badly.

"Now, feed him," the man ordered.

"I'll try, but . . ." She pulled the baby to her breast, trying to make him take her nipple. When little Trevon turned his head and continued to cry, tears gathered in her own eyes. "He won't. He won't take it. I don't have enough milk."

"You have plenty of milk."

To prove it, the man put his hand on her and gently squeezed. She jerked away from his touch, making her and the baby cry all the harder.

"Shut up, Cherise. I'm only trying to help. Sit back, relax, and let your milk come down."

"How — how can I relax? I don't know you! You broke into my house, and you — you . . . Oh, God!" She looked down at his pale fingers against her dark skin. The sight of him kneading and fondling her breast made her feel sick. She bit back another cry.

To her horror, Cherise felt a wet trickle on the underside of her breast.

"See?" the man said. His smile was a mix of good and evil. "You just needed a little encouragement. Try again."

Even with the milk forming again on her nipple, Trevon rejected her offer.

"Don't jump," the man said. "Trust me."

She had to bite her lip not to scream. She tasted blood as the man moistened the end of his pinky with her milk. Almost screamed when she saw him slip his finger into the baby's mouth. Whimpered when her son started to suck.

Moving deftly, the man withdrew his finger and pressed the baby's mouth against his mother. Cherise almost wept with relief when Trevon sucked. Nearly cried in frustration when she felt him withdraw.

"Keep trying," the man insisted.

She didn't protest when he squeezed her breast this time. Milk squirted onto Trevon's upper lip, and he finally rooted for its source. Finding it, he latched on and nursed in earnest.

Tears of joy and relief poured from his mother's eyes. She fearfully glanced toward the man, the question on her face. He nodded with approval.

"Very good, little mama. Very good."

He hummed his lullaby again, and watched mother and child in pure bliss.

It was the best high he could ask for.

CHAPTER TWENTY-SEVEN

Lexi

The dinner party was well underway. I had slipped into the role of Fiona Jackson with ease. No one suspected a thing.

In a brief moment of touch and go, Simon had come into the kitchen and eyed me with scrutiny. I kept my posture demure as I dared a peek at him. "Is — is there something I can do for you, Mr. Brewster?"

"How do you know my name?" he asked sharply.

"You interviewed me, sir. You and your assistant." I knew flattery would give me extra points. I was Sam's assistant, not his, but Fiona wouldn't have known that. She would have assumed Simon Brewster was the boss.

Simon wasn't a man who liked being made a fool. But his question had been foolish, and now, he felt the harsh sting of the truth. "I'm well aware of that!" he snapped. "Get back to work."

"Yes, sir." I dipped my head and went back to filling a tray with hors d'oeuvres.

I had carried the tray into the living area and offered it to the guests, careful not to directly look them in the eyes. The hired help must always know their place.

I moved with ease, my movements slow and graceful. I wasn't doing it for the mysterious Randy's benefit this time; it was the proper way to move among guests. As demurely as possible, I offered appetizers before the main event started. People like those gathered in Sam's penthouse didn't appreciate the help being too visible. They preferred them to blend into the woodwork, as long as they kept the food coming and the drinks flowing.

Another server trailed a few minutes behind to offer a different morsel, while a third took drink orders. A portable bar was set up along one wall of the huge room, staffed by a certified bartender who was overwhelmed with the barrage of orders. This was a drinking crowd, and Sam had spared no expense in serving the finest liquor.

In a scary, revolting kind of way, the guests assembled in her living room were impressive. I knew several of the faces. Some I didn't know by sight, but I knew their names and their reputations. Jack had pegged the three people I wasn't at all familiar with. And he had also been right about Vivian Mann. She was perched carefully at the edge of one sofa, dressed impeccably in a Chanel original and reveling in the attention of two admirers.

So far, there was no sign of Eduardo Diaz. I hoped it stayed that way, but I knew they were waiting for the final guest to arrive. In my former life, Diaz was constantly hitting on me. His lascivious gaze made my skin crawl. My father noticed how I avoided the man, and he reprimanded me for it, but I didn't care. Diaz gave me the creeps.

I had to admit that Sam looked very nice that night. She wore a dark navy tuxedo with a cerulean shirt beneath it. A navy bow tie nestled somewhere beneath her chins. I knew the tux had been made especially for her; an off-the-rack tux didn't come in her size.

I was in the kitchen when Simon stepped inside to say the last guest had arrived, and dinner could be served. As the chef prepared for the main course, we served the soup. In deference to the summer heat, it was a cold gazpacho crafted to be both vegan and gluten-free.

I knew to begin with the person seated to the right of the hostess, and to continue in a counterclockwise movement. Often, the first to be served was the guest of honor. I was dismayed to see that the final guest to arrive was seated there.

Eduardo Diaz.

My disguise didn't seem to thwart his interest in me. I'm certain he didn't recognize me, but I could feel his eyes devouring me, even as I moved down the line. I did my best to ignore him, dutifully serving each guest in a most discreet manner. My slow, meticulous movements gave Randy plenty of time to see all twelve guests in attendance. Simon and Sam occupied the last two seats, making it a full table of fourteen.

My breath stalled for a moment as I served Sam the final bowl of soup. I felt her sharp gaze on my face, but I didn't dare meet her eyes. I murmured a polite, "Here you are, madam," and stepped back. I saw her cut her eyes in my direction before she turned her attention back to her guests. Diaz's eyes followed me back to the kitchen.

When the soup course was done, Raul served salads. It gave me a few moments to gather my scattered thoughts and calm my nerves. So far, my ruse had been successful, and I saw no reason it wouldn't carry through the evening. The key was to remain cool and dispassionate. I need only to concentrate on serving, and the rest would be fine. Jack would get the information he needed, and we would both be one step closer to our goals. I would discover more about my boss and the game she played, and Jack would have the evidence needed to bring her to her knees.

Because each main course was specialized according to personal needs and preferences, the amuse-bouche was served out of its normal sequence. As Patrice served creamy deviled eggs on petite plates, I stood beside Sam's chair to announce dining options. I kept my hands clasped loosely in front of me, and my eyes moving quickly from face to face, not quite meeting anyone's eyes. My voice was friendly and upbeat, even when my gaze crossed Diaz's face. I could have sworn I saw him drooling at me.

"Tonight, the chef is delighted to present to you four meals that will tantalize your taste buds and far exceed your expectations. For a vegan option, he offers a delectable eggplant roti pachadi with saucy tomatoes in a curry paste made with coriander, cumin, and fenugreek seeds.

"If you prefer a gluten-free meal, he has prepared a wonderful salt-crusted seabass that is seared and wrapped in wood paper and served with sauce velouté over lemon bok choy.

"For those of you looking for an over-the-top meal that is sure to delight the palate, please consider a seared duck breast, accompanied by a creamy and tender butternut squash risotto.

"And, finally, the chef has prepared his signature beef Wellington that will literally melt in your mouth. You may select a side of Brussels sprouts broiled with bacon and sweet nuts, or Chef's decadent truffled mashed potatoes. Choose both, if you wish, for the ultimate main course.

"Please give your selection to Raul and Patrice, and the chef will provide you with a dining experience you won't soon forget." My smile was warm and encompassing. Even Sam seemed pleased with my performance.

"Thank you, Fiona. I'm sure it will be difficult to choose from so many tempting options."

"*Si,*" Eduardo Diaz murmured, "but I've already made my choice." His comment was directed at me, as were his eyes. The feel of his hot gaze made my skin crawl, the same way it had all those years ago.

I moved further down the table, prepared to answer any questions the other guests might have. I had to repeat the menu twice and clarify some of the ingredients used in the vegan and gluten-free options.

When it was time to deliver the mouth-watering selections, I turned to Raul. "You take the head of the table; I'll take the foot."

"Are you sure?"

"Quite," I insisted.

As predicted, the talk at the dinner table had already turned to business. For a moment, I wished I had taken the other end of the table, until I overheard a conversation between two men I knew were deeply involved with organized crime while my father was alive. It was highly unlikely they had changed their ways now.

J. Comiskey, known only by his first initial, was hailed for his effective manner in dealing with wayward drug dealers. If deliveries weren't made on time or the take was less than expected, his dealers became an example for others who dared to disobey his strict rules. I had heard rumors of torture and dismemberment, but until now, it was the first time I had seen the man in person. He fit the description I had of him in my mind.

Devarius Mackie had his hand in several endeavors, none of them good. He ran a prostitution ring in Miami and dealt drugs out of his two pool halls in Key West. From what I gathered, he was hoping to expand his operation into Key Largo and further up Florida's eastern coastline.

"Sam is just the woman you want to work with," Comiskey told him. The moment I set his plate before him, he began sawing into his duck breast. "Last year, she set me up with some quality goods coming straight out of Columbia. Pure, top-quality powder. She'll fix you up with the best."

"Yeah, man, that's what I'm looking for," Mackie said. He was having the seabass. "It's hard to get the really good stuff, you know? I have a guy in Honduras, but he's not dependable. To run a money-making venture, you gotta have a reliable supplier, man."

"Then Sam's your man. Well, woman, in this case," Comiskey said with a laugh. "She's come through for me every time."

I hoped my earrings had picked up the conversation, but I couldn't afford to linger. I had to move down the table, delivering another duck entree and a plate of eggplant pachadi.

Vivian Mann was deep in conversation with a man I didn't recognize and whose name I hadn't caught. She dipped into her pachadi as soon as I set it before her.

"I was at my wit's end, trying to make sense of my late husband's records, when a mutual friend introduced me to Sam. She was a lifesaver. With her help, I pulled his business from despair and made it my own. It's amazing what a few substitute ingredients can do for a pharmaceutical company! Her connections and attention to detail are impeccable," Vivian practically gushed. "A lifesaver, I tell you."

Her use of the phrase sent a shiver dancing along my spine. I prayed the tremble in my hand wasn't obvious as I slid the duck entree into place. The minute I stepped into my office on Tuesday morning, I was throwing the entire box of Lifesaver candies into the trash.

My next three deliveries were beef Wellington. As I strayed past the midway point, Eduardo Diaz took advantage of my nearness. Raul was perhaps the same distance away on the same side of the table as Diaz, but Diaz made a point to catch my attention.

I reluctantly walked around the head of the table to inquire demurely, "Yes, sir. How may I help you?"

"*Por favor*," he said, offering what he thought was a beguiling smile, "may I bother you for some pepper?"

"It's no problem, sir. I'll be happy to get that for you."

As I left to retrieve the pepper mill from the buffet, I caught movement out of the corner of my eye. Diaz leaned in to quietly say something to Sam.

I returned and dutifully cranked the pepper mill to produce coarse, black specks across Diaz's plate. When I would have stopped, he encouraged me to continue. He used the opportunity to press his arm inappropriately close. "More," he instructed. "I like things spicy." I had an overwhelming urge to blow some of the pepper into his eyes, but I controlled myself. His plate was practically black before he stopped me.

"Fiona, please stay nearby in case our guests need more water." Sam said the words politely enough, but I heard the warning easily. *Stay nearby for Diaz's enjoyment.*

"Of course, ma'am," I said, stepping back against the wall. Clasping my hands in front of me, my stance was far more guarded than it had been while reciting the menu. I shot Raul a look of apology as our roles suddenly flip-flopped. I now had the head of the table.

Despite my own displeasure over my new assignment, this end of the table had far more interesting conversation. Diaz and Sam dug into their beef Wellington, while Simon the Slippery Snake curled into his seabass. I saw him close his eyes in pleasure as the tastes hit his tongue. Or maybe it was his fangs. No matter, the sight of such obvious gratification was sickening. It was almost sexual in nature.

"I am most eager to work with you, *Senora*," Diaz said to his host. "I think we can achieve great things together."

"I'm certain we can, Mr. Diaz. I deal in very . . . specialized imports/exports. I'm certain we can strike a deal that is beneficial to us both."

I stared straight ahead, trying to look oblivious to the conversation around me. It wouldn't do for Simon to look up from his love affair with his fish and find me actively listening to what Diaz and Sam were saying. Besides, if I kept my head pointed straight ahead, my earrings were more likely to do their job.

"I think Mr. Mackie might also benefit from our endeavor," Sam went on. "I understand he's always looking for new recruits, shall we say."

It took everything I had not to cry out. Sam was involved with human trafficking? She was seriously discussing how she could help Diaz move and sell his victims into bondage with Devarius Mackie? The man would force them to become prostitutes! I literally bit my tongue to keep myself from screaming. I wanted nothing more than to claw Sam's eyes out. She was a monster. Worse, perhaps, than my own father.

I was too furious to listen to the rest of their conversation. I knew the camera's mic would pick up anything else that might be said. I was simply trying to get through the next hour without being sick.

At some point, I felt eyes upon me and realized Eduardo Diaz was speaking to me. "*Querida*," he said, "would you be so kind as to bring me more water?"

"Certainly, sir." I bobbed my head, eager to escape, if only for a moment.

I brought more water and was relieved to see that everyone had finished their meal. "May I take that for you, sir?" I asked, indicating his plate.

"Of course. Give my compliments to the chef." As I reached for his plate and charger, he moved his knee to graze against mine. I ignored his advance and moved to the next guest.

Back in the kitchen, I quickly helped prepare the next-to-last course. I arranged an assortment of cheeses and warm toasted crackers on dessert plates, adding curls of dark chocolate to one side. For those ordering vegan and gluten-free, there was seasonal fruit. Raul and I took a breather, while Patrice and Isabella delivered dessert. Pete, the bartender, joined them to pour the final wine of the night, this time a sweet port.

I dreaded going back out for the mignardises and coffee, but at least the final course signaled the end of the meal. I would have taken the foot of the table again, but Sam wouldn't hear of it. "Fiona," she called quietly. "If you would be so kind . . ." She made a simple hand movement that beckoned me to serve at the head of the table.

I slid a tiny dish of orange sorbet in front of Diaz, accompanied by a madeleine biscuit. My delivery was smooth but quick, allowing him no time for another sly overture.

I wasn't as lucky as I made the coffee round. As I tipped the silver-plated pot over his cup, the man slid his hand up the back of my skirt. Startled by the feeling of his hand on my bare thigh, I jerked mid-stream of the pour. My cry of surprise was drowned by Diaz's bellow of pain. Scalding coffee had poured into his lap.

With steam radiating from his tuxedo pants, Diaz jumped from his chair. He violently cursed in both English and Spanish.

Simon was around the table in a flash. Panicking, he tossed a glass of water onto Diaz's injured flesh. But when he moved toward his groin with a napkin, Diaz's powerful punch sent the smaller man stumbling backward. He fell onto the table, where he groaned and slowly slid to the floor.

The pristine tablecloth came with him.

Chaos ensued. People jumped from their chairs with startled cries. Everyone was talking at once, their words punctuated by curses, screams, and broken china.

Diaz turned to me, his face dark with rage. He backhanded me so violently, I fell to the floor. I felt a trickle of blood escape my nose.

Pain wasn't my biggest concern. To mimic Fiona's nose, I had fashioned one for myself from makeup putty. If it had come loose, I was as good as dead. As I put both hands over my nose, I realized the blood was more than a trickle.

To make my injury look more convincing, I smeared a bit of it on my hand.

Not that anyone was looking. Even Diaz got distracted when the man next to him clipped his leg with the back of his chair.

The other servers and kitchen staff rushed back and forth, scurrying to catch plates and cups before they crashed to the floor. Some brought towels to mop up the mess, or napkins for the guests. With everyone else in motion, I skirted around the wall undetected.

At some point, someone would notice I was missing. Worse yet, they might see my escape. I hovered close to the wall, ducking when I passed behind the portable bar. I kept the same low crouch as I hurried toward the foyer. Making a weak stab at diversion, I untied my once-white apron and flung it in the direction of the kitchen.

I felt an odd vibration on my earlobe, and then I heard Jack's growled whisper coming from the mic. "Front door. Black van."

CHAPTER TWENTY-EIGHT

Lexi

For once, I took no offense at his non-greeting. Those four tersely spoken words said it all. Get the hell out of there. He would be in a black van, waiting for me at the front. He had my back.

Except that at the moment, my back was exposed to a room full of very angry, very dangerous guests.

The entry hall wasn't far ahead. I was glad to see that the French doors were slightly ajar. I wouldn't have to use the handle. Grasping the bottom of one door, I opened it just wide enough to sneak my way through. I gradually straightened as I reached the outer set of double doors. As the heavy doors shut behind me, I heard Diaz's raging voice.

"Where did she go? Where is that bit—"

"The kitchen!" someone else called. "She dropped her apron!"

I knew my diversionary tactic would only buy me a minute or two, at most. I ran into the waiting elevator and jabbed the button. Even though the car was fast, it seemed to take forever to make its descent.

I ran as fast as I could across the second floor. If I saw anything in my path — a small table, a potted plant, chairs intended for customer use, whatever — I pulled it to the floor behind me. Maybe it would slow my pursuers.

Because I knew there would be pursuers. My only chance was to reach the front door before they did.

I reached the public elevators, jumped inside, and hit the down button. After an agonizingly long ride, the doors opened, and I came out on a dead run, where I would have burst free through the front door of the building.

Instead, I face-planted against the glass. The door was locked! I looked frantically around, certain the elevator would open any moment, and Diaz would be breathing down on me. Even if he was unable to come after me in person, there were a dozen other evil men upstairs, and presumably security guards.

Where were the guards, anyway?

I almost panicked when I saw a shadow on the other side of the ornate glass door. Was that the guard? Had he locked the door from outside and stood vigil, to make certain no one interrupted such an important meeting?

My knees sagged with relief when I heard Jack's voice. "Stand back!" he yelled. "Get away from the door!"

I barely had time to react before the blast of his gun shattered the heavy glass. I have no idea of what happened next or how he did it, but somehow, Jack had pulled me through the rubble and was shoving me into a rolling panel van.

I heard shouts behind us and saw a van careening around the corner on two wheels. After that, the only thing I could see was black carpet as Jack bailed in behind me, both of us face down on the floor.

"Hit the locks!" he yelled to the driver. The side door slid shut, and the locks clicked in place. To me, Jack ordered, "Stay down."

I heard more shouting, and gunfire. I flinched at each ping as bullets hit the side of the van. I knew my hands offered no protection against them, but I couldn't help but wrap them around my head.

Without warning, the driver hung a left, and then another left.

"What's happening?" I asked. Rolling around the floor as I was, I couldn't see a thing. "It feels like we're going in a circle."

"We are. Diversion," Jack explained shortly. "We're one of three identical vans in the parking lot. We'll all peel out in opposite directions."

"Hold on," the driver warned. "We're about to burn rubber."

We did a dizzying U-turn in the parking lot, bounced over the curb, and sped off. After a series of screeching tires and blared horns — I assumed we were running red lights and stop signs — Jack said I could sit up. "We lost them. You can move to the seat."

I pushed myself up on my hands and knees. There was one seat in the back, surrounded by flashing grids and gizmos on both sides of the van. I assumed this was the command center for my mic earrings.

As the van whipped around another corner, gravity helped me into the seat.

"Try not to touch any buttons," the driver instructed. "I'm Randy, by the way."

Dryly, I asked, "Any kin to Jake By the Way?"

"Actually, yes. We're cousins."

When I snorted, I felt another bubble of blood come out of my nose. "If your cousin drives anything like you do, remind me to never get in the car with him," I muttered. "Anybody got a napkin or tissue up there?"

"Here," Jake answered, handing me two. As we passed under a streetlight, he got a glimpse of my face. "What happened to you? And why is part of your nose falling off?"

I answered the last question first. "Putty." I used one napkin to wipe the blood away and another to peel off my fake nose. "Diaz backhanded me after I poured coffee in his lap."

"You okay? Did it break your nose?"

"I don't think so. Just knocked it a little out of joint."

"That was quite a scene you created," Jack went on. "Was that part of your plan?"

"No. It really was an accident, but I'm not sorry it happened. The jackass put his hand up my skirt. Given half a chance, he would have tried taking it off me later. Sam would have just stood by and let him."

"Good thing you got out." Jack's voice sounded tight.

"Was the camera working? Could you hear everything okay? Did you get what you needed?"

"And then some," Randy assured me.

"You did good," Jack said.

Belatedly, I noticed where we were. "Hey, my apartment's behind us."

"No way you're going back there tonight," he informed me. "Or anytime this weekend. You're supposed to be out of town until Monday, remember?"

"But I don't think anyone recognized me."

"Doesn't matter. If Sam checks out your story, it has to meet her scrutiny."

I reminded him of a major fault in his logic. "Except that I don't have a friend who got married, and I won't be coming in on a plane Monday morning."

"No, and yes."

He didn't see my frown, but he could hear it in my voice. "You're not making any sense."

"No wedding, but yes, you'll be on an inbound flight Monday."

"What—"

Before I could finish my protest, Randy slowed and turned into a driveway. "We're here."

I saw a large house in the headlights. Judging from the way it sat on huge pillars some ten or twelve feet off the ground, I guessed we were nearer the ocean than we were the bay.

"Where's here?" I asked, curious in spite of myself.

"Home, sweet home. Come in and meet the family."

Jack was already out of his seat and opening the sliding door.

"Wait. Whose house is this? Yours? His? The government's?"

"Randy's," he clarified. "You'll be staying here a couple of nights."

"I don't have any clothes!"

"I have your duffel bag from earlier and the suitcase you call a purse. I assume you put your clothes in one of them when you changed into the uniform?" I nodded and he asked, "Any medicine you need from your apartment?"

"No."

"Then you should be set. Abbie will get you anything else you need."

I did a double-take when I saw Randy in proper lighting. He bore a striking resemblance to his cousin. His hair was darker than Jack's, and he wasn't quite as good-looking, but if they dressed alike, they could easily be mistaken for the same person. I had yet to see Jack in anything but jeans and boots, but his cousin had obviously embraced the island dress code. Khaki shorts, leather sandals, and one of those long-sleeved, UV-protective 'fishing shirts' that seemed all the rage.

Randy's household was loud and boisterous, and I loved it immediately. Abbie had dimples and reddish-brown curls that frizzed in the humid air. She was one of the cutest, friendliest women I had ever met. Chloe, who informed me she had just turned eight, had her mother's hair but looked more like her father, which was to say she looked like her Uncle Jack. Charlie was two years younger and all knees and elbows. He was in constant motion and had the mischievous, snaggle-toothed smile of all boys his age. And if the walls and a chair in the living room were any indication, three-year-old Crissy was well on her way to becoming a budding young artist.

It was the kind of family and the home life I had always wanted. Unfortunately, I had gotten Leonardo Drakos for a father, so neither was possible.

The children were the perfect distraction from the night's events. But when Abbie rounded up her brood and ushered them to bed, the house quietened. The adrenaline from the last few hours had worn off, and my nerves were shattered.

I joined the men in Randy's office and gladly accepted the mixed drink Jack placed in my hand. He didn't ask if I wanted it, and I didn't ask what it was. I took a big gulp and welcomed the warmth sliding down my throat.

"Now what?" I asked.

"Randy will compile the video you took tonight, and we'll identify everyone at the table," Jack replied. "He'll be able to isolate different conversations and home in on what was said. I'll put together a report on Samson Shipping, Lillian Samson, and everything we learned. I'll present it to the DA next week. I think we not only have enough on her, but on several of the others, too, including Eduardo Diaz."

"I have to admit, I tuned out after a while. When I found out they were trafficking people, especially young women, I couldn't listen any longer. Not without finding a sharp knife and attacking them both."

Randy grunted. "Be happy you didn't hear all the details. Let's just say that Mackie prefers to start his harem young, so he can train them to his liking. He specializes in girls, whereas Ismael Garrido, who was seated next to Diaz, deals in young boys. When they've outlived their usefulness, he takes his time in killing them. We should have enough to make a few charges stick."

"Let's hope."

"What you did tonight was very brave," Jack told me. His eyes held mine in a solemn gaze. "You handled yourself well. You are, indeed, a real pro."

His praise had far greater of an effect on me than I wanted. I blamed it on the alcohol and changed the subject. "I do feel guilty about ruining Fiona's stellar reputation. Are you sure she won't talk? If she tells anyone about what we did . . ."

"She won't. She's been handsomely rewarded for her assistance in the matter and will be relocated in a new town with an impressive recommendation."

"At least that's something."

Randy's forehead crunched with concern. "Do you think your disguise slipped enough at the end to incriminate you?"

I spoke with conviction. "No. I kept my hands over my nose, like it was broken. There was just enough blood to be convincing."

"Doesn't look too bad," he said, peering at me closely. "Does your face hurt much?"

I gingerly touched my cheeks, nose, and mouth. "Some, but I haven't had time for it to sink in yet. There's been too much else to think about."

"You need to take it easy tomorrow. Well, as easy as my kids will allow. Abbie can get them out of the house while you sleep."

"I don't sleep in the middle of the day."

"Drink enough of Jack's concoction here, and you will." With a grin, Randy drained his glass. "Our bedrooms are all upstairs, so you get the spare at the end of the hall. I think Abbie laid out everything you'll need for the night. She can go shopping for you tomorrow, or maybe someone can go to your apartment and pick something up. You need to lie low for a couple of days."

I turned toward his cousin. "You mentioned a flight I'll be on?"

"We'll fly you by private jet to Illinois, where you'll make a return trip to Houston via commercial flight. You already have the ticket. For all outward appearances, you'll have spent a fun weekend at your friend's wedding and are just getting back into town."

"I can do that." I nodded. "Well, all except the lying low part. That, I'm not a fan of."

"Fan or not, it's the best way to keep your cover." Jack slapped his hands onto his knees and stood. "I've got a report to type up, so I think I'll call it a night. I think you should, too. Your face may seem fine now, but you may think differently in the middle of the night. I took the liberty of having our medic order you a painkiller. Take it."

I was too tired to argue, and in truth, my nose really did hurt. I hated not to wait up for my hostess and thank her for all she was doing for me, but the bed was calling my name.

I would talk to Abbie in the morning.

CHAPTER TWENTY-NINE

Lexi

Tuesday morning, I had to go into the office and pretend nothing was wrong. I had to hope my makeup covered the lingering bruises on my face. I had to act surprised if anything was said about the disastrous dinner party. I had to remain calm.

What I didn't have to fake was my surprise at seeing the front door. I thought Sam would have taken care of it the day after the party, but the former glass was now covered with a sheet of plywood.

I took the elevator up to the second floor, stopping by the reception desk.

"What's with the wood on the front door?" I asked.

Cindy answered with wide, gullible eyes. "Would you believe a seagull flew into it? Hit it just right, and the whole thing exploded into a gazillion pieces." She mimicked the explosion with her hands.

"Oh, wow," I said, trying to sound convinced by her dramatic tale.

"Did you hear what else happened this weekend?"

I wondered how she knew about Friday night. I had been sure Sam and Simon would keep that under tight wraps.

I pretended not to know. "I've been out of town all weekend. I just got in last night." I knew Cindy wasn't an accurate measuring stick — not if she believed the seagull story — but my lie sounded convincing enough to me.

Cindy leaned in as if telling me something highly confidential. "Well, according to the TV, there's been a home invasion and brutal assault on a brand-new mother here in the city! The baby was unharmed, but the mother was rushed to the hospital. The extent of her injuries is unknown, but, get this. Apparently, this isn't the first time this has happened here! There's been at least two other women come forward after the story aired."

"Really?" I had to wonder when this had happened. I had only seen Jack once since Friday night. That had been yesterday when he drove me to the private jet, but he made no mention of another Milkman attack. Our conversation had centered strictly around his case against Sam.

Randy hadn't mentioned the assault either, but I could think of several reasons he wouldn't. So far, Jack was merely 'looking into' a few random incidents that could be linked to the old Milkman case. Randy might not have clearance for the investigation. Even if he did, I reasoned, it wasn't something he was likely to discuss in front of his young children. Plus, he probably wasn't allowed to share details of an ongoing investigation with his wife.

Cindy was still talking. "Yeah. Crazy, right? I mean, right there in her own home!" She shook her head in amazement.

"There are a lot of sick people in the world," I murmured. "Did I miss anything else this weekend?"

"Not that I can think of."

"Okay. Well, thanks for the update."

I crossed the second floor, noticing that a potted plant and one small table were missing. *Oops. That would be my fault.*

Once inside the second elevator, I practiced my lie. *Went to a wedding, had a great time, just got in last evening. Went to a wedding, had a great time, just got in last evening.*

In case anyone noticed the slight swelling in my nose, I had another lie prepared. *This? Funny story, although my nose didn't think so at the time. When the bride threw the bouquet, one of the women in the crowd was a little too eager to catch it. She pushed the groom's sister aside and elbowed me in the nose. And after all that, she didn't even catch it! Someone else beat her to it.*

I had barely stepped through the French doors when I saw Simon coming my way. He wore a frazzled look on his face. A cold dread seized my heart. Had I been discovered?

I took the initiative, hoping to deflect suspicion. "Simon! What happened to your face? Were you in an accident?" He truly did look terrible. An angry bruise circled his left eye, and his cheek was red. He normally wore his dark hair slicked back in one smooth sweep. Today, there were several stray hairs that would look natural on anyone else, had it not been Simon. He looked less collected than I had ever seen him, which was saying a lot. Afterall, I had seen him sprawled across Sam's dining room table.

Simon winced, and his tone was less than convincing when he said, "Just a minor disagreement."

"I hope the other guy looks worse." It seemed like something I might say if I hadn't known the truth.

Simon seemed horrified at my words. "Are you serious?"

"Of course. Unless . . . did a *woman* give you that shiner?"

"What? Of course not!" My question flustered him, which I found odd. I knew exactly how he had gotten that bruised cheek and black eye, assuming no one else had added insult to injury.

A second thought occurred to me. Could *Sam* have done so?

"As long as you weren't seriously injured . . ." I let the sentence trail off, then interrupted myself as if a new thought had occurred to me. "By the way. How did the dinner party go Friday night?"

His words came out in a hiss. "Whatever you do, *do not* mention Friday night to Sam."

I looked appropriately shocked. "Something went wrong? Please tell me the chef didn't mess up!" I thought putting my hand to my chest was a nice extra touch.

"Oh, no, the food was delicious. He prepared a divine salt-crusted seabass that was to die for! It practically melted in your mouth." I could see he still had that love affair going with the fish. The two were suited for one another; both were cold-blooded creatures. "Enough about the food," he said abruptly. "The staff was horrendous. One of the servers ruined the entire evening!"

I lowered my voice to sound utterly shocked. "You're kidding. But we vetted them so carefully! They all came with glowing recommendations. How could that happen?"

"All I know is that it did, and Sam was mortified. She had important clients and colleagues at that dinner, and the entire night was ruined. I've never seen her so furious. She even locked *me* out this weekend!" he huffed. "She flies out tomorrow morning and will be gone for the rest of the week, trying to repair the damage that one server caused. Just one, mind you, but months of preparation destroyed with a single cup of coffee!"

Simon looked truly aggrieved, so it was prudent I didn't smile. I tried to emulate Cindy in reception and look as guileless as she had. "The coffee was that bad?"

"When it was poured directly into the lap of Sam's most important client, *yes*! It was absolutely horrid."

It was the most Simon had ever confided in me. I must admit, I felt a tiny smidgen of guilt, knowing he was sharing the mortifying scene with the very woman who had created it.

It was a *very* tiny smidgen. I kept up my charade. "I just can't believe it," I said in a shocked tone.

He nodded gravely. "Whatever you do, don't mention the dinner to Sam."

"Won't she think that's odd? I mean, I planned most of the event."

Simon's beady eyes were cold. "Do you really want her blaming *you* for the disastrous night?"

"I see your point." I made the motion of zipping my lips. "Not a word."

"Tread lightly today," Simon warned once again. "Feeling the wrath of Sam Samson is not something you want to experience."

Was Sam suspicious over my portrayal as Fiona? Had I lost my touch when it came to impersonating someone else?

That's not a bad thing, Lex, I told myself. *Maybe there's hope for you yet.*

With absolutely nothing to do once I reached my desk, I turned on my computer and made a final choice on suitcases for the long-timers. I put all fifteen into my virtual cart and continued to browse online.

Just before noon, Sam sent me an email. She had summoned me to her office.

Was I stepping into the lion's den? Was this the day she pounced?

"You needed to see me?" I asked, pleased with how calm my voice came out.

"What's the status on my orphanage project?"

"I'm working on that now. I have several items in my online cart and just need to confirm that I still have a budget of fifteen hundred per child."

"I said two thousand!" she barked in that gruff voice of hers. I had only seen her smoking a cigar twice, but she must have been a heavy smoker at one time to damage her vocal cords so badly.

I wasn't about to argue with the new figure she quoted. With the cost of clothes these days, that extra five hundred dollars would come in handy.

"I grew up in an orphanage, you know. I know exactly what it's like to be forgotten."

What was this, Confide in Lexi Day?

"I'll be gone the rest of the week," she went on. "I want this project completed when I get back. If you need to shop in person, do it. Don't worry about coming to the office that day. Just get it done."

"Yes, ma'am."

She eyed me with her piercing gaze. "What happened to your face?"

I forced myself to look her in the eye. "An over-zealous woman desperate to catch the bouquet. I was in her way." At the blank expression on her face, I reminded her, "A friend from college got married this weekend. I went to her wedding."

"I know that," she snapped. "What did you say her name was?"

"I'm not sure that I did, but her name is Mary Black. Or it was. She married John Smith, so now it's Mary Smith." I had chosen the names because they were almost impossible to trace. There had to be thousands of Marys out there with the same last names. I tried sounding amused. "Can you imagine? She went from one boring name to another. She couldn't sound more generic if she tried!"

Sam narrowed her eyes. I wasn't sure she bought my story, but I didn't fidget. I kept smiling, wondering when and if she would see the humor in my made-up tale.

After a moment that could go either way, she threw her head back and laughed in typical Sam fashion.

I didn't wish her a safe trip. Our interaction had gone better than expected, and I didn't want to jinx it. I wasn't about to remind her of the fiasco this weekend.

Back at my desk, I heard a buzz coming from my purse. I discreetly pulled out my second phone and saw a text from Jack.

Pizza or burgers? Seven o'clock, your place.

He didn't ask if I objected.

Turkey and mozzarella panini from Hahn's. Tomato basil soup.

After these past few days, I need my regular routine more than ever.

He didn't reply. I vowed that if he didn't bring my exact order, he wasn't allowed inside.

Sam hadn't said where to have the donated goods delivered, but I chose my address. Not only would I have to sort the items and fill each suitcase for specific children, but if I were no longer at Samson Shipping, using my address made more sense. I was determined to see this project through.

I left the office a few minutes early, eager to be done for the day. I kept expecting Sam to go off on another of her rants, so the sooner I was gone, the better.

I escaped Sam, but I still had one more encounter with Simon the Slippery Snake when I reached the second floor. I no longer felt that smidgen of guilt where he was concerned. I reminded myself that he was as ruthless and corrupt as Sam. Not only did he make my skin crawl, he made me nauseous. He had sat there listening to Sam and Diaz talk about trafficking young girls and selling them into a life of prostitution, and his eyes had danced with excitement.

Snake was too nice of a description for the man.

"How did it go with Sam?" he asked. For the first time, it occurred to me that he might be afraid of our boss. Was he using me as a scapegoat or to test her mood? I assumed he had already talked with her this morning, but that might not be the case.

It would be too much of an exaggeration to say that she had been pleasant. Sam was never pleasant. Friday night had been the exception, but it hardly counted. It had been a ruse for the sake of her business associates.

I settled on middle of the road. "I only spoke to her for a few minutes, but nothing seemed out of the ordinary."

Simon's shoulders sagged with relief, and I had to wonder again if Sam had slapped him. I didn't put anything past her, and it would make sense that she would take her frustrations out on him. I shuddered to think what might have happened to me if I hadn't escaped when I did.

I offered a glimpse of the brighter side. "Maybe taking a few days off will improve her mood."

"Sam doesn't take days off," he said sharply. "This is hardly a trip for pleasure. She has an intense schedule as she tries to restore her reputation."

"You're not going with her?" I ventured to ask.

A brief shadow crossed his face. Was that a feeling of betrayal? Disappointment? Embarrassment over being left behind? The look was gone in an instant.

"I have my own travel assignments stateside."

I wasn't surprised, but I had to act it. "She'll be traveling abroad?"

"Yes. SSI does a lot of international trade, so keeping good relationships abroad is vital."

It sickened me to think of what that international trade entailed.

"It sounds like it will be a quiet week in the office." My inner Lexi was doing a happy dance. *Yay! A week free from both of them!*

"You'll be allowed access to the apartment." Judging from the I-just-sucked-on-a-sour-lemon look on his face, I assumed he and Sam disagreed on the matter. "Don't take advantage of our trust."

A subtle warning, or acknowledgement of my deceit?

I answered with an indigent sniff. "It's not like I'll raid the liquor cabinet. I'm working on a special project, and Sam wants it completed by the time she returns."

Simon narrowed his eyes. "What kind of special project?"

"One she put me in charge of." I'm sure I sounded smug, but it was true. This was my project. It had become personal to me.

"Don't try to usurp me, Lexi," he warned in an ominous voice. "You'll regret it."

"I have no desire to replace you. This project is far below your pay grade, I'm sure."

"You could never replace me." His words were bold, but I saw a flicker of doubt in his eyes. Was he afraid that, as Sam's biological niece, I might come between them?

"I don't want to be like you, Simon." The sharp words slipped out before I could stop them.

He took offense. What's worse, he looked more suspicious than ever. "What does that mean?" he demanded.

He was the kind of man who liked having his ego stroked. The idea of stroking *anything* of his made my skin crawl, but I had to assuage him. "I don't want the pressure of being Sam's right-hand man. Your job is far too stressful. I'm content being a lowly assistant."

"A highly overpaid one, at that!" he huffed.

"I didn't negotiate the price, Simon." My voice was stiff. "It was offered, and I agreed. And for the record, I agree with you. For what Sam is paying me, I should have more pressing duties than running errands and mailing letters. Planning the dinner party and this special project are the only worthwhile things I've been assigned since being here. Frankly, if I can't be useful, I'd rather not be here at all."

Fed up with his pompous attitude — all the more ridiculous because of the *ick* factor he oozed — I turned on my heel and marched to the elevator.

CHAPTER THIRTY

Lexi

"If there's not a panini in that bag, don't bother coming in."

I met Jack at my door, still clinging to my pissed-off attitude.

Rattling the paper bag, he stepped over the threshold. "Don't you ever get tired of eating the same old thing?"

He would only know my eating habits if he were carrying out his end of the bargain. "Sometimes, I do something wild like change up the soup," I told him as I closed the door.

"Wow. You really like living on the edge, don't you?"

"Been there, done that. I'm comfortable with my routine."

Jack seemed comfortable enough in my apartment to begin laying out our dinner on the coffee table. I wasn't sure how I felt about that as I grabbed us each a bottled water. "I have beer left from the other night," I called over my shoulder. "Want one?"

"Sure."

I added one for each of us. "I take it this is another unofficial visit?" We weren't sharing a pizza this time, but I took a seat on the sofa next to him anyway.

"I generally conduct business at my office."

"Is that your office at *Galveston Gusto* or at your mythical government agency?" I asked saucily.

"I can assure you, it's not mythical. But it's much too stuffy for my tastes, which is why I prefer the coffee shop."

"That, and because you can conduct your stakeouts." I reminded him of my astute observation skills. "Who were you chasing that day, Jack? Someone connected to SSI, or to the Milkman?"

Jack lifted the lid off my soup and set the styrofoam cup in front of me. "Believe it or not, there's more crime on the island than just those two cases."

A hard edge slipped into my voice. "I know all about crime and how rampant it can be."

Glossing over my attitude, he answered my question. "Unofficially, I came to give you an update on my case against SSI and Sam."

"And?"

"The earrings gave us an earful, so to speak. You picked up some very useful information." He tipped his beer bottle to mine for a toast. "The DA is issuing a warrant for her arrest."

"She'll be gone for the rest of the week. I don't know the particulars, but she's taking an international trip to repair the damage I did on Friday." I didn't look remotely apologetic for my part in the fiasco. "You'd better hold off on the warrant until she's back on American soil."

"Good point." He pulled his phone from his pocket and typed out a quick message. We had eaten half our meal before his phone binged in reply. "Done," he said. "She'll return home to a very unpleasant surprise."

"And the others? Diaz? Mackie? What about Vivian Mann? I know she's passing off inferior ingredients, possibly illegal drugs, as the real deal. Do you have enough on them for an arrest?"

"Obviously, the ones in the States will be easier to go after, which we will. The ones abroad and in Mexico will be trickier."

"And the 'invitees' already in prison on other offenses?"

"I'm afraid nothing was said Friday night to directly implicate any of them. There was mention of Phillips, but he's already dead. We didn't hear Pesci, Arenas or Sawyer mentioned."

"What if I could give you confirmation that they were directly involved in my father's crimes? I can't speak to Sam's connection, but it seems like they share the others in common. It stands to reason she's associated with them as well."

"What kind of proof? You've already gone out on a limb for this case. I'm not sure what else you can do."

"Stay here." I was already pushing to my feet. "I'll be back."

"You done eating?" Jack asked.

"Talking about those men made me lose my appetite."

He went about gathering wrappers and empty soup containers. "You want me to save this half of your sandwich?"

"You can put it in the fridge." I was strangely okay with him moving around in my kitchen.

He finished cleaning up as I closed the bedroom door behind me. I went to the closet, moved aside the folded towels, and spun the dial on the safe. I pulled out the red journals and the lone blue sketchpad.

With a heavy sigh, I carried the bundle back to the living room.

"What's this?" As Jack took the stack of books from my arms, he sounded wary.

I answered in one word. "Proof."

"What kind of proof?"

"Have a seat, and I'll show you."

I picked up the first journal, the one labeled 'A–B.' It rested in my lap while I offered a preamble.

"I've kept these for ten years, thinking I might need them one day as leverage. A sort of insurance, if you will. My father kept meticulous records. He recorded his dealings in these journals. This one, A–B, details his business transactions with anyone whose name starts with those letters, including Juan Arenas. Arenas has by far the most entries. I stole these journals the night I disappeared." I gave a bitter laugh. Sometimes, the truth was a nasty-tasting pill to swallow. "My father didn't chase after me out of fatherly concern. He was only concerned with saving his hide."

Understanding dawned in Jack's face. "Hence your many disguises and name changes."

"Yes. But now that he's dead, and if this will put his cohorts away for good, I don't need the journals any longer. You can have them."

Jack reached out for one, then pulled his hand back. "You do realize that even if we lock away the main players, there are plenty of others still out there."

"Of course I know that. But as long as they think I have these journals, I'll always be a target. Take them off my hands, let it be known you have them, and maybe I can finally live in peace."

Jack took the book from my lap and thumbed through it. "You're right. These are very thorough. Unfortunately, these are unsubstantiated documents. They might not stand up in court."

"I recognize my father's handwriting but, again, it's my word against the defense. You can call in an expert to compare samples. It will prove that these are authentic."

"They may prove Leo Drakos' version of the truth, but that may not be enough," he warned. "It will be a dead man's word against men who are very much alive, not to mention adamantly protesting. There's no way to cross-examine a deceased witness."

I leaned back to give him a withering look. "I'm hardly dead, Jack."

His face registered surprise. "You were a witness to these transactions?"

"Some of them. I think if you compare the dates in this sketchbook to those in the red journals, you'll have solid proof. The progression of my handwriting and artistic ability should validate the range of dates."

Jack took the book I offered. He studied the first sketch before looking up at me in amazement. "You drew this?"

"Yes. I was . . . eleven at the time." I leaned over to confirm the date I always scribbled at the top of each entry. "My father was coming off a successful con as a food critic when he first met Arenas. We met him in a greasy spoon in Philly. Definitely not the kind of place a food critic would visit, but the con had run its course, and my father was on to the next one. Juan Arenas offered him a job, and it was the beginning of an entirely new way of life for us."

"You sat in on the meeting?"

"I was at the booth across from them, but I heard enough of what was said to know Arenas was not a nice man. Like I always did to pass the time, I sketched what I saw. The drawing is crude, I admit, but you can see the diner sign through the window. I think you'll find the same name in my father's journal."

"Did you realize what you were documenting at the time?"

I lifted my shoulder. "Sort of. I started keeping a journal of sorts when I learned to write. To remember all the different houses and different towns we lived in, I started drawing pictures of them. Somewhere along the way, I realized I was drawing scenes from our life of crime. I used a blue sketchpad specifically for that. As you flip through the pages, you'll see my skills improved. When I was younger, I was relegated to a corner of the room and told not to make a sound. I never let them know that I was listening, or that I was sketching out what they talked about. Once I learned to sketch faces, I tried to show the people themselves. By the time I was older and hostessing most of my father's events, I drew from memory. The last page was drawn about a month before I disappeared." I reached across his arm to flip to the back of the book. "That's Arenas, that's Diaz, and that's Sawyer. That other man is Dean Henry. I know for a fact that he's connected to Sam. He wasn't at the dinner party, but she sent him a fake invitation, and I saw him coming out of her office one day. If you look through the journals, you'll see this meeting documented in them."

"You drew all these? They're excellent! And there's no doubt who the people are." He looked up at me to ask, "Have you ever considered becoming a composite artist for the police?"

"No. Absolutely not. I don't work with the police."

He tried not to smirk when he pointed out dryly, "Just federal agents."

"Dire circumstances, I can assure you."

Jack thumbed through a couple more red journals. "These are great, Lexi. The drawings, your father's meticulous records . . . It looks like he was using these entries as insurance of his own. I think this is exactly what we need to make a solid case against the men your father was in cahoots with."

"But not Sam." I heard the defeat in my voice.

"That depends. Is her name in here?"

"I don't know. I haven't read the journals in years."

"I'll take the journals with me when I go. Tomorrow, I'll turn them over to the proper chain of command. But remember. We still have the recording from the dinner party. That's compelling enough on its own."

A weight lifted from my shoulders. I was relieved to finally have the journals off my hands.

I was also relieved to know that Jack wasn't leaving just yet. I still had a question for him. "I heard there was another assault by the copycat. When did this happen?"

"Saturday night."

"Why didn't you tell me about it on the way to the airplane?"

"Why should I? You assured me you knew nothing about the original cases." I heard the slight edge in his voice.

"I still would have liked to have known." My voice came out sounding peevish.

Jack shrugged. "Sounds like you found out the same way the rest of the city did. Television."

After working with him on the SSI case, I felt oddly hurt by his snub. "I didn't see the broadcast, obviously, but someone told me this attack was more violent." There was a question in my voice.

"That's true. With this new development, I'm recommending that the Milkman case be re-opened."

"Why would you do that? This is obviously the work of a copycat."

"That may be obvious to you, but it's not obvious to the rest of us. The cases are almost identical. It's not all that unusual for a serial criminal to go dormant for several years and then reemerge after a long hiatus. Usually, there's some sort of event in their lives that triggers renewed activity. Apparently, that's what has happened now."

"But the Milkman never physically hurt his victims. You just said this time was different."

"It was." Jack paused before saying, "You didn't hear this from me, but the woman fought back, and he became angry. Whether intentional or not, he knocked the victim down a flight of stairs. She suffered a broken leg and re-opened the incision from her cesarean birth."

I felt for the unknown woman, but I clung to my convictions. "See? You're obviously dealing with a copycat," I insisted.

My persistent argument drew a sigh. "Did you know that the first reports of the Milkman occurred twenty-nine years ago?" Jack asked. "When he first started his reign of terror in West Virginia, he was obsessed with expectant mothers. He came up to them in public, touching their bellies without permission. Within a few months, it progressed to home invasions. He would stroke the pregnant women's bellies and sing to the babies in their wombs. A few months later, he became obsessed with new mothers, primarily in Ohio and Pennsylvania. At first, he was content watching them hold their babies. Again, over time, his obsession made another shift. He was more interested in lactating mothers, so that he could watch them breastfeed. Over the next several years, he traveled up and down the eastern seaboard, and by that time, he was fondling the mothers while they nursed their babies."

He wasn't telling me anything I didn't already know, but I listened patiently. Hearing the facts all over again made me ill. "There seemed to be a lag in his activity, although that may not be the case. Maybe the location changed, and no one made the connection. Maybe his focus changed or his targeted demographic. It's not clear, but finally, someone made a vague connection here on the island. My point is, the Milkman has evolved over the years. He's moved around. He's become more aggressive. Saturday night's injury may have been an accident; after all, this time, his victim fought back. Or it may be that something else triggered the Milkman, and he took out his frustration on his victim. It may be that he's had another shift in his obsession." Jack's voice hardened. "So no, Lexi, it's not *obviously* a copycat."

Something he said resonated with me. A niggling suspicion had been eating at me recently, and I needed to get this out. "Jack, how much do you know about Simon Brewster?"

My sudden change of topic threw him. His brow wrinkled. "You mean Lillian Samson's right-hand man?"

"Yes."

His tone became wary. "Why do you ask?"

"Please. Just humor me. What do you know about him?"

Jack released a heavy breath. "Surprisingly, very little. Like his boss, his past is riddled with holes. He has no priors, but we both know he's knee-deep in Sam's nefarious business dealings."

"Have you ever met the man?"

"Not really. I arranged to be in the same place as him one day, and we exchanged pleasantries. He was polite enough, but his eyes were soulless."

"Exactly. You may not have noticed, but he exudes a certain *ick* factor."

Jack looked faintly amused. "*Ick* factor?"

"It's a real thing," I assured him. "Even Joy at the flower shop picked up on it. It's that slimy, tacky feeling you get on your hands after touching something repulsive. Except this gets under your skin and travels all over your body. It makes you want to take a shower after being around him." My shoulders shimmied just thinking about the man. "Definitely icky."

"As in sexual?"

My face pulled with indecision. "Not necessarily. It's like you said. His eyes are soulless. He smiles, but it never reaches those dark eyes. It's like looking into a deep void."

Jack understood my meaning. "I get that. I do. But I still don't understand what Simon Brewster has to do with our discussion."

"What if . . ." I moistened my lips and tried again. "What if Simon Brewster is the copycat?"

Jack narrowed his eyes, but he didn't immediately discard my idea. "What makes you think that? The man may have soulless eyes and an *ick* vibe about him, but that doesn't mean he's capable of these assaults."

"He's just strange," I insisted. When I saw the protest forming on Jack's lips, I hurried on. "I've had this feeling of unease around him from the start. I know it's not scientific, but my first impressions about people are usually spot-on. I pegged Simon as creepy from day one. That's why I refer to him in my mind as Simon the Slippery Snake."

That drew another look of amusement.

"Then today," I continued, "the warning bells really went off. Something was up with him. Simon is always dressed impeccably. He always wears his hair slicked back — from all that inner slime, I'm sure — and has a detached, arrogant air about him. Nothing fazes him. Today was totally different. His hair was messed up, his face looked haggard, his clothes were slightly rumpled, and I think he was actually afraid of Sam."

"You don't think it was because of Friday night? He was definitely not composed during the chaos. Especially after Diaz humiliated him that way."

"That could be part of it," I admitted, "but there was something more. He tried to cover it with a concealer, but he obviously had a black eye and a bruise on his cheek." I gingerly touched my own bruised cheek. It felt worse than it looked. "Both could have been from Diaz's punch, but . . . it looked like more than one punch. At the time, I thought maybe Sam had attacked him, which would explain why he seemed to be avoiding her. But now, I wonder if something else happened. You said this latest victim fought back. What if *she* was the one to hit him? What if she was the reason he was so rattled today?"

Twisting his lips, Jack considered my theory. "I suppose after Friday night's disaster — *if* there was a copycat, and *if* he was it — he could have needed the release," he hypothesized aloud. "Despite the fondling, these attacks aren't sexual in nature. But they are about gratification of some sort. Often, situations like this are exasperated by a stressful event in the perpetrator's life."

"Friday night would definitely qualify as stressful."

"All of this may seem like a fit, Lexi, but that doesn't mean Simon Brewster is the missing piece to our puzzle. Plus, I don't think he's old enough to fit the profile. Remember, the first attacks happened almost thirty years ago."

"I'm not talking about the original attacks. I'm talking about the recent ones. The copycat attacks."

Jack wearily hung his head. "Lexi . . ."

"Stop. I know you don't want to hear it, but the Milkman is dead, Jack. I know how, and I know why. Roland's little girl had leukemia, and he couldn't afford to pay for treatments. He needed the money."

My words gave him pause. "That doesn't make sense. Insurance doesn't pay in the case of suicide."

"It wasn't that kind of insurance. An anonymous benefactor came forward and paid for his daughter's treatment. Half when he confessed. The other half when he killed himself. The money was wired straight to the hospital."

His brown eyes narrowed. "That wasn't in any of the files. How do you know about his daughter?"

I had known this was coming, but it was still hard to say. "Because my father was the one who paid that little girl's hospital bills. My father was the one who paid Doyle Roland to commit suicide."

It took a moment for Jack to digest what I said. "That doesn't make any sense," he finally protested. "And that has nothing to do with Simon Brewster. Unless . . ." A gear churned in his head. "Was Roland even the culprit? Was your father paying him to confess to something he didn't do?" Another cog turned. "Is Simon your cousin?"

As much as I vehemently wanted to deny any relation to the snake, I couldn't be certain. Hadn't I suspected Simon might be Sam's son? That would make him my first cousin. Why hadn't I made the connection before?

I shrank at the thought. "Oh, God! It's bad enough that Leo Drakos was my father. Bad enough that Sam is my aunt. But Simon, too? It's . . . too much," I decided, holding my hands up as if to ward away evil spirits. "I can't think about that right now. But Sam knew about my father's shady past, and she obviously confided in Simon. That would explain how he knows so much about the Milkman. How he knows to sing Brahms' 'Lullaby' as he watched the mothers nurse. S—"

Jack cut me short. "I never told you what song he sang."

"I know what song it was, Jack. My father obviously told Sam, and she told Simon. It's the only thing that makes any sense. Simon is the copycat Milkman."

"That doesn't make any sense at all!" Jack argued.

My head was throbbing. My heart was pounding. "You're right. It doesn't make logical sense, and there *was* a cover-up." I spoke just above a whisper. "Roland confessed, sacrificing his own life to save his daughter."

"Why, Lexi? Was your father protecting Simon?"

This was the hard part. This was where I bared my soul. Along with my head and my heart, my stomach ached. But I

234

had to see this through. I had to tell Jack the full truth of my sordid past.

I forced myself to say the words I swore I would never say aloud. "It wasn't Simon he was protecting. My father was protecting himself. My father, Leo Drakos, was the Milkman."

CHAPTER THIRTY-ONE

Lexi

The room grew still. Not even the air conditioner dared to hum.

Still rocking from my bombshell, Jack stared at me in disbelief.

"Your father was *what*?"

"A very sick man. He had a sick, twisted, demented obsession." Whenever I thought about his vile deeds, I hated him all the more. A sense of rage washed over me, soon giving way to shame. "Like mine, his mother abandoned him when he was just a few days old. It . . . did something to him. It broke something inside of him. He . . ." The words were getting harder to say now. Harder to comprehend, much less explain. "He craved that mother/son bond. He obsessed over it. In some psychotic way, he was creating that bond he never had. His assaults weren't sexual. They were emotionally deranged."

I covered my mouth with my hands, sickened all over again by the horrible truths it revealed. I was long past feeling empathy for that little boy who never had a mother. Any tears I cried now were for the victims he left behind.

"You're positive about this?"

My bark of laughter was bitter. "I would never admit to something like this if I weren't absolutely positive." I pushed my hand through my hair. I had left it hanging free, not bothering with a bun or ponytail. "Think about it. His reign of terror started twenty-nine years ago, when he found out my mother was pregnant. It must have triggered something in him. Some deep-seated resentment toward his own mother. I don't know, but it all fits. He was obsessed with pregnant women. When my mother abandoned me the same way his abandoned him, he became fixated on the nursing aspect of our missed chances. If you look in his journals, we lived in or near the same places where all those attacks took place. West Virginia. Pennsylvania. Maine. Massachusetts. Maryland." I closed my eyes as bile rose in my throat. "As much as it horrifies me to say it, my father, Leo Drakos, was the Milkman."

Jack was silent for a moment.

"How long have you known?" he asked quietly.

"When I found his diary. That one was black, like his heart. The man was sick enough to actually write it all down!" I spat in disgust. "That's what pushed me over the edge. That's when I knew I couldn't stay in that house one minute longer."

"And Roland? How do you know your father put him up to taking the fall?" Seeing my eyes flash with fire, he put up one hand. "I'm not saying I don't believe you. I'm just curious."

"When I read in the paper that someone had confessed to being the Milkman, I knew my father was behind it. By that time, he was already in prison. I knew he was behind bars like the animal he was, so even though I had been running from him for five years, I went to visit him. Once, and only once. I told him I knew. That I knew all of it. I told him if he sent his goons after me, I had safeguards in place that would release his journals to the police. It was a bluff. But even though he still kept tabs on me, he never came after me. It kept me alive."

I gave a bitter clap of laughter. "Like I told you. My father always found an angle. When I confronted him about Roland, he said at least that little girl got the treatments she deserved. I didn't bother telling him to go to hell. He was already halfway there. I walked out, and I never spoke to that man again. I didn't even know he had died until the day after I found your file. You told me the Milkman had resurfaced, and for one horrible night, I thought my father may have escaped. So, I flew to the prison the very next day, and the warden told me he had died over three years ago. Complications arising from a prison fight." My voice trembled with emotion, but it wasn't grief. "And I swear, I had never been so relieved in all of my life."

I gave him a moment to absorb everything I had told him. It was a lot to take in.

"Wow." It was the best he could come up with. "I don't even know what to do with that."

"Nothing. Nothing other than to investigate these new crimes as those of a copycat. Someone is out there posing as my father, doing unspeakable things to these poor women, but it's not the Milkman. The Milkman died in prison three years ago."

Jack released another long sigh. "I guess I'm pulling another all-nighter. I need to get back to the office and look up everything I can find on Simon Brewster. We were already planning to press charges against him for his part in Samson's case. I guess this broadens our scope."

We both stood. "I'll put those journals in a bag for you," I offered. "You don't want someone to see you with them."

"What about the black journal? Can I have it as well?" His voice was softer now, as if understanding it could be difficult for me to hand over.

I saw the surprise on his face when I nodded. "Absolutely. I'm so tired of carrying my past around with me. Every time I moved, every time I ran, I took these journals with me. I want them all gone. I'm trying to right the wrongs of my past, and releasing such damning evidence is the best way I can do it."

Jack took me by the shoulders and turned me so that I had no choice but to look at him. The look in his chocolaty eyes was part empathy, part admiration, and part . . . humor? I didn't understand the last until I heard him say, "I mean this in the nicest way possible, but your father would be so ashamed of you right now."

In a moment of weakness — a moment borne of years-long exhaustion and this fragile new hope that maybe, just maybe, the past was behind me — I burst into a laughing sob. Jack pulled me to him and let me cry on his chest. No words were necessary. He just held me when I needed holding the most, and he released me when I had no more tears to cry. The front of his shirt was soaked.

"Thank you," I said softly. "That's the best compliment I could ever receive."

I was purposely ignoring my show of weakness, and he was gracious enough to allow it.

I went to grab the black journal and a duffel bag, and then he was gone.

* * *

Alone in the huge penthouse apartment the next morning, I didn't feel uncomfortable. I felt free.

I didn't bother snooping. I was on a mission. I was ordering clothes for the long-timers. Tomorrow, I would finish buying the personalized items. I might even do it in person. Buying for the children gave me more of a thrill than any five-finger discount ever had.

I left early, planning to visit the hospital. I was stepping into the private elevator when my second phone rang.

It was Jack. I was thinking of renaming him Jack No-Hello Eastwood, but at the sound of his voice I knew now wasn't the time for churlish thoughts. He wasn't calling with good news.

"You're not going to like what I'm about to tell you."

"In that case, do you have to tell me whatever it is I'm not going to like?" The elevator doors closed behind me, but

I didn't think to press the down button. His cryptic statement had me worried.

"Yes. You need to hear it."

My voice was resigned. "Then say it and get it over with."

"I called the prison to ask specifics about your father's death. They didn't have a lot of details, because it turns out your father died in a local hospital."

A pit of dread formed in my stomach. "What aren't you saying, Jack?"

"His body was moved to the morgue, pending the arrival of the funeral home."

I gripped the phone so hard, my fingers turned white. "And?" I knew there was more.

"And his body disappeared."

"*What?*" I shouted.

"There was an internal investigation, of course, but no one solved the mystery of how Leo Drakos' dead body disappeared from the hospital morgue."

"This — this can't be," I whispered. I sagged against the wall of the elevator. My legs threatened to give way beneath me.

"I'm sorry, Lexi," he said with compassion, "but I'm afraid it's true."

"He's still alive, Jack." I spoke with certainty.

"We don't know that," he was quick to say. "A doctor pronounced him dead. He recorded the exact time. I plan to call him the moment I hang up with you."

"It won't matter. If the doctor is still alive, which is doubtful, my father paid him to fake the death certificate. Even if he can, the man won't talk. No one turns on my father." It went unsaid that I had done just that. A chill stole over me. "I'm telling you, Jack," I said with quiet conviction, "my father is still alive, and he's here on the island."

"We'll find him. We won't let him hurt you."

I was too upset to answer. I hit the *End* button and let the wall support me. *My father was still alive.* The knowledge filled me with terror.

When I realized the elevator hadn't yet moved, I jabbed the button to take me down. Suddenly desperate to get out of the building — *Sam's* building, the one that held too many secrets and too many references to my father — I stabbed the button again. Three short jabs of frustration, fear, and an overwhelming sense of entrapment.

The elevator glided to a stop, and I got out.

Except I wasn't where I was supposed to be. I had never seen this floor before. It seemed to be a parking garage.

That's weird, I thought. Employees parked out back in the open lot. *Deliveries, maybe?* But that didn't make sense. The loading docks were also out back.

I ventured a few feet away from the elevator. I couldn't say why, but my heart was racing. Something didn't feel right. I counted at least a dozen vehicles. Red truck. White panel van. Snazzy little convertible. Mid-sized gray pickup. Silver sports car. Blue minivan. Plain green sedan. Black SUV with heavily tinted windows. What looked like a mail truck, but something was odd about its logo. Another brown delivery truck, easily recognizable even without the usual writing. Two more panel vans, one white, the other dark blue.

There were others parked further down, but I had seen enough. I stepped back into the elevator and punched the top button. Remembering that three jabs had brought me here, I repeated the action. Even the penthouse was better than this, wherever *this* was.

I hit the redial button on the phone I still held, but my call went to voicemail. For reasons I couldn't explain, I whispered my message. "Jack. Something weird is going on. The elevator stopped on a floor I've never seen before. Maybe the basement, I don't know. There were all these cars . . . Ones I've seen around town. Like the truck that was following me. I'm headed back up again, I assume to the penthouse. I hit the button an extra three . . . oh, never mind. I-I just wanted you to know I'm still in the building."

I stuffed the phone inside my pants pocket and waited for the doors to open. When they did, I would punch the down button *one* time only, and I'd get out of there as quickly as possible.

Except, once again, I wasn't where I was supposed to be. I was inside a . . . closet?

Judging from the clothes all around me, I would say this was definitely a closet. And it was huge. I had been in boutiques that were smaller than this room.

A large dressing table sat in the middle of the space, surrounded by drawers and doors. The table contained enough lighted mirrors to rival a movie set's hair and makeup trailer. An array of wigs sat atop styrofoam heads, each labeled. The heads weren't unusual, but they glowed an eerie white in this strange space. I didn't bother reading the labels or the binders in front of each one. My eyes traveled to the clothes.

They, too, could have come from a movie wardrobe set. There was a mix of styles, sizes, and genders, all neatly organized and separated into sections.

I easily recognized Sam's clothes. The bold patterns were her trademark. The extended plus sizes were her fit.

The clothes next to hers seemed to be two different sizes, both significantly smaller. Were these her old clothes, before she became morbidly obese? Some of them looked familiar, but I couldn't quite place them. Not until my gaze fell upon a hideous blue blouse.

Why on earth were Grandma Gail's clothes in Sam's closet? Warning signs flashed all around me.

Yet, like in a teenage slasher movie where the girl knows a killer lurks somewhere in the shadows and goes outside anyway, I moved further into the closet. My feet felt leaden, but some invisible force reeled me in.

I came to the men's clothing. A couple of black hoodies. A dozen dark suits, with shirts and ties in cerulean blue.

My father's clothes? These were my father's *clothes?*

It was too much for me to absorb.

Had Jack been right? Were my father and Sam in a relationship? It seemed impossible, but why else would his clothes be here in her closet?

242

I knew I should turn around, get back on the elevator, and get the hell out of there. Was I above or below the penthouse? It didn't matter, because I was done with the triple jabbing thing. One single press of a button would take me to a floor I recognized and away from this insanity.

My brain told me to run, but my feet dragged me deeper into the lion's den.

That's what this is, I suddenly realized. This was Sam's house of horrors, filled with props she thought would drive me to the point of breaking. My father's clothes. Grandma Gail's blouse. I should have trusted my first instincts and known the older woman was indeed following me. She was part of Sam's sick game. This was just another elaborate prop.

It wasn't until I rounded a corner in the closet that I realized a terrible truth. This wasn't her house of horror, and these weren't props.

This was the lion's den, and a half-dozen carcasses hung in front of me.

Warning signs glowed around me. I heard sirens in my head, the kind that warned of nuclear danger. The flashing lights were blinding. I pushed through the red haze, unsure if it was all in my mind or literally in the room with me. I moved toward the carcasses, which weren't really carcasses at all.

They were fat suits.

My hands trembled as I reached out to touch the first one. The outer layer had the convincing texture of skin. A twist of my hand revealed the layers of padding beneath. The sagging pouch around the middle and the fullness at the hips and breasts were the very image of any pudgy, overweight woman. Yet one woman in particular came to mind. Grandma Gail.

My stomach churned as I touched the second body suit. This one was made for a slimmer woman, with small breasts and a trim silhouette. Miss Sally?

Something was terribly, terribly wrong.

Almost frantic now, I moved to the next fat suit. This one, along with three others, belonged to Sam's persona. The padding was thick and globby, creating roll after roll of disgusting 'fat.' The suit fit from the chin to the wrist to the ankle.

Something clicked into place. Sam always wore long sleeves that were either cuffed and buttoned, or else clung to her wrists with elastic bands. In comparison to her body, it always struck me that her hands were surprisingly small.

It was because those were her *real* hands! I realized. But what about the rest of her? What about Grandma Gail and Miss Sally and the costumes filling the closet?

Were those women even real?

I felt sick. I was about to lose what little lunch I had eaten. My mind spun with the enormity of my discovery, but it balked when it came to assimilating the undeniable facts.

Even when I closed my eyes, I still saw them. The fat suits. The wigs. The clothes.

The warning signs.

I backed away in horror. I bumped against the wall as it turned into the larger closet. I couldn't get out of there fast enough.

Yet when I spun around, I found myself staring into the face of the lion.

CHAPTER THIRTY-TWO

Lexi

"Hello, Michaela," my father said. His Greek accent bled through the somber greeting.

"What — what are you doing here?" I asked in a weak voice.

His was patronizing. "Come, now. Haven't you figured it out yet? I thought I raised you better than that. I thought I had taught you to recognize the best of scams, no matter how good they are."

I closed my eyes again, letting it all sink in.

Of course.

That explained how Sam had known things she couldn't possibly know. Why he 'confided' in her.

That explained the way she watched me. The way she taunted me. The lion-about-to-pounce look.

That explained this crazy closet, and all the different personas within it.

That explained my father's supposed death, and the body missing from the morgue.

That explained the re-emergence of the Milkman.

Lillian 'Sam' Samson had been my father's biggest and most brilliant scam of all.

"You became Lillian Samson," I murmured.

"I invented Lillian Samson," he corrected. "George Samson's untimely death was the perfect opportunity for his estranged wife to take control. A shipping company was the perfect fit for my latest venture."

My voice was surprisingly flat. "You had George killed and reincarnated yourself as Sam Samson."

"Brilliant, was it not?"

"You," I spat in disgust, "are a sick man."

"Sick? Or stunningly clever? You knew a prison cell could never contain me, Michaela. You knew I would find a way out. And you have to admit, it was the perfect disguise," he boasted. "Leo Drakos posing as a woman? Even the mafia was fooled. It wiped my slate clean, but they have no control over Sam Samson. She creates her own deals. Keeps her own profits. Makes her own fortune."

"She isn't real," I reminded him.

"My life of luxury is very real." His smirk turned sour. "But you? I'm disappointed in you, Michaela," he chided. "You never saw through my guise. I groomed you to be my protégé. To be as resourceful and astute as I am. Yes, I admit you did well at running away from home and starting a new life for yourself. Your first cons were actually quite good."

I interrupted him with a fervent cry. "They weren't cons! I didn't do it for money. I did it to escape you!"

He continued as if I hadn't spoken. "I thought you held real promise. I thought that, in time, you would see we were still a great team. I facilitated your move here to Galveston, and your job within SSI." He allowed me no chance to ask what 'facilitated' meant. I knew the details didn't matter in the long run, because it was exactly like something my father would do.

"I gave you hints, Michaela. The lemon tree. The cerulean. My favorite roast beef sandwich. The cigar box. Hint after hint, but you never put it together." His voice turned hard. "You failed your test."

246

"I knew something was wrong, but not even I thought you were evil enough to do something like this!" I spat.

"How to Run a Con 101," he ground out. "Never underestimate your opponent."

My mind had been numbed with shock, but now that it was wearing off, I realized I was in a dangerous predicament. I was trapped here, alone, with a man who thought of me as an opponent, not his daughter.

"Why blonde, Michaela?" he asked abruptly. "Your dark hair was one of your best features."

It was a backhanded compliment. "I needed a change," was my only answer. "But you didn't change, did you? The Milkman is back."

He flashed an evil smile. "You have no idea how stressful it is to run a multi-million-dollar business. A man needs some form of pleasure in his life."

"You scar those women for life, yet all you think about is your own pleasure? You're despicable. And sick," I added. I motioned to his closet of horrors. "Is this how you did it? You created alternate personas to work at the hospital? To get the names and addresses of new mothers so that you could molest them?"

"I never molested them, Michaela. I helped them. I showed them the proper way to breastfeed their child."

"You fondled them!"

"I was helping their milk come down," he insisted. "I was massaging them for the good of their sons, not me."

He was sick enough to believe his own words. "You were reliving your own pathetic childhood." My voice was cold. "Apparently, you targeted mothers of little boys, and you pretended they were *your* mother, and it was *your* mouth feeding at their breasts." I gave a bitter laugh. "And to think I pegged Simon for your crimes! I thought he was a copycat Milkman."

"*I* am the one helping those women," he thundered, jabbing his chest with his thumb, "not him. *I* am the Milkman. I'm helping them to be better mothers to their sons than my mother was to me. Than yours was to you. Your mother ran out on you, Michaela, and don't you forget it. *I* was the one who raised you! *I* was the one who was there for you."

He was pathetic and not worth the argument. With a weary voice, I shook my head. "No. You were the one who used me."

"I was the one who taught you," he countered. "I taught you how to fend for yourself in this world. How to be resourceful. How to use your wits. How to win."

"You know the best lesson I learned from you?"

He expected a compliment. I saw the smile forming on his lips, thinking he had won this round. "What is that?"

I lifted my chin. "You taught me that I never wanted to be like you. That if doing things your way was the only way to win, I'd rather be a loser. At least I can finally look myself in the mirror."

When I would have stormed past him, he caught my arm with a steel grip.

"You're hurting me!" I protested.

His dark eyes flashed with a dangerous gleam. "Like your betrayal did not hurt? You walked away from me, Michaela. My own daughter left me!" As always when he was angry, his accent was more pronounced.

I saw the lie for what it was. "I only hurt your pride. You said it often enough. No one walks away from Leonardo Drakos." My chin came up another notch. "But I did."

"You think you're better than me? You think you can just walk away from everything I've given you, everything I've done for you?"

I stared him in the eyes. "I've done it once. And I'm doing it again."

He let me push around him before his words stopped me in my tracks. "If you dare walk away from me again, I swear I'll kill you."

Somewhere in my heart, I always knew he was capable of killing me. *Willing* to kill me, if it meant saving himself.

It was still a shock to hear. No father should ever say those words to his own flesh and blood.

I kept my voice even. I didn't bother turning to face him. "If you want the journals back, it's too late. I no longer have them."

"You're lying."

I turned around, amazed at how calm I felt. "Am I?"

"You would never do that. You would lose your leverage. You called it your insurance."

"You know another lesson you taught me, Leo?" I would no longer call this monster my father. "The art of bargaining. You taught me that every single one of us has something that someone else wants. You said that if another person wants it badly enough, it gives us bargaining power. I took the lesson to heart. I finally found something I wanted more than insurance. Something that was better than my own safety."

"And what would that be, *sciocco*?" He called me a fool, but for once in my life, I felt powerful.

I leaned in closer so that he had no trouble understanding my very distinct, very softly spoken word. "Justice."

His face turned beet red. "Justice for who? For yourself? You ratted your old man out to make your own sentence lighter?"

"I told the truth to make my soul lighter," I ground out. "You, Leo Drakos, are a sick, evil monster. When I turned the journals over to the feds, I truly believed you were dead. I wanted everyone to know what a sorry excuse of a human being you were. I wanted the world to know what you had done. What you were still doing, through Sam. But it turns out, you *are* Sam, and you are still alive."

My chest heaved with the venom of my words. I forced myself to breathe naturally. I wanted my next words to be clear and strong.

"And you know what, Leo?" I leaned in again, my voice hard and low. "Getting justice while you're alive? Is. So. Much. Better."

With the roar of a lion, it finally happened.

He pounced.

Inner Lexi screamed at me. How to Escape a Madman 101. *Run!*

I broke for the door.

Leo came from behind to tackle me, and I went down hard.

I groaned as he flipped me over to my back. Fury distorted his face. He cursed me in Greek and then in English. His chest heaved, and the veins in his neck stood out. When his hands came toward my neck, I knew he planned to choke me to death. He was trying to straddle me and hold me down.

As his leg came across my body, I jerked my knee up, catching him in the groin.

Just for a moment, he gave in to the pain. It gave me the few seconds I needed to shift forward and to the left. In those few seconds he had held me to the floor, something silver under the dressing table had caught my eye. It looked like scissors. I knew I didn't stand a chance of escape. But I had a chance to fight back.

"Do you know what you've done?" he bellowed, scrambling toward me again. "The mafia believed I was dead. Now, they'll come after me."

He managed to trap my body between his legs. He was too busy with his rant to worry about my flailing arm.

"Now, I'm a dead man! And you," he spat, slapping my face hard enough to push my other cheek against the carpet. It gave me a clear view of the scissors. They were small and tapered, the kind used for sewing. The kind of scissors that were pointed and extremely sharp. "You are as worthless as your mother!"

Spittle flew from his mouth as he closed his hands around my throat. "She left when you were hours old. No mother should ever leave her child behind. That's why I tracked her down, and that's why I killed her. And now, I'm going to kill you. You're as deceitful and weak as she was!"

I couldn't let his admission about my mother slow me down. I would deal with that discovery later. Right then, I was fighting for my life.

I swept my hand along the carpet and felt a sharp prick on my finger. The fine tip of the blades had drawn blood. *Good. The sharper the better.*

Leo's hands tightened, and I found it harder to breathe, especially with him sitting on me. I knew it was now or never.

Clutching the scissors firmly in my hand, I aimed for the side of his throat. I jabbed, thrusting the sharp tip in with all my might.

It took a moment for his grip to slacken. It felt like forever, but only a few seconds had passed. I felt his fingers slip away from my neck. Jerking my body to one side, Leo tumbled to the floor beside me. Blood spurted from his neck.

"Help — help me," he gasped. He put a shaky hand to his wound, but blood flooded around his fingers. I had hit his jugular vein. He was dying before my very eyes, and I felt nothing. No sadness. No regret. Nothing.

His voice was fading. "Michaela . . ."

My voice was gaining strength. "My name is Lexi." I managed to get unsteadily to my feet. "And you were right, Leo." I stared down at him with no emotion. "You're a dead man."

I stumbled toward the elevator. I pushed the call button to open the doors, but nothing happened. For a moment, I panicked. I knew I was safe from Leo Drakos. Amid a pool of his life's blood, his eyes were already glassy and blank. Sam wasn't real, so I was in no danger there. But what about Simon? Had this been some sort of trap? Both he and Sam — correction, Leo — had said they were going out of town, yet there Leo was, bleeding out in this house of horrors. Was Simon on his way up at this very moment?

The elevator's cables were almost silent. I hadn't even known when it went down. Only a faint light alerted me to the car's return. Any moment now, the doors would open, and I would find out if Simon was friend or foe.

I ducked behind a rack of dresses, daring to peek as the elevator doors slid open.

"Lexi?" I heard Jack's whisper.

I had never been so happy to see a lawman in all my life. "Jack!" There was no reason to keep my voice down as I stepped from my hiding place.

"I got your message." He still had his weapon drawn. "Are you—" He stopped mid-sentence when he spotted Leo's body. "Who's that? What happened?"

"That," I said without emotion, "is Leo Drakos. I killed him."

Speechless, Jack's eyes darted between me and the body, the body and me.

It took far longer to tell the story than it had to live it in real time.

He found an undercounter refrigerator and handed me a bottle of water. "You're sure you don't need to see a doctor?"

I guzzled down the offering before answering. "I'm sure," I said, even though my throat was aching.

I spotted a small sink I hadn't noticed before. "I guess this is where he washed his hands after applying all that makeup," I muttered. I turned on the water. Leo's blood washed from my hands and disappeared down the drain. "How did you get up here?" I asked Jack. "How did you find me?"

"There's a ramp around back that goes to an underground parking garage."

I knew the one he spoke of. I had seen it the day I applied for the job. The day the madness began.

Unaware of my mind's wandering, he explained, "You said something about 'hitting the button an extra three.' I assumed you were talking about the elevator, and that you meant hitting the button an extra three times. I acted on the assumption, and here I am."

I was still unclear if we were above or below the penthouse, and I didn't care. I never intended to come back again.

While Jack used his phone to document photos of Leo's body, I flipped through the binders I had seen earlier. It came as no surprise that Leo kept such meticulous notes. The folders contained full descriptions of his different personas. They included instructions on wigs, contact lenses, makeup application, mannerisms, even personality quirks. It read like a character bible used by authors. He even had pictures of himself in costume.

The sound of Jack's voice startled me. I hadn't realized he was through taking pictures. "We need to have a talk." He put his hands on my shoulders and turned me to face him.

He took a decisive breath, and then his words wound around my brain, cutting off circulation. That was the only explanation for my utter confusion.

"You were never here," he said. "I received a tip from a confidential informant that Leo Drakos was still alive and here in this apartment. When I encountered the escapee, he confessed to his elaborate hoax as Sam Samson and his identity as the Milkman. A fight ensued, at which time I used a pair of scissors to fend him off. He died here in this room."

Too stunned to speak, my head rattled on my shoulders in protest.

Jack's voice was firm. "It's the report I'm filing."

"Why?" I managed to whisper.

He didn't answer immediately. He studied a loose thread at my shoulder, bringing the ripped sleeve to my attention.

His voice was slightly rough. "I would be seen as carrying out my duties as an officer of the law. You, on the other hand . . ." He left the thought dangling but added, "There would be a formal investigation. A deep dive into your past. Your true identity would come out, Lexi."

"But I did this. I killed him."

"In self-defense, which I'm sure the DA would take into consideration. But it's not the law you have to worry about. It's the outlaws. If we do it my way, I'll say I discovered the red journals here. But if there's a trial and you have to authenticate them and confess your part in all this, there will be a target on your back. Do you really want the mafia knowing who you are and what you did?"

"Of course not. But I can't let you take the blame for this."

"We made a deal, Lexi," he reminded me. "You would get me the information I needed, and I would watch your back. The case against Sam Samson is obviously a moot point, but Simon Brewster will be the first to fall. Mann, Comiskey, Mackie, and half the people at that dinner party will be right behind him. Arenas will be held responsible for his crimes. You did that, Lexi. You came through in a big way, and now, it's my turn. This is me watching your back."

Tears and indecision swam around in my eyes. He sounded so sure this would work. But wasn't this, too, just another scam?

"If I do this," I whispered brokenly, "I'll be no better than him." My eyes darted over his shoulder to the body of Leonardo Drakos.

"You, Lexi Graham, are a thousand times better than that man. You turned in the evidence needed to bring down a major crime syndicate. You stopped your father from ever scamming or hurting another soul ever again. Because of you, the Milkman is no more. You didn't do any of that for money. You didn't do it to get ahead in life. You did it because it was the right thing to do. You did it for justice. And today, justice was served."

My eyes still lingered on Leo's prone form.

"Hey, look at me," Jack said quietly. He put a finger under my chin and directed my gaze up to his. "You stood up to him. You stood up for what was right. You're a good person, Lexi Graham. You're nothing like him. And if the past ten years didn't convince you of that, this past week surely does."

It was always easier for me to believe the worst about myself than it was to believe I had redeeming qualities. I think Jack was the only person who had ever pointed those out to me.

"I have a lot to do here," he said gently. "You should go."

"But . . ." The word was more symbolic than it was argumentative.

Jack gently squeezed my shoulders. "You're free now, Lexi. No more looking over your shoulder. No more living in your father's shadow. Just go. Go live your life. Let someone have your back for a change."

I bit my lip, overwhelmed by the beautiful picture he painted. Could it really be so simple?

He gave my shoulders a final squeeze. "Please. Let me do this for you. It's no less than you deserve."

"No one's ever believed in me before," I whispered. "How — how can I ever repay you?"

His voice no longer sounded so smooth. "By letting go. By being free." He dropped his hands from my shoulders and took a step back. "Go, Lexi. I've got your back."

CHAPTER THIRTY-THREE

After

Afternoons were always slow at The Coffee Gallery, but they were quickly becoming my favorite part of the day. I did my best work then, coming down from the adrenaline rush of a busy lunch hour. Sketching relaxed me. It was the best therapy I could think of, and cheaper than all of those self-help books still cluttering my bookcase.

I settled at my favorite table with a cup of coffee and my sketchpad. I was putting the final touches on a new piece for the gallery.

It had been a little over a year since my *Big Moment*. That fateful day when my life splintered into Before, and After.

After was so much better.

The official story was that Lexi Graham, the personal assistant to Sam Samson, was completely in the dark about her boss' nefarious deeds. When she learned the truth, she packed up and moved away from Galveston as quickly as possible.

The truth was that I had stayed in town for another three weeks. Randy and Abbie were gracious enough to let me stay with them, and with Abbie's help, I was able to fill fifteen suitcases with some very special gifts for the group home long-timers. She even went with me to deliver the gifts in person.

I was tempted by Joy's offer to work for her, but after all that had happened here, Galveston wasn't the fresh start I needed. With my final project completed, I had done the one thing I swore I would never do again: I moved.

As it turned out, Texas had grown on me. Maybe it was that slow, honey-flavored drawl. Maybe it was the sea of cowboy hats, or the diverse regions and demographics contained within its borders. I ended up in what was known as the Prairies and Lakes Region of the state. Dublin was a good five hours from the coast, located in the rolling plains of North Central Texas. I had gone back to my natural hair color, and without the chemical relaxer, the wavy curls brushed against my shoulders. I thought it was a nice touch that a Greek girl settled in the official 'Irish Capital of Texas.'

Without Leo Drakos' shadow hanging over me, I was finally happy. My life was normal, if such a thing exists. Best of all, I had found a way to combine my two favorite things: coffee, and art. Hence, The Coffee Gallery.

I, Lexi Graham, was now a legitimate business owner. Legit in every sense of the word. I even had the red numbers in my ledger to prove it.

Leo may have lived lavishly, but I knew how to hoard my cash. Over the past several years, I had scrimped and saved for the proverbial rainy day. I had arrived in Texas with a small but decent amount of savings. Thanks to my frugal ways and the generous salaries from both Janine and 'Sam,' I was able to buy a formerly empty storefront and bring new life not just to *it*, but to me. I was in my element here.

With the shop now quiet, I critiqued the drawing in front of me. It still needed something. More shadows? The hint of breaking light? I twisted my lips as I studied my latest creation.

Lost in thought, I didn't hear the approaching footsteps. I had bought the old building at below-market price, probably because it was quickly slipping from *historic* to *decrepit*. I put in a lot of sweat equity into making it functional, but I had left the bare wood floors and the exposed brick walls as they were. That telltale floor was better than any bell. It announced visitors the moment they stepped through the door, especially those wearing cowboy boots.

A slow Texas drawl startled me from behind.

"I think a pink elephant would look good in your sketch."

A small stuffed animal appeared on the table, delivered by a hand bearing pearl snaps on its cuff.

"Jack." It wasn't a question.

"May I?" he asked, stepping around me to indicate the chair next to mine.

My lips itched with a smile, but I did my best to hide it. With a nonchalant shrug, I bumped the chair toward him with my foot so he could have a seat.

He looked good. I hadn't seen him since leaving the island, and I had to admit I missed those chocolate-brown eyes and his corny jokes. Through texts and the occasional card, Abbie would casually mention how Jack was doing or what he was up to these days. I had a feeling she told him the same about me.

"Nice place you have here," he said, looking around the rustic chic atmosphere.

I couldn't keep the pride from my voice. "Thanks. I've worked hard on it."

"I hear that's not the only thing you've worked hard on. I understand Safe Harbor is nearly finished."

That was another source of great pride, and it filled me with as much satisfaction as The Coffee Gallery.

Leo may have invented the role of George Samson's estranged widow so that he could outsmart the mafia, but it turned out he had quietly purchased the business months before. He even paid for it with clean money, if winnings from an Atlantic City casino could be called that. Then, for whatever reason, he left George's original upstart operating as a legitimate business. I had no delusions about it being a noble gesture, more like an attempt to throw off suspicion.

I didn't hide my smile. "As my father's sole heir, what better way to spend the liquidation proceeds than to reopen the old warehouse as The Safe Harbor Home for Children?"

"From what Abbie tells me, it comes complete with an indoor gym, game room, and a big common room for everyone to hang out in."

"There was that long hallway and all those confusing doors on the ground floor," I said with a shrug. "Can you think of a better use for them?"

"Not a one."

I had found a worthy organization to rent the facilities to for a very reasonable one thousand dollars a month. My only stipulation was that the long-timers be moved to the penthouse suites overlooking the harbor. I hoped it would become a sort of badge of honor, and a reminder that no matter how long they lived in the home, they were worthy and not forgotten. I wanted them to believe in themselves and know that they had redeeming qualities.

"You did a good thing, Lexi." Jack's voice was filled with admiration, and those chocolaty-brown eyes were doing weird things to my emotions. He nodded to the plush elephant in front of me. "You deserve your pink elephant."

I picked up the silly animal that looked better suited for a carnival game. Then I hugged it to me, and the craziest thing happened. Tears filled my eyes. "Thank you, Jack," I whispered.

Allowing me time to compose myself, Jack looked around again. "So, tell me. What's good to eat in this place?"

Tears wiped away, I replied saucily, "Everything, of course."

"Any house specials?"

"For breakfast, we have a wonderful sausage and chorizo croissant." I felt the twinkle in my eyes. "Our lunch specialties are salads, paninis, and soups."

"You really are a creature of habit, aren't you?"

I imagined his astute gaze saw through my casual shrug. "I find a steady routine is comforting."

"You serve tomato basil soup, I presume?"

"Of course."

"Good to know. I'll need a good spot to eat." I saw the smile hovering around the edges of his mouth. "By the way. Do you have any tables to rent for office space?"

I lifted my brows. "Tell me why," I asked slowly, "you would need an office in Dublin?" I put a hand over my chest and faked a sudden revelation. "Don't tell me you're homeless again!"

"Nope, I have an apartment. And a stuffy office that I share with a bunch of other agents. But I like Dublin's small-town atmosphere better than that of a bigger town."

"What are you talking about, Jack? Galveston is over three hundred miles from here."

"I've transferred to the Stephenville office. It's only twenty minutes or so away."

I stared at him in genuine shock. "You transferred to Stephenville?"

"I needed a change in scenery. It took a while to clean up the mess your father left behind, but now that I've wrapped that up, I'm ready for a new challenge."

I put my hand up to correct him. "I no longer refer to Leo as my father, and I'd appreciate it if you would do the same." My voice was as hard as my heart when it came to that man. "If I thought a complete blood transfusion would cleanse me of his DNA, I'd do it in a minute."

"DNA and morals are two very different things," he pointed out. "You definitely got the better end of the bargain."

He did have a point. I hadn't inherited Leo's wicked ways.

When Jack placed his hand over mine, I felt the zing again. It traveled all the way to my toes.

"What do you say, Lexi? Think you could put up with me hanging around here every day?"

My breath caught in my throat. It sounded tempting, but . . .

"You're still a lawman, Jack," I whispered.

"And you're a law-abiding citizen. We're good together. And I know you just felt that zap of electricity, the same way I did."

I didn't try denying it. But change didn't come easy to me, even though I had spent the last eleven years trying. Starting a relationship with an officer of the law was completely out of my box. It scared me.

"I—"

As he often did, Jack injected a sense of humor into the tense moment. "It's the nine-toe thing, isn't it?"

His comment was so ridiculous, and so predictably Jack. The lawman with the quirky sense of humor. The lawman I couldn't quite get out of my head this past year. The lawman who made me see my own value as a person.

The lawman who delivered the prize Leo always promised but never gave.

I felt the edges of my mouth lift. "Well," I drawled, "I suppose the pink elephant does kinda make up for it."

He squeezed my fingers as a smile spread across his face. "So, can you think of any reason we shouldn't give this a try?"

His smile was contagious. I was probably smiling like a fool.

Was I being foolish? I wondered. My sperm donor was a criminal. He was evil.

Inner Lexi rebuked my doubts. *Yet you prevailed, didn't you, Lex? You survived a damaged childhood. You survived a sick, deranged father. You survived all his twisted morals and blurry lines between right and wrong. You survived running from the law, running from the mob, and running from him. Leo Drakos tried breaking you, but you were stronger than him.*

She was right. I had vowed to never be anything like him, and this was the ultimate proof.

I, Lexi Graham, was my own woman. I wasn't corrupt. I wasn't crippled by my past.

I was worthy of happiness.

I was ready to take a chance. And with a lawman, of all people.

I was living my *after*.

Leaning over to bump my shoulder against Jack's, I felt that foolish smile spreading even wider. "Give me a while," I said, "and let's see if I come up with one."

THE END

THE JOFFE BOOKS STORY

We began in 2014 when Jasper agreed to publish his mum's much-rejected romance novel and it became a bestseller.

Since then we've grown into the largest independent publisher in the UK. We're extremely proud to publish some of the very best writers in the world, including Joy Ellis, Faith Martin, Caro Ramsay, Helen Forrester, Simon Brett and Robert Goddard. Everyone at Joffe Books loves reading and we never forget that it all begins with the magic of an author telling a story.

We are proud to publish talented first-time authors, as well as established writers whose books we love introducing to a new generation of readers.

We won Trade Publisher of the Year at the Independent Publishing Awards in 2023. We have been shortlisted for Independent Publisher of the Year at the British Book Awards for the last four years, and were shortlisted for the Diversity and Inclusivity Award at the 2022 Independent Publishing Awards. In 2023 we were shortlisted for Publisher of the Year at the RNA Industry Awards.

We built this company with your help, and we love to hear from you, so please email us about absolutely anything bookish at feedback@joffebooks.com

If you want to receive free books every Friday and hear about all our new releases, join our mailing list: www.joffebooks.com/contact

And when you tell your friends about us, just remember: it's pronounced Joffe as in coffee or toffee!